ONE-WAY TICKET TO DEATH

"If you ask me, there's something fishy here."

"I agree," Daisy said. The decision was easy. Yielding to the temptation of years, Daisy reached up and yanked on the emergency brake chain.

Brakes squealed. Shuddering, the Flying Scotsman slowed.

As the train came to rest in a jolting clash of buffers, Dr. Jagai entered the compartment.

"So the poor old fellow's gone," he said sadly, reaching for the bony wrist. "No sign of a pulse. Well, at his age it was to be expected. The heart simply wears out."

As he leaned forward to close his benefactor's staring eyes, Daisy said sharply, "Don't!" She exchanged a glance with the manservant, who nodded. "I'm afraid Weekes and I suspect dirty work. Nothing must be touched until the police arrive."

"Police!"

Weekes nodded. "Where's the master's pillow, sir, I ask you? You know as well as I do that he never would have laid down flat like that. Not with his stomach trouble."

"True." Dr. Jagai's forehead wrinkled. "But why should anyone dispose of his pillow?"

"The only reason I can think of," Daisy said tentatively, "is that he was smothered with it and the murderer disposed of the murder weapon. . . ."

Daisy Dalrymple Mysteries by Carola Dunn

DEATH AT WENTWATER COURT

THE WINTER GARDEN MYSTERY

REQUIEM FOR A MEZZO

MURDER ON THE FLYING SCOTSMAN

DAMSEL IN DISTRESS
(coming soon)

Published by Kensington Publishing Corporation

A DAISY DALRYMPLE MYSTERY

MURDER ON THE FLYING SCOTSMAN

CAROLA DUNN

KENSINGTON BOOKS
Kensington Publishing Corp.
http://www.kensingtonbooks.com

KENSINGTON BOOKS are published by

Kensington Publishing Corp.
850 Third Avenue
New York, NY 10022

First Printing: November 2001
10 9 8 7 6 5 4 3 2

Printed in the United States of America

ACKNOWLEDGMENTS

My particular thanks to Peter N. Hall, LNER Steward and member of the Historical Model Railway Society, for his extensive research on the Flying Scotsman of 1923. Any errors made or facts altered to suit the story are solely my responsibility.

Thanks also to the librarians of Berwick-on-Tweed. Their patience in demonstrating (more than once) the microfiche machine enabled me to discover, in the *Berwick Journal* of 1923, Superintendent Halliday and his officers.

And I must both thank and apologize to Beryl Houghton of the Berwick Walls Hotel, which resembles the Raven's Nest Hotel only in its location and exterior. The discomforts of the latter emanate entirely from my imagination.

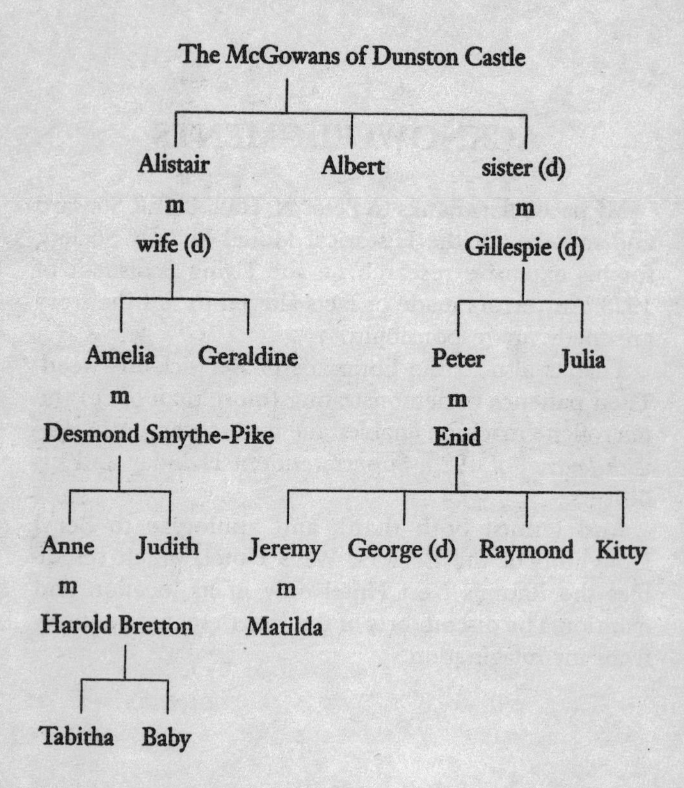
The McGowans of Dunston Castle
Alistair
m
wife (d)
Albert
sister (d)
m
Gillespie (d)
Amelia
m
Desmond Smythe-Pike
Geraldine
Peter
m
Enid
Julia
Anne
m
Harold Bretton
Judith
Jeremy
m
Matilda
George (d)
Raymond
Kitty
Tabitha
Baby

PROLOGUE

"A month, hey, Doctor?"

"I'll no gi' ye more than five weeks, Mr. McGowan, nor promise the end willna come sooner."

"Bah!" The old man snorted with surprising vigour, considering his cadaverous face and the skeletal hand plucking at the patched counterpane. "Niver kenned a doctor yet wha'd commit himsel' one way or t'ither."

His lips pursed, the doctor picked up his black bag and turned to the grey-haired, dowdy woman who stood at the foot of the four-poster bed. "I s'll write twa prescriptions, Miss Gillespie, for the pain and to help your uncle sleep. And I'll drop by next week . . ."

"That ye'll not!" Alistair McGowan snapped. "If there's nowt to be done, I'll no pay a guinea to hae ye not do't."

The doctor shrugged. "Verra weel. I'll see ye again when I write oot the death certificate. Good-day tae ye, sir."

Julia Gillespie led the way out of the gloomy, chilly, cavernous bedchamber into the equally gloomy and chilly if less cavernous passage with its threadbare carpet. As they descended the magnificent Jacobean staircase, she noted with distress a thin layer of dust on the carved oak balusters. It was impossible to keep the house decent when Uncle Alistair refused to hire more than an absolute minimum of staff, but at least the front stairs should be clean.

"A month?" she said, the news at last beginning to sink in.

"Thereabouts. Ye'll be sending for the family?"

"Not unless Uncle Alistair tells me to. I shouldn't dare. A month!" A tiny smile lightened her careworn face. "It's a shocking thing to say, Doctor, but I can't wait to shake the dust of Dunston Castle from my feet. I shan't stay a moment longer than I must."

"Ye're provided for?" he asked gruffly.

"A hundred a year, enough to live on if I'm careful, and I've practice enough at that."

"Imphm."

Julia saw the look in his eyes: genteel poverty, it said, but was that not how she had lived for nearly a quarter of a century now, in this year of 1923? Twenty-five years ago, before the turn of the century, the family had collectively made up its mind she was the one to be sacrificed on the altar of duty. Uncle Alistair's older daughter, Amelia, was married. The younger, Geraldine, had run away, disappeared beyond all ken. Somehow Julia had had no choice.

"The wife sent her greetings," the doctor said now, "and she expects ye for coffee the morn's morn as usual."

"Thank you. Yes, I'll try to be there."

He wrote out the prescriptions and took his leave. Julia hurried back up to her uncle's bedroom.

"Whaur the de'il hae ye been?" he greeted her. "I'm cauld. Draw the bed-curtains and bring anither quilt."

"I'll have a fire lit, Uncle."

"In April? Hae I no taught ye yet that a bawbee saved is a bawbee earned?"

Under her breath, Julia rebelliously muttered his other favourite maxim, "Take care of the pennies and the pounds will take care of themselves." But in this case he was the only one to suffer, so she did not make even the feeblest effort to persuade him.

She drew the faded brocade draperies on both sides, handling the worn, fragile material with care. As she reached for the curtain at the foot, he stopped her with a gesture of one claw-like hand.

"Wait. Write to my solicitor today and tell him I want to see him. Donald Braeburn o' Braeburn, Braeburn, Tiddle and Plunkett. Ye'll find the address in my desk."

"You want Mr. Braeburn to come all the way from London?"

"I pay him, don't I?" the old man snarled. "And a pretty penny it costs to keep a Scottish lawyer in London, but almost worth it sin' he's bound to outwit the Sassenachs. Then write to a' the family and tell them to be here next Monday wi'out fail. Every single one, mind."

"But suppose they cannot get away?"

"They'll come, if ye tell 'em Braeburn's on his way." He chuckled nastily. "Half o' them'll hope I'm going to change my will, and t'ither half'll hope I shan't. Dinna fash yersel', they'll come running all right."

1

The vast vault of King's Cross Station echoed and reechoed to the thunder of pneumatic hammers. The air was thick with dust. Daisy tucked her extravagant first-class ticket into her handbag, hitched up the camera's strap securely on her shoulder, stuck her fingers in her ears, and looked about her.

The unification of three railway companies into one, the new London and North Eastern, was responsible for the current chaos. Why the merger necessitated the complete rebuilding of King's Cross escaped Daisy, but one result was that the clerk at the ticket window had not been able to tell her with any assurance which platform the Flying Scotsman would leave from today.

Another result was that the usual swarms of people were confined within a variety of barricades and temporary walls. Not only was the W. H. Smith's bookstall out of bounds, so were the slot machines, and Alec was not there this morning to see her off with a box of chocs. He was already in the North, the Northumberland police having called in Scotland Yard to solve some difficult case for them. Daisy was not even likely to see him, since she was going still further north. She was on her way to a stately home near Edinburgh to collect information for her next *Town and Country* article.

Her porter reappeared, battling through the crowd towards her with her bags and the portable typewriter. She removed one finger from one ear and he bellowed into it, "Platform Five, miss.

He led the way to the ticket barrier, where a reassuring sign announced *The Flying Scotsman: London–York–Edinburgh dep. 10:00 A.M.* A harassed ticket-inspector was trying to deal with a long queue at the same time as fielding queries from anxious passengers who had expected *their* train to leave from Platform 5.

Daisy's porter went ahead with her luggage and she joined the slow-moving queue. It looked as if the train was going to be pretty full and she was glad she had blown the extra three quid odd on the first-class ticket. She could just about afford it since getting the American magazine commission for the series on London's museums. For short trips third class was good enough; for over eight hours, the extra comfort and space was worth the money.

All the same, it was a pity she had not been able to buy something to read, she thought as she walked along the platform beside the varnished teak coaches. Passengers in first tended to be less chatty, more standoffish, than their lower-class fellow-travelers. It was going to be a long, dull journey. Oh well, she could always buzz along and try to bag a seat in third for a while when the scenery palled.

She did want a window-seat, though. Coming to the first-class carriage, she stepped up into the train and walked along the corridor. Some of the first few compartments were smokers, others had both window-seats taken, but at last she came to an empty one with a *No Smoking* sign.

"To face the engine or not to face the engine," she mused. "That is the question."

Reluctantly she put down her handbag and Lucy's camera on the backwards seat. She preferred traveling forwards, especially when she had nothing to read. However, she wanted to arrive looking reasonably professional, and the frightful smuts which always floated in through the window invariably landed on one's face. The window was bound to be opened, since the weather forecast prophesied another unseasonably warm day.

In fact, it was jolly hot in the train already. Why the steam heating was always on at full blast on warm days and left one shivering on cold days was another of life's little unsolvable mysteries.

Brought up on "Ne'er cast a clout till May be out" (May month or May blossom? she had always wondered), Daisy was wearing her green tweed winter coat. As she unbuttoned it, from the corridor came a male voice in rising tones of desperation.

"Oh God, oh God, oh God, I can't stand it much longer! Some of the fellows think the mud's the worst, but to me its a hot day when all you want is to play cricket or laze in a punt. I tell you, I can't . . ."

"Hush, Raymond." A girl's voice, its superficial languid drawl seemed to Daisy to have an undertone of tenderness, a blend of love and pity. "Come and sit down, darling. We'll close the window and door, and you can put your hands over your ears."

"I'm sorry, Judith," he said brokenly. "It's those damned hammers. They sound just like . . . Oh God, why doesn't the bloody train start?"

Shell-shock. Daisy knew the attacks of memories too vivid to be ignored were often set off by loud noises. Wilfred Owen's words drifted through her head:

What passing-bells for these who die as cattle?
  Only the monstrous anger of the guns.
  Only the stuttering rifles' rapid rattle
Can patter out their hasty orisons.

Owen had been a friend of Michael's. He was dead, along with Michael, and Gervaise, and uncountable others. At least they were at peace, she thought with a lump in her throat, unlike those poor souls who still suffered five years after the Armistice.

"Shell-shock, poor chap." The porter popped up again like the genie of the lamp. "Me sister's lad's the same way. Takes him something awful, it does. I put your big bags in the luggage van, miss, and warned the guard to mind the FRAGILE labels on the one with your photographical stuff in, like you said."

"Thank you. Yes, the typewriter and the small bag up in the rack, and would you put the camera up, too, please." She tipped him and he departed.

It was really too unbearably hot in the compartment, yet opening the window would let in all the noise and dirt of the station's demolition. Daisy took off her cotton gloves, stuffed them in her pocket, then took off her coat.

Thank heaven she had trusted the forecast enough to wear a summer frock. It was a rather nice new one, short-sleeved, in blue voile patterned with white and yellow daisies, with a blue sash at the low waist. She looked quite pretty in it even if her figure was far from the fashionable ideal of no bosom and no hips. A pity Alec was not there to notice that the blue was the same shade as her eyes—not that he was given to compliments. About all he had ever said on the subject of her eyes was to blame their guileless depths for leading him into indiscreet disclosures about his investigations.

She bundled the coat up onto the rack, forced to stand on tiptoe though she was not particularly short. The world was designed for men, she thought darkly. Perhaps that would change now that women at last had the vote.

The hat came off next, the prized emerald green cloche from Selfridge's Bargain Basement. Her mother would be simply aghast to see her traveling without gloves and a hat, but Mother was far away. It was too ridiculous to die of heat stroke for the sake of convention. Besides, she had the compartment to herself so far, and the train must be about to start off.

Kneeling on the seat, she peered in the mirror to tidy her hair. The short, honey brown curls still took her by surprise when she wasn't thinking. She had not told her mother she'd had practically all her hair cut off. What a row there'd be when she found out!

Alec said the shingle cut made her look like Lady Caroline Lamb. He also said the little mole by her mouth, the one face-powder never quite hid, looked like an eighteenth-century face-patch called the "Kissing"—but he had not kissed her yet.

Perhaps he never would, Daisy thought gloomily. When she went to tea at his house, his mother had made it plain, without ever putting it into words, that she disapproved of the middle classes mixing with the aristocracy. Of course Daisy's mother, the Dowager Lady Dalrymple, felt just the same, or would if she knew about her daughter's friendship with Detective Chief Inspector Alec Fletcher. As though having an Honourable in front of one's name translated one to a different plane from ordinary humanity!

At least Alec's daughter, Belinda, jolly well liked her.

The freckles on Daisy's nose were showing. She powdered them into submission and refreshed her lipstick. Sitting down, she leaned her shingled head back on the antimacassar covering the padded headrest. The fawn and red patterned seat was indeed comfortable, softer than third class. She might even manage to snooze away part of the journey.

Outside, whistles blew and doors slammed. The Flying Scotsman slid slowly along the platform, rattled with increasing speed over the points, and settled down to a steady clickety-clack. Signals and signal-boxes, reverberating tunnels and shunting trains gave way to the smoke-blackened backs of terraced houses, their tiny gardens abloom with Monday morning's wash. Daisy stood up to slide open the window and let in the cool morning air.

"M-Miss Dalrymple?"

She swung round. In the open door to the corridor stood a small, skinny girl with gingerish pigtails, wearing a navy blue school uniform coat and hat, and black stockings. She looked hot and bothered and on the edge of tears.

"Belinda! Good gracious heavens!"

"I thought I'd never find you. I thought I'd got on the wrong train, or you weren't . . ." A sob interrupted.

"My dear!" Daisy opened her arms. Belinda flew into them.

A hug and a handkerchief later, when the child was sufficiently restored to calm to start unbuttoning her coat, Daisy's tone changed.

"It's a jolly good job you found me," she said severely, "but what on earth are you doing here in the first place?"

"I ran away," said Belinda in a small voice, her gaze firmly fixed on the button she was fiddling with.

"From school?"

"No, it's the Easter hols. This is my best coat and hat, that's why I'm wearing them."

"So you ran away from . . . ?"

"From Gran. My grandmother."

Her fingers crossed for luck, Daisy prayed it might be the maternal grandmother, of whom she knew nothing. "Mrs. Fletcher?" she asked with foreboding. She groaned beneath her breath as Belinda nodded.

"Granny wouldn't let me go to Deva's house," she said passionately, "or ask her over, or even meet her in the park to play, only because she's Indian. So I decided to go and ask Daddy if I may. Daddy says you mustn't judge someone by where they come from or what they look like or how they talk, 'cause everyone's equal before the law. Anyway, I play with Deva at school, so why shouldn't I at home?"

"I can't imagine," Daisy lied. "But the point is, it was very wicked of you to run away. Your grandmother will be fearfully worried. And what made you think this train would take you to your father?"

"I looked it up in the atlas my other gran and grand-dad gave me for Christmas. Daddy's in Northumberland, and you left that message for him saying you were catching the Flying Scotsman to Scotland today, and they're right next to each other."

"Northumberland's a big county, and Scotland's a whole country. I don't even know whereabouts your father is, and we have no plans to meet."

"Oh." Belinda's eyes, a greener grey than Alec's, were huge in her freckled face (more freckles than Daisy had ever possessed). "Oh dearie, dearie me."

"What *am* I to do with you, for pity's sake?" Daisy's

eyes wandered to the emergency brake pull above the window. She had always wanted an excuse to yank down that red chain. *Penalty for Improper Use Forty Shillings* she read, and came back to earth with a bump. Money—ticket—"How did you get onto the train?"

"I bought a platform ticket from a machine. It's only a penny. I've only got tuppence left of my pocket money, though, 'cause the bus fare was thruppence. The child's fare."

"Child's fare? Of course, thank heaven. I was just thinking I haven't enough money on me to pay your train fare when the ticket-collector comes round."

"I could get off at the next station and go home," said Belinda unhappily.

"This is an express train," Daisy informed her with asperity. "The next station is York. We don't get there till after lunch, and your father—to say nothing of your grandmother—would have my head if I sent you home alone. They may anyway, since it seems to be my telephone call which gave you the idiotic idea of running away."

"I'm awfully, awfully, *awfully* sorry."

"Well, it's no use crying over spilt milk. Cheer up, darling, and take your coat and hat off before you expire from this frightful heat. Tell me about your friend Deva."

"She's got a sari! That's a sort of Indian dress you wrap round you. She wears an ordinary uniform to school every day, but she put it on for our Christmas pageant. It's blue silk with gold stars and gold along the edges. She said I can try it on if I go to her house. I don't see why Granny won't let me. Deva's daddy works for the India Office, so she's perfickly respectable. You'd let me, wouldn't you, Miss Dalrymple?"

"That's beside the point. It's for your grandmother to decide, and she only wants what's best for you."

Belinda sighed. "I wish you'd marry Daddy."

"Mr. Fletcher and I are just friends," Daisy said firmly, hoping her face-powder hid her blushes. She welcomed the interruption of a smart young woman who appeared in the doorway with a sleeping baby in her arms and a little girl in tow.

"Daisy, it is you! I thought I saw you in the station but the crowd was so frightful I couldn't be sure."

"Anne Smythe-Pike—no, of course you're married now. It's ages since we last ran into each other, and you were engaged then."

"Bretton. Mrs. Harold Bretton," said her one-time schoolfellow complacently. At twenty-six, a year older than Daisy, Anne Bretton's pretty face already bore marks of petulance, so it was no surprise when she added in a querulous tone, "Harold is being disagreeable."

"How difficult for you," Daisy said with a sympathetic smile.

"He says children should be seen and not heard, and preferably not seen either, but I want my little darlings with me. I'll join you. You won't mind the children." It was a statement, not a question.

"No, of course not. I see you, too, have succumbed to the heat. The sun shining in doesn't help. Aren't you glad you wore a summer frock?"

"Rather! Except it will probably be freezing in Scotland." Sitting down, the infant in her lap, she gave Daisy's bare head an envious look. "Mother would have forty fits if I took off my hat."

"Mrs. Smythe-Pike is with you?"

"She and Father have a compartment to themselves, because of Father's gout. The whole family's on the train, believe it or not. We're . . . Oh, is this your daughter? No, surely not. She's too old."

Anne's little girl, who had been staring at Belinda, now announced, "I'm five. How old are you?"

"Nine and three quarters. Nearly ten."

"This is Belinda Fletcher, Anne. She's the daughter of a friend."

"How do you do, Mrs. Bretton," Belinda said politely. "What is your little girl's name?"

"Tabitha, dear. How nice, you two can play together." She smiled fondly as the child, clutching her doll, clambered up onto the seat beside Belinda. Anne glanced at Daisy's left hand. "You're not married, then, Daisy? That time we bumped into each other—at the Savoy, wasn't it?—you were engaged, too. Oh! Oh dear, I suppose . . . ?"

"Yes, Michael was killed in the War." Daisy did not elaborate. Anne had never been a close friend, had in fact been regarded as fearfully soppy by Daisy's set. She changed the subject. "Did you say all your family is on the train?"

"That's my bruvver," said Tabitha, pointing at the baby. "He's in my family. He's called Astair."

"After Fred Astaire?" Daisy queried, surprised.

"No, no," Anne assured her. "His name is Alistair. Alistair McGowan Bretton, in honour of my grandfather. He's Grandfather's first direct male descendent. Don't you think he's bound to change his will in Baby's favour?"

"Good heavens, Anne, how can I possibly guess? Surely it depends on who else has claims upon him."

"If only it did," Anne said peevishly, "I'm sure we have a better claim than anyone. The trouble is, Grandfather is frightfully prejudiced. In the first place, he loathes the English, and of course Father is as English as can be, and so is Harold."

"So are you, aren't you? And your children."

"Well, yes, but Mother is Scottish, being his daughter."

"If he—Mr. McGowan, is it?—has left his money to your mother, will it not come to you in time?" Daisy asked.

"To me and Judith, but he hasn't. Hasn't left it to Mother. That's the other thing. Grandfather has left everything to Great-Uncle Albert, even though they haven't spoken to each other for decades, only because he believes in inheritance through the male line."

"Not really! How fearfully Victorian."

"Isn't it?" Anne agreed. "What's more, as they're twins Uncle Albert is just as ancient, and everyone was sure he'd die first."

"Why?"

"He spent most of his life in India, ruining his health with the climate and curries and too many chota pegs—isn't that what they call whisky? Yet Grandfather Alistair is on his deathbed and Uncle Albert's here in this very train, summoned along with the rest of us, *and* the solicitor. The only possible reason for Uncle Albert to go is to gloat over being the survivor. *He* doesn't need the money."

Daisy was beginning to get interested in the ramifications. "Who gets Uncle Albert's money?" she enquired. "His children, I imagine?"

"He has none. He never married. There's a family legend that Grandfather pinched his fiancée, though I don't know if it's true. His own fortune, the one he made in India, dies with him. Would you believe he spent every penny to purchase an annuity just to spite the family?"

"So he'd leave practically nothing."

"That's what it looked like. No one expected him to outlive Grandfather, to inherit Dunston Castle and the family fortune. Hush, Baby," Anne interrupted herself as little Alistair began to whimper. "Don't start fussing again, my little sweetypie doodums. Be good and your great-grandfather will leave you lots of money."

"As he has sent for his lawyer, I should think he might," Daisy said, "since the money would presumably have come to you, or at least to your mother if Albert McGowan had died before Alistair as expected."

"Not at all. It's terribly unfair. The next heir is Uncle Peter, who's the son of their younger sister. She married a Scot, you see, and Uncle Peter was born in Scotland. So were his wife and children, though the Gillespies live in London now. What with that, and there being only one female generation on that side, they get the preference over Grandfather's own . . . Hush!"

The baby wailed. Screwing up his little red face, he hiccuped, and then let loose a full-throated bawl. Daisy tried not to wince too obviously.

"Oh, do be quiet, you horrid little monkey," Anne snapped at her sweetypie doodums. "If you're going to be naughty, you'll have to go to Nanny. You too, Tabitha. Come along."

"No!" screeched Tabitha. "I'm being good. I want to stay with B'linda."

"She really is being good," Belinda said gravely. "I'll look after her for you, Mrs. Bretton. If Miss Dalrymple doesn't mind."

"Not at all." Daisy swallowed a sigh. What had happened to her long, dull, but peaceful journey?

2

"Where's my wife?"

The man at the open doorway of the compartment wore a pearl grey lounge suit of obvious Savile Row cut and a club tie with a rather too flashy gold pin. His thin, fair hair was pomaded back from a prematurely receding hairline. He looked hot enough to begin steaming at the ears any moment. Pitying him for being too gentlemanly to take off his jacket, or even loosen his tie, Daisy almost forgave the scowl he bent upon her.

"Where is she?" he demanded impatiently. "That's my daughter. Where's my wife?"

"I'm being *good,* Daddy," Tabitha wailed. He ignored her.

"You must be Mr. Bretton," Daisy said, her tone frigid. "I'm Daisy Dalrymple. I was at school with Anne. How do you do?"

He nodded an ungracious acknowledgement. "Where . . ." he began again, then thought better of it. "Oh lord, I beg your pardon," he said, flashing her a weak smile. "The Honourable Miss Dalrymple? Anne mentioned spotting you at King's Cross. My humble apologies for my curtness, but honestly, what with one thing and another, it's enough to try the patience of a saint."

"Do come in and sit down." She spoke with slightly less coolness, but on first acquaintance she didn't much care for Harold Bretton. "I expect Anne will be back any minute. She took the baby to his nanny, in third class, I presume. My young friend Belinda Fletcher offered to take care of Tabitha for her."

"How do you do, sir," said Belinda. Daisy was proud of her manners, particularly as Tabitha, used to being dismissed and determined not to be parted from her, was clinging like grim death around her neck.

Belinda might as well not have spoken for all the notice Bretton took of her. "You're going to Scotland?" he asked Daisy with the air of a man prepared to make polite small talk though his mind was on more important matters.

"Yes, I have a job to do near Roslin."

"A job?" He stared, his protuberant blue eyes shocked. "You work?"

"I'm a writer," Daisy said shortly. "What do you do?"

"Me? Oh, I, er, I help my father-in-law run the jolly old family acres in Kent. At least, he'd like me to," Bretton corrected himself in a burst of candour, "but it's a mug's game if you ask me. Since the War, there's no money in farming. Not at all what I expected when I married Anne. We'll all be on our uppers if things don't look up."

It really was very odd, Daisy thought, the way the most unlikely people insisted on confiding in her. "My cousin, the present Lord Dalrymple, seems to be doing reasonably well with Fairacres," she said.

"Actually, the truth of the matter is Smythe-Pike's let the estate go to rack and ruin," the disillusioned son-in-law said resentfully. "All he ever cared for was his huntin', shootin', and fishin', though his gout's put a stop to all that, which doesn't help his temper, I can tell you. It's only cash will save the place now, a big win on the gee-gees or Anne's grandfather coming round."

"Anne told me you hope Mr. McGowan will relent in favour of your son."

"The old skinflint! Never spends a penny where a farthing'll serve, so there must be plenty to go around, but what does he do? Leaves the lot to Great-Uncle Albert, who's already rolling in it. I must say Albert knows how to live," Bretton said with envy and grudging admiration. "He won't loan a fellow a fiver, let alone anything useful, but it's nothing but the best for him, no expense spared. Though how much joy he gets of it with his dyspepsia is another matter."

"I gather Albert McGowan's in a parlous state of health."

"Ha! He's been at death's door since before I married Anne. Still, even if he had popped off, it wouldn't have done *us* any good. Old Alistair's next heir is Anne's uncle, that crook Peter Gillespie."

"Crook?" Daisy pricked up her ears.

"Inherited a thriving boot factory—rather infra dig, of course, but a real money-spinner—and he goes and kills the goose that laid the golden eggs by selling shoddy boots to the Army in wartime. They couldn't prove it was deliberate fraud. He wasn't convicted, but the business had to pay enormous fines and it went under."

"Does Alistair McGowan know?"

"Oh yes, Smythe-Pike—Anne's father—made sure of that! Would you believe it, the old miser apparently considered it praiseworthy to have saved money by buying the cheapest leather available. If that didn't make him change his will, I don't know what would. I suppose if we can't talk Alistair into providing for his great-grandson, we'll have to tackle Albert next."

Daisy was dying to find out who was Uncle Albert's present heir. Before she could ask, a sandy-haired young man in light tweeds appeared in the open doorway.

"Tackle Uncle Albert?" he said. "Rather you than me, old bean. His man announced in no uncertain terms that the old curmudgeon doesn't want to see hide nor hair of any of us. I just walked past his compartment and he's got the blinds drawn. We'll get nowhere if we set the ogre's back up. Hello there, Tabby."

" 'Lo, Uncle Jemmy. Not Tabby, Tabiffa."

"Right-ho." He glanced at Daisy with a frown, of puzzlement rather than annoyance. "Excuse me for butting in, I assumed Bretton was talking to one of the family."

"This is Jeremy Gillespie, Anne's cousin," Bretton explained to her. "Miss Dalrymple is a friend of Anne's, Gillespie. She's on the same train by sheer coincidence."

"Oh, I see. I *thought* I knew all the relatives, except Aunt-Geraldine-who-ran-away, of course, and you're much too young and pretty to be her." He studied her with an appraising eye, and gave her a smile of approval. "How d'ye do, Miss Dalrymple. I don't know how it is, but my cousin Anne—second cousin, by the way—seems to be friends with all the prettiest girls."

Daisy smiled back. He was quite good-looking in a sturdy, sandy, Scottish way, and older than she had thought at first sight. In his early thirties, she thought, about the same as Harold Bretton, who looked older because of the thinning hair.

"You make a point of meeting Anne's friends, Mr. Gillespie?" she teased.

"As many as possible," he said with an exaggerated leer. "But please, the name's Jeremy."

"Where have you left Mattie?" Bretton enquired nastily.

Jeremy Gillespie flushed. "She's with Ray and Judith and Kitty. My wife Matilda, Miss Dalrymple," he said, rueful now, "being great with child, as they say in the Bible, tends to stay where she's put."

"How fortunate for you," said Daisy sweetly, her opinion of Gillespie taking a nose-dive.

His point made, Bretton dropped the subject. "How is Raymond?" he asked.

"Judith's calmed him down. Your sis-in-law has a way with the poor chap, but unless one of the great-uncles comes through, they haven't a hope in Hades of getting married."

Raymond and Judith—Daisy had heard those names recently. Oh yes, the shell-shock victim. And "Judith Smythe-Pike, of course, Anne's sister. She was a couple of forms below me at school."

Gillespie laughed. "If you remember Judith as a scrubby schoolgirl in a gym tunic, you'll never recognize her. She's a flapper now, the epitome of the bright young thing, all drawl and 'darling.' "

"And 'too, too frightfully boring,' " added a scornful young voice, "and she smokes gaspers when Uncle Desmond's not around."

A plump, plain girl of about fifteen, the newcomer had Jeremy Gillespie's sandy colouring. She wore a buttercup yellow summer frock that suited her not at all, and a bottle green school-uniform hat. Her direct, almost challenging hazel eyes went straight to Daisy. "Hallo, are you a friend of Jeremy's?"

"No!" said Daisy with more emphasis than she intended. "I'm a friend of Anne Bretton's."

"My little sister, Kitty," Gillespie said condescendingly. "With any luck she'll learn a few manners before she leaves school. This is Miss Dalrymple, Kitten."

"Don't call me Kitten!"

"Then pull in your claws."

Pulling a face at her brother, Kitty Gillespie turned her back on him. "Howjerdo, Miss Dalrymple," she said rapidly, then addressed Bretton. "Cousin Harold, Daddy told me to find you. He wants to talk to you about Great-Uncle Albert's will."

"A fat lot of good that'll do him. I haven't the foggiest who's his heir, any more than anyone else." Nonetheless, Bretton departed.

Kitty at once took his seat. "Hallo, young Tabiffa. Who is your friend?"

"It's B'linda." Tabitha, relaxing as her father left, now moved closer to Kitty and clutched her arm. "Have you got any sweeties?"

"Not here. They're in my coat pocket." She and Belinda regarded each other with interest. "Are you traveling with Miss Dalrymple?" Kitty wanted to know.

"Yes," said Belinda guardedly. "Sort of."

"What do you mean?"

"Don't be a Nosey Parker," Jeremy Gillespie advised her.

"It's good practice. I'll have to be nosy when I'm a reporter."

"Ha! You know perfectly well the parents will never let you get a job."

"I'll probably have to, since it looks as if Gruncle Alistair is going to die before Gruncle Albert," Kitty pointed out. "Anyway, I'm not like you. I *want* to work."

"Good for you," said Daisy, who had listened with

amusement to the would-be ladykiller squabbling with his little sister.

He saw her amusement and flushed. It must be difficult carrying on clandestine flirtations when his fair skin coloured so readily. "I'd better go and see what that ass Bretton and the pater are saying to each other," he said with dignity, and he went off.

Kitty turned eagerly to Daisy. "You don't think it's wrong for a lady to work, do you, Miss Dalrymple?"

"I work myself. I write, as you want to, but for magazines, not newspapers. I'm a journalist rather than a reporter."

"I wouldn't mind that. Or I might be a nurse, then I could help Judith take care of my brother Raymond. He's got shell-shock, you see, from the War, so he can't get a decent job, and Judith's a silly flapper, with no idea how to do anything practical. But he's in love with her so I think he'll be happiest if they get married, don't you?"

"Perhaps," Daisy said cautiously.

"I do want him to be happy. He's my best brother by miles. He's the nearest my age, though he's ten years older than me, and he never bossed me around or teased me like Jeremy and George. Well, hardly ever. Not," she hastened to add, "that I'm not sorry George died in the War."

Daisy assured her she quite understood. "My brother used to tease, and try to boss me," she said, "but I still miss him frightfully."

"He was killed in the War, too? I can't exactly say I *miss* George," Kitty candidly admitted.

"I miss my Mummy sometimes," Belinda said in a woebegone little voice. "She died of flu when I was four."

"So did my father," Daisy told her, pushing up the

folding arm-rest and patting the seat at her side. Belinda slipped across and nestled beside her. "In the flu epidemic, that is, not when I was four. But what a fearfully depressing subject. Tell me, Kitty, what makes you think you'd like to be a reporter?"

"I get jolly good marks in English, and writing a book would take much too long. I don't really care what I do, though, as long as it's interesting. I wish I was a man, they can do anything."

"Just about."

"Jeremy works for a shipping company. He wanted to stop at the end of the War—he has flat feet so he couldn't be a soldier—and he's still mad as fire that he has to go on working because Daddy lost lots of money. *I* don't mind. I think it'll be fun being a reporter." Turning to Belinda, she asked in a stern tone more suited to a cross-examining barrister than a newshound, "What did you mean when you said you're *sort of* traveling with Miss Dalrymple?"

"I stowed away," Belinda confessed.

Kitty gawked. "Golly," she breathed, "did you really? Tell me all about it!" She swung over to sit next to Belinda.

Left alone on the opposite seat, Tabitha opened her mouth wide to protest. A preliminary squawk was cut short when her mother returned, sans Baby, to Daisy's relief.

"Sorry I've been so long," Anne apologised. "Mother saw me pass and called me in. She agrees Grandfather's most likely to bequeath the money directly to Baby, but Father's being difficult. He wants to try to talk Grandfather into leaving it to Mother. Harold says if we don't all try for the same result, we won't get anywhere."

"I should think he's right as far as Alistair McGowan

is concerned," Daisy agreed. "The baby's the only new factor, after all. But if he won't change his will in his namesake's favour, Albert might be more easily persuaded to leave at least part of the family fortune to your mother rather than your son. A niece is closer han a great-great-nephew."

'Oh, Uncle Albert! I don't believe the selfish beast has the slightest spark of family feeling. Uncle Peter's found out he's leaving the lot to that ghastly little Indian. All very well when it was nothing but his flat and his bits and pieces—though what a savage wants with a London flat is beyond me—but to let a rank outsider get his grubby hands on the McGowan fortune is more than a bit thick!"

Abandoning her tête-à-tête with Kitty, Belinda turned with an indignant protest obviously hovering on her lips. Daisy glared her to silence and said hastily, "The Indians aren't exactly savages, Anne. They were writing books and building cities when our ancestors lived in mud huts and painted themselves with woad."

"Even if this Chandra Jagai person had written a hundred books, he has no right to our money. What is it, darling?" she asked as Tabitha tugged on her arm.

"I need to tinkle, Mummy," demanded the little girl in an urgent whisper. "Now."

"Oh botheration! Well, we must go anyway. My mother wants to show off Tabitha to Aunt Enid and Mattie," she explained to Daisy, "while Father and Harold are in confab with Uncle Peter and Jeremy."

As Anne and Tabitha departed, a voice was heard calling "Tickets, please." Daisy scrabbled in her handbag for her ticket, and took out her purse to pay Belinda's fare.

"I'm really sorry, Miss Dalrymple," Belinda said guiltily, "but Daddy will pay you back." She heaved a sigh. "I expect I shan't get any pocket money for *years* and *years.*"

"Golly, how frightful!" said Kitty. "I'll tell you what, I'll give you some of my sweets and if you hoard them p'raps you can make them last for a while. Not a whole year, though."

"Gosh, you are a brick!"

"I can always buy some more. Daddy will always give me half a crown if I ask, just to make me go away. Everyone talks about not having any money but . . . Hallo, Ray. Oh, you've brought my ticket, jolly good. I was about to dash back to Mummy to get it."

"She sent me after you."

The tall young man was darker than his brother and sister, his hair a decided brown rather than sandy. Daisy thought he'd be better looking than Jeremy if he wasn't so painfully thin, almost gaunt. He at least had bowed to the interior climate of the train: he was in his shirtsleeves, the cuffs rolled up to his elbows, his tie discarded. Those who had suffered in the trenches tended either to cling more tightly to the conventions or to consider them utterly irrelevant.

Raymond Gillespie had not dispensed with manners. With a charming, hopeful-small-boy smile, he said to Daisy, "Do you mind if we come in for a minute? The ticket-man's coming and we're rather in his way."

"Not at all."

"I'm Raymond Gillespie, and if you're Miss Dalrymple, as I assume, I gather you already know Judith." As he spoke, he stood aside and Anne's sister entered the compartment.

Judith Smythe-Pike had taken off her hat, revealing shingled ash-blond hair like a dandelion puff. Her plucked eyebrows were thin, pencilled lines, her lashes darkened, lengthened, and thickened with mascara.

Her mouth was a scarlet bow against her powder-white face, touched with rouge at the cheekbones. Though not gaunt like Raymond, she was boyishly slender, flat front and back as fashion demanded. Her lilac silk-chiffon frock hung straight from shoulder to hem as its designer intended, the line scarcely indented by the darker purple belt about her nonexistent hips.

The belt matched the embroidery at the neckline. An expensive frock, Daisy noted. As Kitty had said, everyone talked about not having any money but . . .

"Hallo, Judith," Daisy said as the bright young thing subsided languidly onto the seat opposite her. "I wouldn't have recognized you."

"I should jolly well hope not," Judith drawled. "Let's see, you stayed into the upper sixth, didn't you? When you left school, I must have been in the fifth form, and covered with spots. Too, too tiresome."

"I remember the spots," Raymond said reminiscently.

Judith flashed him a glance full of sparkling mischief and affection. "As a gentleman, darling, you are honour bound to forget them. That's the sort of thing that gives marriage between cousins a bad name."

"Second cousins," said Kitty. "Ray, this is my new friend Belinda. Guess what, she's a stowaway!"

"Tickets, please." The inspector stepped in, a small man with a fierce cavalry mustache to complement his quasi-military railway uniform. "What's this I hear about a stowaway?" he asked sternly.

Belinda looked frightened. Daisy took her hand in a comforting clasp and said, "My young friend bought a platform ticket and somehow didn't manage to get off the train in time. I shall pay for her ticket, of course."

"Come to see you off, did she, miss? Well, it happens

now and then, though not half as often as it's claimed." He winked as he took out his pad of forms and book of fare prices. "York or Edinburgh?"

"Edinburgh, single, child's fare." She would worry about paying Belinda's return fare if and when she could not get hold of Alec. "Does the train stop long enough at York for me to make a telephone call or send a cable to her grandmother?" she asked as he made out a ticket for Belinda.

"Six minutes, miss. Even if the exchange put you through quick, you'd be cutting it fine. If you was to write down a cable and give me the money, I'll see it's sent off all right and tight. I get off at York."

"Thank you, that would be very kind." Daisy was glad of an excuse not to 'phone Mrs. Fletcher.

"Right-oh, miss, I'll come back for it when I'm done with me round." He clipped their tickets and backed out into the corridor. "Want the door left open for air, do you? This heat's a bit much, innit? They'll be taking orders for morning coffee soon, but you can always ask for lemon-squash instead." He saluted and disappeared.

"If I hadn't found you, Miss Dalrymple," Belinda said timorously, "could the inspector have arrested me and put me in prison for not having a ticket?"

"That I could, young lady!" Unexpectedly reappearing, the man stuck his head in. "So mind you don't get up to such-like tricks again."

"I won't," the child promised with a shudder.

For the present, Daisy decided, it was just as well if Belinda believed in the railway official's powers of summary arrest and imprisonment.

3

After lemon-squash all round, Kitty took Belinda off to find her sweets and a book to borrow. Judith and Raymond stayed in Daisy's compartment with her.

"I expect Anne told you why we're all traipsing up to Scotland," Judith said. "It's a frightful bore. Dunston Castle is a positive mausoleum, and I don't imagine there's the least chance of Grandfather changing his will."

"If he does," said Raymond, "he ought to change it in poor Aunt Julia's favour. She's suffered the mausoleum and his filthy temper for a lifetime—my lifetime, anyway—and she deserves a comfortable old age. Great-Uncle Alistair doesn't owe the rest of us anything."

"But do stop saying so to Daddy and Uncle Peter, darling. It's bad for their blood pressure. Aunt Julia is Uncle Peter's sister, Daisy. The poor old thing has been Grandfather's housekeeper and general skivvy forever, and now I suppose his nurse as well, since he's far too stingy to hire one. Anyone would think he intended to take every penny he's ever saved with him to the grave."

"Perhaps we can talk Uncle Albert into doing something for her," Raymond proposed, "even if he loathes and despises the rest of us."

"He's about as unlikely to do that as to leave the lot to Aunt-Geraldine-who-ran-away."

Daisy gave up her noble effort to restrain her curiosity. "Jeremy mentioned Aunt-Geraldine-who-ran-away," she said. "Where does she fit in?"

"She's Mummy's younger sister," Judith told her.

"Great-Uncle Alistair's younger daughter," Raymond amplified. "When Aunt Amelia married, Geraldine foresaw being stuck in the mausoleum looking after her father for life, so she hopped it—and who can blame her? No one's heard from her since. That's how her cousin, my Aunt Julia, got stuck with the job. Please refer to family tree in frontispiece."

"I need to," said Daisy, laughing. "It's all the honorary aunts and uncles who complicate matters. My family's the same. The 'aunt' who remembered me in her will was actually some sort of second or third cousin several times removed. I never did work it out exactly."

"That's the kind of aunt we need if we're ever to get married," Judith said enviously.

"Oh, it's not enough to live on. I write for a living."

Judith was distinctly taken aback. "You work? But I thought at school . . . That is, isn't your father a peer?"

"He was. A cousin inherited the title and Fairacres. I could live with him, or with my mother in the Dower House, but I decided I'd rather be independent. During the War, after I left school, I worked in a hospital office. It wasn't bad, so later I took typing and shorthand classes, but I must admit I hated being a stenographer. Then I helped my friend Lucy in her photography studio. I still give her a hand when she needs me, but mostly I write magazine articles."

"Gosh! And Lady Dalrymple doesn't mind?"

"Mother can't stop me," Daisy said firmly.

"I bet Daddy would find a way to stop me." Judith sounded almost wistful.

Raymond clutched her hand. "There's no need for you to work," he said in a harsh voice. His face was pale. "I'm almost well. I'll soon be able to get a decent job."

"If only you'd try in the country, darling. The city noises are not good for you."

"But I couldn't earn as much, and besides, you loathe the country. I've heard you say it often enough."

"Darling, that's just something one says. I was brought up in the country and I can easily turn back into a tweeds-and-pearls type just like Mummy."

"I won't have you making sacrifices for me!" he cried.

"You're hurting my hand, darling," Judith said softly.

He let go at once. "I'm sorry I'm sorry I'm sorry. Oh God, I'm sorry."

His eyes were screwed shut and he was breathing very fast and shallowly. Daisy, trying to pretend to be suddenly fascinated by the view outside, was afraid he was going to cry. From the corner of her eye, she saw Judith put her arms around him and kiss him full on the mouth. He clung to her, his head bowed to rest his forehead on her shoulder.

After a moment, he said on a long, shuddering breath, "I'm all right now."

"That's good," she said lightly. "I don't suppose my lipstick is." She stood up and turned to the mirror to repair the damage.

"Ah, there you are, Raymond." The short, portly man in the doorway had a face like a sulky bulldog, incongruously adorned with a bristling soup-strainer mustache which belonged to some other breed of dog. The mustache was russet-red, whereas his hair was that indeterminate salt-and-pepperish shade to which sandy hair tends to fade with age. Peter Gillespie, Daisy guessed, the would-be war profiteer. He looked uncomfortable in his too-new tweeds, the townsman making concessions to a country visit.

Raymond stood up. "Exactly, sir. Here I am."

"Sit down, sit down, my boy. You don't look at all well."

In the mirror, Daisy saw Judith's scarlet lips tighten. Catching Daisy's eye, she raised her eyebrows and rolled her eyes in exasperation. "Raymond is perfectly well, Uncle Peter," she said, turning. "Hallo, Daddy. Where are you two off to then? Going to beard the lion in his den?"

Over Gillespie *père's* shoulder loomed a florid face with silver-white hair, a beak of a nose, and a sweeping white cavalry mustache which put the other's rusty brush to shame. Daisy vaguely recognized it from school Open Days. Desmond Smythe-Pike was a large man, as corpulent as his wife's cousin but solid rather than flabby. He tended to speak as if addressing foxhounds in full cry.

"Lion? Stuff and nonsense! Your Great-Uncle Albert's no more dangerous than a badger in its sett, Judith, but we're not ready to sick the terriers onto him yet. No, Gillespie and I are going to consult old Alistair's solicitor, Braeburn. He's in the next compartment, between this and Albert's."

"You're hoping he'll tell you Great-Uncle Alistair's plans, sir?" Raymond asked.

His father answered. "That's part of it."

"But we also want to know," Smythe-Pike barked, "what are the chances of shooting down Albert's will."

"Then you'd better keep your voice down when you get next door, Daddy," Judith advised pertly. "Contesting a will is hardly a respectful thing to do and won't endear you to the old gentleman."

"Bah!" With a ferocious scowl, Smythe-Pike limped off down the corridor, leaning heavily on his silver-headed cane. In his aged tweed shooting jacket and knickerbockers, he was the image of the gouty country squire.

"It's for you children we're going to all this trouble," Peter Gillespie said, belligerent yet defensive. Daisy imagined that was the attitude he had taken when charged with defrauding the government. He scurried off after his cousin's forceful husband.

A moment later, the door of the next compartment slammed shut, privacy being more important than comfort for their business. The rumble of Smythe-Pike's voice came through the wall, but no words were distinguishable.

"Amazing," said Judith. "Daddy must be whispering."

"Oh blast," said Kitty, "the chocolate's melted. Look, it's all squishy. We could scoop it up with our fingers, but Mummy will be livid if I get it on my frock."

"I don't think Miss Dalrymple would be livid, but I haven't got any other clothes with me," Belinda said regretfully. "I didn't know it would take so long to get to Scotland."

"She's nice, isn't she, your Miss Dalrymple? Was she a friend of your mother's?"

"No, she's Daddy's friend."

"Gosh, are they in love?"

"I don't know," Belinda admitted. "When I said I wished she'd marry him, she said they're just friends, but her face went all pink."

"She might just have been embarrassed," said Kitty with all the worldly wisdom of fifteen years. "You shouldn't say things like that. We'd better have aniseed balls or liquorice bootlaces instead of the choc. Or there's Dolly Mixture. Which d'you like best?"

"Dolly Mixture, please. They last longest." She held out her cupped hands and Kitty filled them with the tiny sweeties, pink and orange and yellow, white and red and brown, all different shapes, some hard and some soft. "Do they let you eat sweets at school?"

"Only on Saturdays. It's a boarding school."

Belinda was fascinated. Popping Dolly Mixtures into her mouth, one by one, she plied her new friend with questions, until a small, thin woman came in. She had greying hair, elaborately marcelled, and she looked cross.

"Kitty, you're not eating sweets again! How do you expect ever to have a decent figure?"

"I don't care. I'm not going to be a deb, after all. I'm going to work and make pots of money. Anyway," she went on hastily as her mother frowned, "I'm giving half . . . most of my sweets to Belinda. This is Belinda, Mummy."

"I'd better go," Belinda said even more hastily as the frown turned on her. "Miss Dalrymple must be wondering where I am."

"Here." Kitty thrust the paper bag of sweets into her hands. "If I don't see you before, let's sit together at lunch."

"If I can." Making her escape, Belinda worried about lunch. She was already costing Miss Dalrymple an awful lot of money but she had a feeling even such a nice grown-up would not let her eat liquorice instead of a good, nourishing meal.

She glanced into the next compartment. Kitty's brother Jeremy was there, with a lady who was either very fat or going to have a baby. She was crying. Tabitha's mummy and daddy were there, too, but not Tabitha, so Belinda went on.

As she passed she heard one of the gentlemen say loudly, "Albert McGowan is a rotten blighter who's dashed well letting the side down."

"Calm down, Bretton," said the other. "Slanging the old ba . . . boy won't get us anywhere. We need to put our heads together and decide what to do." The noise of the train cut off his voice as Belinda moved on.

The door of the next compartment was shut, the blinds pulled down; then there was one with strangers in it. After that came Miss Dalrymple's. Kitty's other brother, the nice one, Raymond, was still there with Judith, the lady he wanted to marry. There was an old lady, too, a plump, comfortable sort of old lady who reminded Belinda of Granny.

She bit her lip. Granny must be awfully upset, wondering where she had got to. She shouldn't have run away—but Kitty said it was a simply ripping adventure, and some bits were exciting and fun.

The old lady was talking. "Father always was unreasonable," she said, "but Uncle Albert is utterly unnatural, leaving everything to a stranger. Desmond is furious. You know how your father is, Judith, always liable to fly off the handle even at the best of times." She went on about Desmond's temper.

Belinda didn't like to interrupt by going in. As she hesitated in the corridor, Miss Dalrymple saw her and smiled. Belinda pointed forward to indicate she was going to the lavatory at the end of the coach. Miss Dalrymple nodded.

The next compartment had its door shut but its blinds up. The three men in it all looked hot and angry. Belinda wondered if one of them was Judith's bad-tempered father. The one nearest the door had a red mustache almost the same colour as his face. Next to him, by the window, was a stringy man in gold-rimmed glasses with a long, thin neck and a sticking-out Adam's apple. He was bald as a coot and he kept wiping his glistening head with a large white handkerchief. Opposite sat a large man with a white mustache and a purple face with a big nose. Belinda could hear him right through the closed door.

"I don't care if he is in the next compartment," he roared. "There must be a law to stop a bloody fool chucking away his ancestors' wealth on a demned native!"

The bald man shook his head and said something inaudible. Belinda moved on. Everyone was angry with Uncle Albert McGowan for leaving his money to an Indian, though she couldn't see why he shouldn't if he wanted to. She hadn't understood everything she had heard, but it sounded as if they were all afraid even to go and talk to Mr. McGowan because he said he didn't want to see them. He must be a real ogre.

To her disappointment, the next door was closed and the blinds down. She went to the lavatory, then started back to rejoin Miss Dalrymple.

In front of her, a small man in black came out of Mr. McGowan's compartment. Turning back, he gave a sort of stiff little bow and said, "Very good, sir. I shall convey your message to Dr. Jagai."

He slid the door shut. Belinda stepped back into the carriage-end vestibule to let him pass. As she set off again, the train jolted, clattering over some points, and she saw the door slide back an inch. The man in black hadn't closed it far enough to latch properly.

Belinda promptly applied her eye to the gap. Mr. McGowan looked more like a goblin than an ogre, she decided. She must remember to tell Kitty he ought to be called Mr. McGoblin. His long, narrow face was yellowish and covered with hundreds and hundreds of wrinkles. His yellowish scalp showed through lank strands of yellow-grey hair, but his eyebrows were even bushier than Daddy's. He sat hunched in the corner, a rug over his legs though the window was shut and stifling hot air wafted through the crack onto Belinda's face.

It was hard to tell with all those wrinkles, but she thought he looked bored and miserable. She felt sorry for him. It must be horrid having everyone hate him, even if it was his own fault.

Belinda would have liked to talk to him about India. What a pity he was an ogre! She was about to leave her peephole when the train rattled over another set of points and to her horror the door slid all the way open.

4

"Ha!" snapped the goblin in a far from feeble voice. "Who're you, hey? A Gillespie? A Smythe-Pike? A Briton, or whatever the fellow calls himself?"

"I'm a Fletcher," Belinda squeaked.

"Not family?"

"No, sir."

"Good. Come in, then, Miss Fletcher, and close the door before I catch my death. There's a terrible draught. Come in, come in, I don't bite. At least, not pretty little girls."

He didn't look strong enough to kidnap her, Belinda thought. Besides, he couldn't very well on a moving train. "I'll come in," she temporized, "if I can put one of the blinds up, so if Miss Dalrymple comes looking she can see me."

"Very well, very well," he grumbled. "Anything for company that doesn't come to sponge. This Dalrymple woman, she's your governess?"

"No, just a friend. I don't have a governess, I go to school." Stepping in, Belinda wrestled the door shut and let up a blind. "Are you Mr. Albert McGowan, sir?" she asked.

"That's right. Talking about me, are they, hey?" He

laughed, a peculiar, creaky sound. "And not a good word among 'em, I'll be bound."

Uncertain how to answer, she proffered her bag of sweeties. "Would you like some aniseed balls?"

"No, thank you, Miss Fletcher. I am obliged to watch what I eat or suffer appalling consequences. Do you play chess?"

"Sort of. Daddy's taught me the moves. But I'm not very good."

Pale, washed-out eyes peered at her from under the shaggy brows. He nodded. "I like an honest woman. Perhaps we'd better stick to draughts, then, Miss Fletcher. Can you climb up and get down my camp-stool to put the board on?"

Standing on the seat, Belinda took down the green canvas stool from the rack. She opened it and set it on the floor in front of him, and he laid on it the traveling chequer-board he had had on his knees. The pieces were round and flat like draughts counters, with inlaid pictures of chessmen so you could play either game. They had little holes in their tops, and pegs underneath to fit into each other or the holes in the board.

"Gosh, what a spiffing set," said Belinda, helping him lay out the men.

"Spiffing?" His hands were like claws, bony, with long yellow nails, the backs blotchy. They trembled slightly as he handled the pieces.

"I used to say topping, but Miss Dalrymple says spiffing. It means wonderful."

"You like it, hey? Ivory and ebony it is, and other woods I forget the names of. I had it specially made for me in India."

"I've got an Indian friend at school. Would you,

could you *please*, tell me about India? Deva's just a girl like me, and she doesn't remember much."

So as they played, he told her about playing chess—with this very set—with a maharajah in a howdah on an elephant, on the way to a tiger hunt in the jungle. He described hot blue skies, and cool marble fountains, and temples, and festivals where gleaming, glittering gods, garlanded with marigolds, paraded through streets smelling of aromatic spices. Belinda forgot to take her turn. Soon she gave up even trying to play.

At the end of a story about a temple monkey which stole his watch right out of his waistcoat pocket, Mr. McGowan said firmly, "That's enough now. I don't want you suffering from intellectual indigestion. The pains of the real thing are bad enough."

Belinda wasn't sure what he meant, but there was one more thing she really wanted to know. "Couldn't you just please tell me about the Indian you've left your money to in your will?"

"Little busybody," he growled, but his eyes twinkled at her. "So they've found out, have they? That must have set the cat among the pigeons."

"Rather! They're awfully angry, 'cause of him being Indian and 'cause of it being the family's money."

"Bah! It belongs to that old miser, my brother Alistair, now, and it'll be mine when he pops off the hooks. I'll do with it as I please. Let them earn their own. Now who's this, hey?" he went on, glancing towards the corridor. "One of 'em come to try to change my mind?"

"No, it's my Miss Dalrymple. Oh dear, I've been gone an awfully long time," Belinda said guiltily.

Peering through the window, Daisy wondered what on earth the child was doing in there with the misanthrope. Good gracious, it looked as if they had been playing a game together! She opened the door.

"Come in," he said at once, glaring at her beneath beetling brows. "Come in, don't stand there letting the draught in. So you're Miss Fletcher's friend, hey?"

'Miss Dalrymple, this is Mr. McGowan. Mr. *Albert* McGowan, not Alistair. He's nice."

Daisy pulled the door to behind her. "How do you do, Mr. McGowan. I must apologize for this young imp's intrusion."

"Not at all, not at all. It's been a pleasure making Miss Fletcher's acquaintance. Won't you sit down, young lady? I don't dislike company, only that tribe of would-be spongers I'm forced to acknowledge as relatives."

With a smile, Daisy returned frankness for frankness. "They believe you *don't* acknowledge them, sir."

He cackled. "As little as possible," he admitted. "The way they treated me when I was in India. No 'Dear Uncle Albert, How's life and is there anything we can send out to make it easier?' They didn't even bother to notify me of weddings and births and such."

"The mean beasts!" Belinda said indignantly.

"Their loss, my dear. I didn't have to send wedding and christening presents. Of course, when I came home they found out I wasn't the indigent younger brother any longer."

"I suppose they camped on your doorstep," said Daisy.

"Descended like a flock of vultures. All of a sudden I was 'dearest Uncle,' " he spat out, his lined face twisted. "That was when I decided I wasn't going to leave much, and what I did leave was not going to my beloved family."

"Mr. McGowan was just going to tell me about the Indian who's going to get it all," said Belinda.

"I was, was I?" The old man sounded amused. "I don't remember agreeing."

"Please, sir."

"Oh, as you please. It all started a long, long time ago. I fell in love with an Indian girl, which wasn't as easy as you might think, for they keep their women shut up out of sight. But she was the daughter of a man who had adopted many English ways and among his friends she went unveiled."

"Was she very beautiful?" Belinda asked, all agog.

"Very beautiful, and charming, and intelligent, too. Just as my little friend Miss Fletcher will be when she grows up."

"Did you marry her?"

Daisy frowned at this impertinence, but McGowan was unoffended. He sighed.

"No, my dear, I did not. For a start, I was more than twice her age. Still more important, life is very difficult for Asian women married to white men. Belonging to neither side they are despised by both, and I could not allow her to suffer so, though she and her father were willing. So she was married to one of her own, a good enough fellow. They had one child, a boy. I was invited to be his godfather, or as near as their religion comes to that office. Though they prayed for more children, perhaps it is as well their prayers were not answered. He was five when his parents and many of his relatives died in a typhoid epidemic."

"Poor little boy," Belinda cried, wide eyes filling with tears. She held on tight to Daisy's hand, and Daisy knew she was thinking of her own mother.

"Not so poor," said Albert McGowan dryly. "I took him into my house, and when he was seven I sent him to school in Scotland. He did well, went on to university, and he has just finished his medical training. He's a houseman now at St. Thomas's Hospital in London. He is my heir."

"Naturally," Daisy approved.

"I set aside funds enough to see him through his education and to purchase a partnership in a medical practice when he's ready. I see no reason to change my Last Will and Testament merely because my penny-pinching brother Alistair seems to be about to pop off before me after all! Chandra Jagai is . . . Where is the boy?" he interrupted himself fretfully. "I told Weekes I want to see him."

Daisy was afraid Belinda's visit, however welcome, had tired him. He was very old, eighty at least she thought, since Peter Gillespie, his younger sister's son, was in his fifties. She was about to take leave of him when the door slid open a few inches and a round, dark, serious face appeared.

"Sir? Weekes told me . . . Oh, I beg your pardon, you have company."

Chandra Jagai spoke English with a slight Lowland Scots accent. Only the faintest hint of a foreign lilt suggested it was not his native tongue. A stocky man in his mid-twenties, he was neatly dressed in a dark suit, buff waistcoat, dazzlingly white shirt, and maroon tie. Catching Belinda's disappointed look, Daisy smiled. She recalled her own disillusionment when Alec took her to the Cathay for dinner and the Chinese proprietor wore tails and spoke with a Cockney accent.

"Come in, my boy, come in and shut the door." McGowan raised his bushy eyebrows at Daisy and she nodded. "Miss Dalrymple, Miss Fletcher, allow me to introduce Dr. Jagai."

After an exchange of courtesies, Daisy said, "We'll

leave you to your business, gentlemen. Come, Belinda."

"Thank you very much for the stories, sir," said Belinda, "and the game, and everything."

"Not at all, young lady. Come back and have tea with me this afternoon at half past four and we'll see if I can come up with some more stories. Make sure you're on time, now, I have to eat at regular intervals. And take this, my dear." He folded the chequer-board with the men inside, fumblingly fastened the little brass catch, and handed it to her. "It's yours. I shan't be taking many more journeys."

"Golly, thanks! And I'd love to come to tea. May I, Miss Dalrymple?"

Seeing no harm in the unlikely friendship, Daisy assented—then wondered what Mrs. Fletcher would say if she found out.

Belinda impulsively kissed the old man's wrinkled cheek. "Off with you, baggage!" he said, beaming. "And off with your jacket, Chandra," he was saying as Daisy closed the door after Belinda. "I know your blood has grown accustomed to Scottish temperatures."

"He's *not* an ogre," said Belinda. "I like him, don't you?"

"Yes, but I can imagine him being quite ogreish to people he dislikes!"

"P'raps. What's indigent mean?"

"Poor."

"Mr. McGowan was poor when he went to India, even though his twin brother's rich? That's not fair! He had more fun, though. He told me some ripping stories about India. What's intexual indigestion?"

"Intexual?"

"Something like that. He said he didn't want me to get it from too many stories."

"Intellectual indigestion? It's what your mind gets from too many new ideas at once." Particularly if they were hard to swallow, Daisy thought.

Their compartment was now empty. Daisy proposed a game of draughts, but Belinda was tired of sitting.

"May I stand in the corridor for a while?" she begged.

"To watch the cows and trees on that side for a change? Yes, but don't wander off again, please! Oh, wait a minute, you have a smut on your cheek. Here, let me get it off." Daisy delved in her handbag for a handkerchief, spat on the corner the way her nanny used to, and wiped away the fleck of soot, feeling very motherly. "That's better."

Belinda hugged her, blushed, and went out to the corridor.

Anne had lent Daisy two or three magazines. Now and then she glanced up from the glossy pages of the *Tatler* to check the whereabouts of her impetuous charge. A quarter of an hour or so later, she heard Belinda say, "Hallo, Dr. Jagai."

The young doctor joined her, shrugging into his jacket. "Hallo, Miss . . . Fletcher, is it?"

"Yes, but you can call me Belinda. I'm not really quite old enough to be Miss Fletcher yet."

"I'll tell you a secret, Belinda: I'm such a new doctor that whenever someone addresses me as doctor, I still look round to see to whom they are talking."

Belinda laughed. So the earnest Dr. Jagai had a sense of humour, Daisy thought. With a quirk of the lips for her own impetuosity, not to mention curiosity, she invited him in.

Now that she saw him properly, he looked tired.

From her hospital days during the War, she remembered witnessing the exhausting life of a lowly houseman, always on call.

"I shouldn't really be in first class," he said.

"Oh, never mind. The ticket inspector won't come again till after York. Do come and sit down. Are you going to Edinburgh?"

"Yes, ma'am. I have friends there, and since I must go as far as York, I might as well go on to see them. Mr. McGowan told me to catch this train. I've been on duty since he learnt of his brother's illness, and he wanted to speak to me."

"A dictatorial gentleman!"

Jagai smiled. "Undeniably, but who am I to complain after all his kindness and generosity? Especially in this instance." His solemn face lit up and he leaned forward in his enthusiasm. "Mr. McGowan summoned me to tell me he's going to rewrite his will to leave his brother's wealth to found a medical clinic in India!"

"Not to you?"

"I shall be named as director of the charitable trust, and of the clinic. It's my dearest dream, but I thought I should have to work and save for years before I could afford it. He'll set it up that way, rather than as a personal bequest, to make it more difficult for his family to contest the will."

"Clever!" Daisy applauded. "It must be much harder to find grounds to object to a charity inheriting than a non-relative."

"So he hopes. He's going to consult brother Alistair's solicitor this afternoon about the best way to do it. I gather Mr. Braeburn is on his way to Dunston Castle with the rest."

"So I've heard. You have considered, haven't you, that Alistair McGowan may change *his* will first?"

"Yes." Jagai's face lost its brightness and settled back into lines of tiredness. He shrugged his shoulders. "If so, if old Alistair disinherits his brother, I shan't be any worse off than I was before."

"I hope you get it *all,*" said Belinda, who had been listening in silence.

"So do I," said Chandra Jagai, giving her a weary smile, "but after all, Alistair has as much right as Albert to do what he wants with what's his."

5

"Bel!" Kitty appeared in the doorway. "It's nearly . . . Oh, hallo. Who are you? Never say you're the infamous Chandra Jagai?"

"Kitty, really!" Daisy exclaimed.

"Oops, sorry. I didn't mean to be rude." She studied the Indian with interest. "But are you?"

Jagai laughed. "I am. You are a McGowan descendant, I take it."

"Yes, I'm a Gillespie. Kitty Gillespie. How do you do?" She shook hands. "You aren't a bit like I expected."

"He's a doctor, Kitty," Belinda informed her.

"Golly, really? And everyone's been saying . . ." She caught Daisy's admonitory eye and cut herself short. "Yes, well, I'm happy to make your acquaintance, Dr. Jagai." Her momentary grand manner evaporated. "But it's time for lunch and I came to see if Bel may sit with me. Please, Miss Dalrymple?"

The steward's voice sounded in the corridor. "Lunch is now being served. Lunch now being served!"

"Have you asked your mother, Kitty?" Daisy asked.

"At first she said no, but then Raymond told her you're an Honourable so she changed her mind," Kitty said with her usual devastating frankness.

"Oh dear!" Daisy had never understood why her courtesy title should be regarded as a guarantee of respectability. It was no more reasonable than Mrs. Fletcher's antipathy.

"Now she's just glad I've found a friend to keep me from pestering her," said Kitty.

Daisy laughed. "Right-oh, run along, Belinda. I'll come in a minute."

"I shan't eat much," Belinda said anxiously. "I know it's awfully expensive eating on a train."

"You eat as much as you want, darling. We can't have your grandmother accusing me of starving you. Just don't order the smoked salmon!"

The girls said good-bye to the doctor and went off.

"If you are short of funds, Miss Dalrymple," the young Indian said hesitantly, "I should be happy to lend you . . ."

"That's very kind of you, Dr. Jagai, but I can manage a few shillings for lunch. I wasn't expecting Belinda to travel with me, you see, or I should have gone third class and brought sandwiches."

"As I have." He grinned, his teeth gleaming in his dark face. "And more than ready for them I am."

"Good-bye, then. Perhaps we shall see you again later."

Daisy powdered her nose and regretfully put on her hat. The restaurant car was altogether too public to be seen without one. She made her way thither.

Belinda, solemnly studying the menu, sat with Kitty at a table set with white napery, silver cutlery, sparkling glasses, and a small vase of spring flowers. Peter and Jeremy Gillespie, at the next pair of tables, introduced their respective wives to Daisy. She felt sorry for Matilda, who was very pregnant and whose blotched face and red eyes suggested recent tears. Beyond them were Anne and Harold Bretton, without Tabitha and the baby.

Anne waved to Daisy, pointing to the table across the aisle from them, but Daisy shook her head and mouthed a polite refusal. She took a seat directly opposite Belinda, so that she could help in case of difficulties. Belinda gave her a relieved smile.

A steward in railway uniform and bow tie brought Daisy a menu. As she looked it over, the other tables gradually filled. The Smythe-Pikes sat across from the Brettons.

"Blasted lawyer says we'll come a cropper," boomed Desmond Smythe-Pike, "haven't a leg to stand on. Sneaky sort of fella, wouldn't look a man straight in the eye."

The thin, bald man just coming along the aisle turned to glare at him. Braeburn, the solicitor, Daisy thought. She had seen him in the compartment next to hers when she was hunting for Belinda. Stalking stiffly like an offended heron, he continued to the only remaining empty table.

Smythe-Pike lowered his voice minimally. "I'll have to set my own chap on the scent when we get back to town."

"It may be unnecessary, sir," Harold pointed out. "Alistair McGowan may have already decided to change his will in our favour."

Peter Gillespie, at the next table, turned and said coldly, "Or ours. I am, after all, already his heir after Uncle Albert."

"Bah!" snorted Smythe-Pike.

"Hush, Desmond," Mrs. Smythe-Pike said soothingly. "We shall all have our chance to persuade Father."

"And Uncle Albert," Anne put in.

"A bit off, don't you think," Jeremy said, quite loud enough to be heard at the next table, "pestering Uncle Albert about Uncle Alistair's money with Uncle Alistair dying upstairs."

Daisy missed the next bit of the squabble. A frightfully smart woman in a black costume, with a simply heavenly little black hat which Daisy's fashionable friend Lucy would have killed for, stopped beside her table. *"Pardonnez-moi, madame,"* she said, "is this seat taken? May I join you?"

"No, please do. I mean," Daisy corrected herself in careful French, *"ce n'est pas occupé. Asseyez-vous madame, je vous prie."*

"Thank you." The woman smiled as she sat down. She was expertly made up, her dark hair slashed with silver set in soft, Marcel waves only just too perfect to be natural. "It's all right, English is my native tongue, though I've lived so long in France that French tends to slip out first."

"If you are used to French food, I hope you will find English railway food edible!"

"I rarely eat a large luncheon. Do you think an omelette would be safe?"

"I couldn't guarantee it, but I shall have the same so we can both complain if it's too dreadful."

The steward came to take their order, and Daisy told him to add Belinda's bill to her own. Over lunch, she and the woman from France chatted about Paris. She caught odd bits and pieces of the argument raging further along the aisle but she had heard most of it before and took little notice.

The last thing she heard, as she paid her bill, collected Belinda, and started back to the compartment, was Harold Bretton announcing, "Well, *I'm* not afraid to tackle old Albert. I shall go straight after lunch."

Immediately a dispute broke out over who had the right to see Uncle Albert first. Daisy shook her head in amused disgust. Never in her life had she met such a quarrelsome family!

Just before the train stopped at York, the friendly ticket-inspector popped his head into the compartment.

"Never fear, miss, I haven't forgotten your wire," he told Daisy, patting his breast-pocket. "It'll be on its way soon as I've turned in me numbers and signed off."

Daisy thanked him. The train rumbled into the station with a squeal of brakes and the hiss of let-off steam. Opening doors thudded against the carriage sides, porters shouted, barrowboys cried their newspapers and magazines for sale, as the ticket-man saluted and trotted off. At once Daisy began to wonder if the telegram message was sufficient to reassure Mrs. Fletcher.

"Belinda safe with me will telephone from Edinburgh." She hadn't used the full allowance of twelve words for a shilling, but what else could she have said?

Ought she to get off and take Belinda straight home? Surely Alec wouldn't expect her to let his daughter's naughtiness disrupt her work. His mother might, though—probably would, in fact. Mrs. Fletcher disapproved of her employment almost as strongly as of her aristocratic background, and she did want to get on Mrs. Fletcher's right side.

Too late. Daisy sat back with a sigh as whistles and slamming doors announced that the Flying Scotsman was once more on its way.

Through the window, Daisy pointed out to Belinda the towers of York Minster. Then they settled down to look at borrowed books and magazines. Though she owed her reading matter to the McGowan family, Daisy was thoroughly fed up with their fusses. She avoided raising her eyes from the pages of *Punch* as feet tramped back and forth in the corridor.

She didn't care who saw Albert McGowan first, second or last; she was only sorry the poor old man was being disturbed. He hadn't come to lunch in the dining car. She hoped it was because he was rich enough to pay to have his meal brought to him, not because Belinda had exhausted him.

Belinda grew bored with Kitty's *School Friend* magazine and she'd already finished *Beano* and *Dandy*. "May I go and see Kitty?" she asked. "And Tabitha, if she's with her mummy?"

"Yes, go ahead. Just don't go anywhere else without telling me."

Daisy was left in peace for some time. She read *Punch*, occasionally glancing out at the green, rolling countryside, patched with buttercup yellow meadows. The sun still shone, but it no longer hit the window, and the air coming in was still cool here in the North, however warm it was by now in London. Though the heating was still on at full blast, Daisy was quite comfortable in her short-sleeved frock.

The atmosphere in Mr. McGowan's compartment must be unbearable by now, she thought as more footsteps went by. The angry men succeeding each other in the airless space must exude heat. Perhaps he'd invite his unwanted visitors to take off their jackets as he had Dr. Jagai.

"They're all in such a stew." Belinda had returned to echo Daisy's thoughts. "Please, Miss Dalrymple, may I go along to third class and see if I can find Dr. Jagai?"

"I don't think that's a very good idea."

"*Pleeease!* I expect he's bored, too. I'll take my draught board and see if he wants to play."

"Oh, all right. But don't wake him if he's dozing, don't pester him, and not more than one game, then you come straight back here."

Belinda hurried off before Miss Dalrymple could change her mind. Gran would never have let her go, but then, Gran would not have let her talk to an Indian man at all, and anyway they would have been in third class in the first place.

From Mr. McGowan's compartment came an irritable roar which could only be Mr. Smythe-Pike. ". . . No loyalty to the family . . ." Belinda heard as she scurried past. She hated all the loud, angry voices and red, scowling faces. Daddy never shouted however cross he got. He got quieter instead, and his eyes looked as if they would go right through you like a spear, and then you knew he really meant it, but it wasn't frightening.

She found Dr. Jagai. Luckily his compartment wasn't full. He was glad to see her and let her win at draughts, which was jolly decent of him even though Daddy always said she'd never learn to play better if she didn't really have to try.

While they played, Belinda told the doctor about stowing away on the Flying Scotsman because she wasn't allowed to meet Deva during the hols.

"I'm afraid your grandmother would not like your talking to me," he said, looking sad.

"She might, 'cause you're a doctor, after all. Anyway, Miss Dalrymple said I could, and Daddy would've let me. Daddy's a detective at Scotland Yard and he says everyone's the same before the law, Chinamen and Hindus and Africans and Red Indians and *every*one. So you see!"

Dr. Jagai smiled. "I see."

Belinda smiled back. Moving a counter, she glanced out of the window while he took his turn. "Oh, look!" she cried. "A castle."

Perched atop a steep hill, castle ramparts towered over the roofs of a town. "Durham," said the doctor. "The tallest towers are not part of the castle, they're the cathedral, one of the oldest in Britain."

"Golly, it's simply enormous. D-u-r-h-a-m," she read out as the train sped through a station without stopping. "But you said Durrem. It's spelt funny."

"You never can tell with English."

They finished the game. "I've got to go now," Belinda said regretfully. "Miss Dalrymple said only one game. Thank you very much for playing with me."

"Thank *you*, Belinda. I hope you won't get into too much trouble for running away, and I hope you will never do such a thing again, or you might really find yourself in the soup."

"I won't. It was scary till I found Miss Dalrymple."

She made her way back to the first-class carriage. It was fun—and a little bit scary—crossing between carriages on her own. The floor shuddered and shifted under her feet and the noise of the wheels was so loud she could hardly hear herself think. One of the doors was extra stiff. She was afraid she wouldn't be able to open it, but the ticket man came along just then and did it for her.

It was a different man, fat, red-faced, and cheerful. "Hallo, young miss, you must be our stowaway," he said, winking at her. "Your friend showed me your ticket."

"Does it say stowaway on it?"

"No, but it shows it was issued on the train, and the King's Cross inspector told me about you at York. You mind you behave yourself now, miss."

"I will. Thank you for opening the door."

Belinda went on. Outside Mr. McGowan's compartment she heard a raised voice again, and she was shocked to realize it was her kind goblin friend himself who was shouting now. Miss Dalrymple had said he might be ogreish to people he didn't like, she remembered. She didn't understand what he was saying, but he sounded absolutely livid.

The door started to open. Head down, Belinda sped onwards. Past one more door, and then, thank goodness, there was Miss Dalrymple, unruffled, pretty as ever, and smiling at her.

"How is Dr. Jagai?"

"He let me win. He's ever so nice. But I heard Mr. McGowan screeching at someone. I don't want to go to tea with him after all."

"Poor Mr. McGowan has had a lot to bear this afternoon. It would be a wonder if he hadn't reached screeching point. You must go, darling; you accepted his invitation, but you need not stay long."

Belinda heaved a sigh. "All right, but I wish he'd invited you, too. Miss Dalrymple, what does 'norbit' mean?"

" 'Norbit'?"

"Yes, a 'norbit.' "

"An orbit, I suppose."

"I think I've heard of that. What is it?"

"It's something to do with the earth going round the sun. I'm not sure exactly what; we didn't do much science at school. Why?"

"That's what Mr. McGowan shouted out."

"How peculiar!"

"And about someone called Miss . . . Miss Probation. Do you know who she is?"

"Another relative, one we haven't met, perhaps,"

said Miss Dalrymple, laughing, "but I suspect you heard wrong. 'Approbation' means approval. 'Disapprobation' means disapproval."

"He certainly sounded jolly disapproving!" Belinda admitted.

"Don't worry about it. He has no reason to disapprove of you, darling."

Belinda hoped not.

She didn't want Miss Dalrymple to disapprove of her, either, so she'd better stop pestering her. Outside the window, she saw, was now a grimy, smoky city, ugly but quite interesting. The train rumbled through a station with a sign saying *Gateshead,* then across a bridge, high over a river. Next came another station, Newcastle-upon-Tyne, then more dingy city, on and on. Belinda picked up the book Kitty had lent her, which was stories about horses. The trouble was, she had read *Black Beauty* not long ago and it made her so sad that now she felt sad whenever she read about horses.

Finishing a story, she returned to the view outside the window. The sun had gone in. There were hardly any houses now, just an occasional isolated farm-house and sometimes, right beside the track, a level-crossing keeper's cottage. Now and then, in the distance, Belinda glimpsed a dark grey line she guessed must be the sea. The fields and trees were still quite wintry this far north. She was an awfully long way from home.

She shivered.

"Are you getting chilly, Belinda? Close the window a bit, or put on your coat. We may yet be glad of the heating."

Belinda struggled with the window. As Miss Dalrymple stood up to help her, Mrs. Bretton came in, with Tabitha and the baby.

"It is cooling down a bit at last, isn't it?" Mrs. Bretton said, sitting down. "Thank heaven. Baby is so fretful when he's too hot, I've had to leave him with Nanny almost all the way."

Baby Alistair whimpered.

"He doesn't seem frightfully happy now," said Miss Dalrymple.

"Nanny thinks he's teething. I'll take him back in a minute. I only fetched him because Harold hoped Uncle Albert might take pity on the poor mite."

"He didn't?"

"We didn't go after all, and after I'd walked all the way along the train to fetch him, and Tabitha insisting on coming, too!"

"Why not?" Miss Dalrymple asked.

"Daddy started creating. He said a bawling baby was as likely to win Uncle Albert over as presenting the fox's brush to a farmer whose fields have just been trampled by the hunt. Particularly as Baby was named for Grandfather, not him. He really is the most disagreeable old man. Belinda, dear, will you look after Tabitha for me while I take Baby back to Nanny?"

"Of course, Mrs. Bretton."

Belinda was very soon sorry she had agreed. Tabitha was being difficult. She didn't want to listen to stories, or look at pictures in *School Friend,* or undress her dolly and dress it again, or do any of the things Belinda had amused her with before. When Miss Dalrymple said it was time to go to tea with Mr. McGowan, Belinda was actually glad.

"Just tidy your hair, darling. One of your ribbons is coming undone. Here's a comb. I'll keep an eye on Tabitha till Mrs. Bretton comes back." Miss Dalrymple looked as if she wished that would be soon! "Off you go, then, and I hope he gives you a good tea."

Remembering the shouting, Belinda thought she'd

better knock on Mr. McGowan's door. There was no answer—but he might not have heard over the noise of the train, and she *had* been invited. She opened the door.

He was lying down. Belinda saw the yellowish, blotchy top of his head with its few strands of hair. His face was turned to the seat back so she couldn't be sure if he was asleep. He had said she must be on time, though, because he needed to eat at the right time. Perhaps he wanted her to wake him up? Or should she just sit there till someone brought their tea?

Stepping into the compartment, she conscientiously closed the door. Something moved on the floor and she bent down to pick up a feather. While she tried to decide what to do, she inspected it. It was quite a pretty one, curly and speckled white and brown, so she put it into her pocket to show Tabitha.

Mr. McGowan hadn't moved. His arm was hanging down off the seat, looking awfully uncomfortable. Granny always woke up with a stiff neck if she fell asleep in a chair in an awkward position. Belinda decided to make Mr. McGowan more comfy—if he woke up when she moved his arm, she could explain and he wouldn't be angry.

She took his hand. It was cold and clammy. His arm seemed very heavy, considering how skinny he was. She folded it across his chest so it wouldn't fall again.

He didn't wake up, didn't even stir. He must be awfully sound asleep. Leaning forward, she glanced at his face.

His pale eyes were wide open, staring at her.

But she could tell he didn't see her.

6

Belinda's freckles stood out against her stark white face.

"What is it, darling?" Daisy asked, holding out her hand. "What's wrong?"

"It's him." The child's whisper trembled.

"Mr. McGowan? Is he ill?"

"I think he's dead." With a dry sob, Belinda launched herself into the shelter of Daisy's arms. She was shaking all over. "His eyes are open, but . . . I touched him. I moved his arm, to make him comf'table, 'cause I didn't realize . . . I feel sick."

Daisy stroked her hair. "Are you going to *be* sick?" she enquired, deciding a matter-of-fact tone was most useful in the circumstances.

"N-no, I don't think so."

"I was sick once," Tabitha announced with unwarranted satisfaction, "when I ate too many sweeties."

"I'm cold," said Belinda.

"Then let's get your coat on." Taking it down from the rack, she steered Belinda's arm into the sleeve. "He was a very old man, you know, darling. You've had a frightful shock, but it's not really very surprising. Oh, Anne, thank heaven you're back. Belinda's found Mr. McGowan dead, or at least very ill. Could you . . ."

"Dead?" Anne shrieked, hands clapped to her horror-stricken face. Tabitha promptly began to cry.

"For pity's sake, pull yourself together! It might be a paralytic stroke, I don't know. I must go and see, so could you please take care of Belinda—she's had a nasty shock—and arrange for someone to go and find Dr. Jagai?"

"That man!"

"I'll go," Belinda said with a disdainful glance at Anne. Daisy scrutinized her, mistrusting her rapid recovery. "Honestly, Miss Dalrymple, I'm all right now, and I know where he is. It won't take a minute."

"Bless you, darling. Don't tell anyone else, please, Anne," Daisy added sharply. "Not until I've found out what's happened."

When they reached the open door of Mr. McGowan's compartment, Belinda turned away her head but she went on without faltering. Steeling herself, Daisy turned in.

Albert McGowan certainly appeared dead. His chest was not rising and falling. Stretched out on his back on the seat, with his head towards the door, his body looked lifelessly limp, untenanted. Shoeless feet in black silk socks stuck out from the tartan lap rug which covered him to the waist. Daisy bent to see his face. The open eyes glared at her. The blind mask of fear and fury made her flinch.

As she reached for his wrist to try for a pulse, a neat little man in black, carrying a tea tray, arrived in the doorway.

"What's up?" he demanded. " 'Ere, miss, what's 'appened?"

"You're his manservant?"

"Weekes is the name."

"I'm afraid Mr. McGowan seems to have died in his

sleep." In spite of the ghastly eyes, it seemed the correct, soothing thing to say.

"In 'is sleep? Not bloody likely, if you'll excuse me saying so, miss. The master wouldn't never've laid 'isself down flat like that without 'is pillow. Arsking for trouble that'd be, with 'is dyspepsia."

"Are you sure?"

"Sure as bloody eggs is eggs." The gentleman's gentleman recollected himself. "Yes, miss, I'm quite sure. I took his pillow down from the rack for him myself, after luncheon, so's he could nap whenever he wanted."

Daisy looked around the compartment. "Then where is it?"

"That's what I'd like to know, miss. Nor he wouldn't have laid down with his head to the door. See the camp-stool there under the window? I put his medicine and that glass of water there for him with me own two hands. Bismuth, it is, for his stomach. He always had it within reach."

There was a small puddle on the floor beside the stool. Daisy moved to look at the glass, her hands behind her back to avoid the temptation of touching it. Fingerprints on glass had played a considerable part in the dreadful business of the Albert Hall murder.

The tumbler was upright but empty. She frowned.

Her frown deepened as she felt the chilly breeze from the open window playing on her hair.

"He was afraid of draughts," she stated.

"Gorlummecharlie," gasped Weekes, "the master wouldn't never in a million years've opened that winder!"

"That's what I thought."

"If you ask me, miss, there's something fishy here."

"Positively piscatorial." The decision was easy. Yielding to the temptation of years, Daisy reached up and yanked on the emergency brake chain.

Brakes squealed. Shuddering, the Flying Scotsman slowed.

As the train came to rest in a jolting clash of buffers, Dr. Jagai entered the compartment.

"So the poor old fellow's gone," he said sadly, reaching for the bony wrist. "No sign of a pulse. Well, at his age it was to be expected. The heart simply wears out."

As he leaned forward to close his benefactor's staring eyes, Daisy said sharply, "Don't!" She exchanged a glance with the manservant, who nodded. "I'm afraid Weekes and I suspect dirty work. Nothing must be touched until the police arrive."

"Police!"

"Where's the master's pillow, sir, I ask you? You know as well as I do he wouldn't never have laid down flat like that, not with his stomach trouble."

"True." Dr. Jagai's forehead wrinkled. "But why should anyone dispose of his pillow?"

"The only reason I can think of," Daisy said tentatively, "is that he was smothered with it and the murderer disposed of the murder weapon in a panic. Is it possible?"

The doctor's frown deepened as he peered at the dead man's face. "I don't know. I'm no forensic expert. His lips are bluish, which could indicate asphyxiation, but could equally well be simple heart failure. An autopsy might be able to tell the difference. I imagine there will be an autopsy if there's the slightest suspicion of murder."

"Murder?" bleated someone in the corridor. The stout ticket-inspector was now neither florid nor cheerful.

Another railway official elbowed him aside. "All right, all right, all right, what's going on in here now? I'm the guard. Who was it stopped my train?"

"I did." Daisy squeezed past Jagai and Weekes.

"Are you aware, madam," the burly guard enquired, scowling down at her, "that to engage the emergency braking system without good cause is a punishable offence under the Railways Act?"

"I have good cause." She drew herself up to her full height, wishing she were as tall as Lucy, and as capable of withering hauteur. "A man has died, and I am very much inclined to believe it was murder."

"Murder!" Daisy heard the horrified murmur run down the corridor, by now crowded with curious travelers. She wished she had spoken more quietly.

"Murder, madam?" The big man gazed sceptically over her head. "I don't see no blood."

"For a number of reasons, which I shall be happy to relay to the police," she said in a hushed voice, "his manservant and I fear Mr. McGowan was smothered to death. Dr. Jagai—this gentleman is a doctor—agrees that it's possible. I happen to know there are a number of people on this train who may hope to benefit by Mr. McGowan's death."

No sooner were the words out of her mouth than Daisy, appalled, realized their truth. That was why she had taken Weekes's qualms seriously. In the back of her mind had lurked the knowledge that the Gillespies especially, but also the Smythe-Pikes and Brettons, all had their hopes of wealth from Alistair McGowan vastly increased by his brother's death.

She must have paled, for the guard asked with concern, "You all right, madam?"

She nodded. "What are you going to do?"

"Well, madam," he said, resigned, "if you claim it's

murder I've got no choice but to call in the busies. Seeing the old gentleman died in England, I reckon we'll have to stop in Berwick, afore we cross the border. Ah well, my schedule's already all bug . . . shot to pieces." He gave a martyred sigh.

"Don't let anyone get off the train. And no one must touch anything in here."

"Right, madam. You'd better find yourself a seat elsewhere in this carriage, and these gentlemen, too. I'll lock this compartment and all the exit doors." He turned to the corridor. "All right, all right, all right, ladies and gentlemen! There's nothing to see. Everyone return to your seats *if* you please."

Daisy took Dr. Jagai and Weekes back to her compartment. They were both down in the mouth, and she was glad to think poor Albert McGowan had at least two genuine mourners.

Anne had gone, thank heaven. Belinda sat huddled in a corner, white and frightened. The *sangfroid* she had displayed in fetching the doctor had vanished.

"They said it's murder." She looked at Daisy with imploring eyes. "They won't think I killed him, will they?"

"Of course not, darling." Sitting down beside her, Daisy put her arm round the child's thin shoulders. "Do you know, I bet they have to call in Scotland Yard, because they can't be sure which county poor Mr. McGowan died in. And your daddy—Belinda's father is a detective, Dr. Jagai—as he's already in Northumberland, he'll be in charge of the investigation."

Belinda let out her breath in a shuddering sigh. "I hope so."

She seemed slightly reassured, but still—not unnaturally in the circumstances—frightfully pale. Daisy tried to distract her. Fortunately the Flying Scotsman had stopped at an interesting spot, close to the sea. There were sand dunes, and then miles of sands crossed by watery channels, with a long, low, rocky mound beyond.

"Look at that island," she said, pointing past Belinda at the window. "Or perhaps it isn't an island, what do you think? The beach goes all the way there."

"That's Lindisfarne." Dr. Jagai, seated opposite, exchanged a glance of understanding with Daisy. "Also known as Holy Island. At low tide, one can drive there on a causeway across the sands."

"Have you been there?" Belinda asked with more politeness than interest.

"No, but I have read about it. I like to know something of the places I pass. There are ruins worth a visit, a monastery nine hundred years old replacing an earlier monastery destroyed by the Danes. St. Cuthbert was buried there and when the Danes attacked, the monks fled the island, taking his coffin. . . ." The doctor pulled himself up as Belinda flinched. "Look at all the seagulls. They must have good fishing in the shallows when the tide begins to cover the sands."

"Miss Dalrymple, do trains sometimes hit birds?"

"Oh dear, I expect they must, but hardly ever I should think. The engine makes such a noise, they can hear it coming a long way off."

"Yes, I s'pose so. Only, I found a feather on the floor in . . . *there.*" Belinda took a small, curly plume from her pocket and showed it to Daisy.

Daisy caught Weekes's eye. Mr. McGowan's pillow, it said. He opened his mouth. She frowned at him.

"Birds are always leaving feathers around," she told Belinda, "like dogs shedding hair. You know how one finds them on the ground. I expect the wind blew it in." She held out her hand and Belinda automatically gave it to her. "I'll keep it safe for you."

She tucked the feather into her handbag. It didn't seem likely to be a significant bit of evidence, but one never could tell.

The train started off again, rumbling slowly northwards. Belinda remained alarmingly subdued, and Daisy started to worry about her. She hoped it was true that Alec would be called in on the case. She would suggest it to the Berwick police, and ask them to try to get in touch with him even if they didn't request his help.

Chandra Jagai continued to talk to Belinda, asking questions about school and home in an evident effort to divert her thoughts from Albert McGowan's death. She answered politely but listlessly, not to be diverted until he said, "May I beg a favour? You beat me handily at draughts and I'd like my revenge."

She gave him a proper smile. "I only won because you let me. I'll play another game if you promise not to."

"I promise," he said, laughing, and she went to sit beside him.

As Belinda turned her serious attention to the game, Daisy silently blessed the kind young man.

She moved over to the window, and to give the players more room, Weekes crossed to sit next to her. The small manservant sat stiffly upright, looking uncomfortable, his gaze fixed on a rather wishy-washy sepia print of Durham Cathedral on the opposite wall. Daisy decided she could talk to him as long as they spoke in low voices and she kept an eye on Belinda to make sure she was concentrating on the game.

"Had you been with Mr. McGowan long?" she enquired softly.

"Ever since he came home from India, miss, and

that's going on twenty years. It's not right, miss," he burst out. Daisy, expecting a peroration on the wickedness of doing away with an aged gentleman, put her finger to her lips and glanced at Belinda. But he went on, "I know my place. I didn't ought to be sitting here with my betters whatever that guard said."

"Bosh, of course you ought," Daisy soothed him. "The police will want everyone associated in any way with Mr. McGowan to stay in this coach, I expect, so that the rest of the train can proceed to Edinburgh. The suspects won't want to do without their servants so we'll all have to squeeze as best we can."

Weekes relaxed a bit, then looked nervously over his shoulder at the door to the corridor. "The suspects, miss—who d'you reckon they are?"

Daisy pondered. Not Weekes, or he would not have drawn attention to the possibility of murder. Not Chandra Jagai, who stood to gain a great deal if Albert had survived Alistair. But all the Gillespies, Smythe-Pikes, and Brettons had both motive and opportunity, and she rather thought even the women must be strong enough to overwhelm a feeble old man.

"All his relatives, I should think," she said, "though it's for the police to decide. Just how frail was he?"

"There was nothing wrong with his heart, miss. Dr. Jagai wasn't his doctor, so he wouldn't know. Dr. Frost in Harley Street he went to. 'The old ticker's still going strong,' he used to tell me when he came back from an appointment. Which isn't to say he was uncommonly spry for his age, though he did walk to his club most days, with a cane and slow, like. 'Slow and steady' he used to say."

"What about his arms?" Daisy asked. His arms would be more important than his legs in fighting off an attacker, she thought.

"He had a touch of trouble with rheumatics in his hands, and a bit of a tremble recently. Couldn't manage an umbrella anymore. That bothered him, but the worst was the dyspepsia. Made him suffer something dreadful, it did. He wouldn't have laid down flat on his back, miss, nor yet so he couldn't reach his tablets."

"I believe you. You liked working for him, I take it, or you wouldn't have stayed so long."

"Very particular he was. I won't say he didn't have a temper when things weren't done quite to suit him, or if he was crossed. But he never took it out on you for things that weren't your fault—like a shirt gone missing at the laundry, as it might be. He knew what he wanted and he was willing to pay for it. You couldn't ask for a more generous master."

"Generous?" said Daisy, taken aback.

"Generous, and don't you let them tell you otherwise. I'll never find another position that pays as well," Weekes continued, with regret and a hint of disgruntlement. "Only he couldn't abide his family, that ignored him all those years then came fawning around when they heard he was well off after all. You're right, miss, it was one of them did it."

But which one? Daisy was rather surprised that none of them had popped in to see her since the discovery of Albert McGowan's death. Did they realize they must all be under suspicion? Were they closing ranks, or wildly swapping accusations?

She decided it was time to put her thoughts in order so as to be ready to explain the situation to the Berwick police—in such a way as to persuade them to send for Alec.

7

The Flying Scotsman made a brief, unscheduled stop at Tweedmouth station.

Belinda lost interest in the game of draughts. "I'm sorry, I just can't concentrate," she said miserably.

"That's all right," Dr. Jagai assured her in the gentle voice Daisy was sure would bring patients flocking to him once he had his own practice.

"But you haven't had your revenge properly yet, though you're winning by miles."

"Perhaps we'll have another chance to play later. Here, let me help you pack up the set. You don't want to lose any pieces."

Through the open compartment door and the opposite corridor window, Daisy saw the guard in confab with the station master. No doubt he was explaining the ruination of the LNER timetable. If he had any sense, he would also ask for the Berwick police to be telephoned with advance warning of their coming.

Ought she to suggest it? Before she had made up her mind, the guard strode back to the train, blew his whistle and waved his flag, and swung aboard.

Slowly the train moved off again. Clattering over the points, it puffed at a snail's pace around a bend, and rumbled across thc railway's Royal Border Bridge high above the Tweed estuary. Downstream stood the old stone bridge with its multitude of low arches. On the far side, beyond the riverside embankment, the red-tiled, pinkish brown stone houses of Berwick spread up the hillside, presided over by a tall clock tower.

"What a pretty town," said Daisy. "Look, Belinda, wouldn't it be nice to walk along the river wall?"

Belinda slipped across to sit beside her. "What's going to happen now?" she asked, sounding apprehensive.

Daisy took her cold little hand. "Nothing too frightful, darling. I expect the policemen will want to ask you exactly what you saw, but I'll be right there beside you." Just let them try to stop her!

"I wish Daddy was here."

"I'll do my very best to get him here, I promise."

"S'pose he's awfully busy?"

"No matter how busy he is, I'm sure he'll come as soon as he finds out that you're here."

"Yes, I 'spect so." Belinda hesitated. "Miss Dalrymple, can lawyers put people in prison?"

"Lawyers are part of the legal system, like policemen," Daisy said reassuringly. "But don't worry about it, we don't have to rely on Mr. McGowan's lawyer. Even if your daddy can't come, the Berwick police will . . . Ah, here we are already."

Belinda read the station sign. "Ber-wick-on-Tweed. But it's pronounced *Berrick*, isn't it? Sometimes people think you understand words when you don't really."

"Remember Durham," said Dr. Jagai.

"English spelling is frightfully erratic," Daisy agreed. She paused as a heavy tread was heard in the corridor. "This must be the police, I imagine."

The brawny guard appeared in the doorway. Then he moved aside and pointed. "That's the lady which stopped my train, Superintendent, sir," he said to the blue-uniformed police officer at his side, "and them there's the deceased gentleman's vally and the foreign doctor."

The officer nodded his thanks. In spite of the uniform, he looked like a prosperous farmer, solidly built with a ruddy face, bluff and hearty. Daisy could imagine him leaning on a five-barred gate, a muddy-booted foot on the lowest bar, directing the shrewdness in his china blue eyes at a prize bull—instead of at her.

"Superintendent Halliday, head of Berwick police, ma'am. I understand you are the person who claims that the old gentleman's death was not natural?"

"That's right, Mr. Halliday. I'll be glad to give you my reasons, though . . ."

"Beg pardon, Superintendent, sir," the guard interrupted, "but I've got a train full of passengers 'specting to arrive in Edinburgh any minute now and what the company's going to say I don't like to think."

"Then don't think," said Halliday sharply. "You must see I can't let you proceed until I know what's going on."

"It's not like it was any ordin'ry train. This here's the Flying Scotsman express, always on time to the minute."

"Not quite always." The policeman stepped into the compartment and shoved the door closed behind him, right in the persistent guard's face. "You were saying, ma'am?"

"I was going to say, it was Mr. Weekes who drew my attention to the suspicious circumstances."

The manservant shrank back as the Superintendent's scrutiny turned upon him. "You go ahead, miss," he bleated.

"Right-oh. My name's Dalrymple, by the way, Daisy

Dalrymple." She decided to keep the Honourable up her sleeve in case of need. "Won't you sit down, Mr. Halliday?"

"Thank you, Miss Dalrymple, but I'd appreciate it if you'd keep it short as you can. The other passengers *will* be up in arms." He winced as a stentorian roar came from the corridor.

Recognizing Desmond Smythe-Pike's bellow, Daisy said sympathetically, "I'm afraid that's one of those you'll have to ask to stay to help with your enquiries. I'll be as quick as I can. For a start, Mr. McGowan . . ."

"The deceased?"

"Yes. He was dyspeptic. His medicine was on the stool by the window, and he'd not have lain down where he couldn't reach it easily, nor flat on his back, as he was found. He carried his own pillow with him, which has disappeared. And the window was wide open. Mr. McGowan lived most of his life in India. He liked it hot and he was terrified of draughts."

"It's true, sir," Weekes put in anxiously. "Every word Miss says."

"What is more," Daisy continued, "not only are his relatives angry with him, they all might hope to gain financially by his death. And they are all on this train!"

Superintendent Halliday was sceptical. "All?"

"Well, lots of them. There must be at least a dozen if you count the children."

"Might I enquire how you . . ." He cocked an ear to the increasing clamour in the corridor. "No, it'll have to wait. One more question, for now. Just what do you imagine was the method of . . ."

Daisy interrupted firmly, "I see no need to go into that in front of my young friend, Superintendent. We have come up with a plausible possibility, as I'm sure Dr. Jagai and Mr. Weekes will confirm." The two men nodded. "You may pursue the subject with them elsewhere, but first I have a point to make and a request for your assistance."

"Yes, Miss Dalrymple?" Halliday sounded resigned, but he looked amused, and even a trifle admiring.

Reminded of her friend Tom Tring, Alec's sergeant, Daisy was emboldened. "The thing is, we have no idea whether Albert McGowan died in Yorkshire, Durham, or Northumberland. I'm not absolutely certain, but doesn't that raise the question of jurisdiction?"

"Possibly," the policeman admitted with caution. "And what is your request?"

"It's for Belinda. She's had a fearful shock and she wants her father. He's on a temporary assignment in Northumberland at present, though I'm not sure exactly where. I hoped you might be able to trace him, because, you see, he just happens to be Detective Chief Inspector Fletcher of Scotland Yard."

Halliday was indubitably startled. "Just happens, eh?" he said, with a thoughtful glance at Belinda. Standing up, he gave a decisive nod. "Right, Miss Dalrymple, I'll see what I can do, though it's up to the Chief Constable—as I expect you know," he added dryly.

"Yes," she said, smiling at him.

"I'll have to ask you all to stay put in here. This carriage will be uncoupled from the train and shunted into a siding, but we'll have accommodations in the town arranged for you as soon as possible. Oh, and one of my officers will be here in a moment to take the names of those passengers you know to be associated with the deceased. It remains to be seen, Miss Dalrymple, whether I shall later thank you for your cooperation or . . ." His voice trailed off meaningfully.

"Or curse me for meddling," she obligingly completed.

Grinning, he saluted and departed.

"Well," said Daisy with a sigh, "what a relief that he turned out to be both reasonable and intelligent, and with a sense of humour into the bargain."

"I believe I'll treat myself to a whisky," said Alec Fletcher, the Newcastle Chief Super's glowing words of grateful praise still echoing in his ears. The Customs man had been no less appreciative. "What's yours, Tom?"

"I'll take the usual, ta, Chief," rumbled his massive sergeant, subsiding onto a dark-oak settle built solidly enough barely to creak under his weight.

"A pint of bitter it is. Ernie?"

"Half of mild, please, Chief," young Piper requested modestly. He took out the packet of Woodbines which lurked alongside his notebook and an endless supply of well-sharpened pencils in the pocket of his brown serge suit.

"Never trust a half-pint man," Tom Tring teased. One thick forefinger preened the walrus mustache which compensated for the vastly hairless dome of his head.

"A half's the same to me as what a pint is to you, Sarge," the wiry Detective Constable retorted, tapping a cigarette on the table-top.

"Hark to our numbers expert."

Alec laughed. "Don't slight mathematical genius. It was Ernie's noticing the discrepancy in those manifest numbers that started us on the right track to break up the smuggling ring. He's earned a pint—so I'll see if they have a quart pot for you, Tom!"

He crossed to the bar. It was still early, and the three

detectives were the only customers in the hotel residents' bar parlour. A sharp rap on the countertop brought the proprietess herself through from the next room to serve him.

"What can I do for you, Mr. Fletcher?" A veneer of refinement overlaid her native Geordie twang.

Alec gave his order. As beer foamed into tankards, he went on, "We'll be leaving in the morning, catching the early train up to London, so . . . Isn't that your telephone ringing?"

She cocked her head. "Yes. Drat that girl! Might as well run the place single-handed," she threw over her shoulder as she hurried out to the lobby to answer the insistent bell.

Taking his men their drinks, Alec returned to the bar to await his own. The landlady reappeared and announced, "It's for you, sir."

With a sigh, he went out to the telephone, picked up the apparatus, and applied the dangling earpiece to his ear.

"Fletcher here."

"Chief Inspector," said a faintly Scottish voice, "this is Superintendent Halliday, Berwick-on-Tweed police. The Newcastle department put me onto you. I've a wee bittie problem up here."

Alec swallowed a second sigh. "Sir?"

"A matter of a dead body on a train, and . . ." A resounding crash came over the wire, drowning out the next few words. "Did you hear? Sorry about that, I'm at the station. There's odds and ends of the Flying Scotsman being shunted around outside. I said, I've a dead body on a train and a young lady who claims it's a case of murder. Her name's Miss . . ."

"Don't tell me," Alec groaned. "Let me guess. Not, by any mischance, Miss Daisy Dalrymple?"

"Right first time, Chief Inspector." Halliday sounded amused. "An old acquaintance?"

"Miss Dalrymple has a positive genius for falling over bodies, sir. I have to admit, if she says murder she's very likely right. But I'm sure the Berwick police are perfectly competent to handle a murder investigation without calling in the Yard."

"Indeed I hope so, though misplaced cattle and motors without rear lights are more our mark. However, there's some doubt about which county the death took place in. More to the point—are you sitting down, Fletcher?—it seems your daughter is a material witness."

"My daughter?" As the words sank in, Alec sank onto the nearest chair. *"Belinda?"* he yelped. "A witness? But she's in London."

"Not she. I've not had time to get the details, but she appears to be traveling with Miss Dalrymple."

"What the devil . . . ? I'll wring Daisy's neck!"

"After we've caught our murderer and sewn up the case."

"Belinda's all right? She's not hurt?"

"Not hurt. Shocked, naturally. Miss Dalrymple assumed you'd wish to come, whether my C.C. agrees to call in Scotland Yard or not. Newcastle have offered to provide a car."

"Thank you, sir. I'm on my way!" Hanging up, he put down the set on the table and clutched his head. "Oh Lord," he groaned aloud. "How the devil am I going to tell Tom and Piper that Daisy's done it again?"

8

A frigid wind whistled up the Tweed estuary and swirled about the station built upon the foundations of Berwick's demolished castle. On this very spot, Edward I refused the throne of Scotland to the Bruce family; here, having crowned Robert the Bruce king despite Edward's choice, Isabella, Countess of Buchan, spent six years in a cage in the courtyard.

"Or possibly in a turret," said Dr. Jagai as they followed the rest of the waylaid travelers down the platform. "The accounts differ."

"I hope in a turret," Daisy exclaimed, burying her hands in her pockets. "It might have been just a trifle warmer."

Hanging on Daisy's arm, Belinda asked wide-eyed, "Did she die?"

"No, no. First she was sent to a convent, and then set free. A brave woman."

Belinda nodded solemnly. "What happened to the castle?"

"The stones were used to build Stephenson's great railway viaduct, and this was erected in its place."

Daisy regarded with disfavour the towered and turreted mock-Gothic station. It was in poor repair, the frivolous battlements visibly crumbling and half of one of the turrets missing. Her disapprobation increased when the station-master announced apologetically that the main waiting-room was unusable as part of its chimney—the tottering turret—had recently fallen through the roof.

Were they to have no shelter until the police found lodgings for them all in the town?

However, the ladies' waiting-room was available. On hearing this, Jeremy Gillespie at once supported his swollen-bellied, swollen-eyed wife towards it.

"Come on, old dear, you'll feel better sitting down out of the wind," he said, full of solicitude. As he spoke, he cast a sidelong glance at Daisy, as if to make sure she noticed what a considerate husband he really was. She wondered whether he hoped to persuade her he was much too nice to have killed an old man for money.

His mother joined them. "There's no need to pamper Matilda, Jeremy," she said sharply. "Pregnancy is not an illness. She really must pull herself together."

"I'm sure we're all upset," said Mrs. Smythe-Pike, coming up on Matilda's other side, "and getting out of this dreadful wind is hardly pampering. Anne, dear, do bring the children in before they take cold."

"Come along, Kitty," the elder Mrs. Gillespie snapped at her daughter who showed a disposition to linger with Raymond and Judith.

Raymond was in a bad way again. The way he hugged his overcoat about him suggested it was a protection against imaginary terrors as well as the biting chill. Daisy didn't know how the news of the murder had affected him, but the crashing clashes of shunting engines and coaches would have been enough to shake him.

"Judith, go with your mother!" barked Desmond Smythe-Pike. For him, it was a subdued bark. They were all decidedly subdued.

"But, Daddy," Judith started to protest. A ferocious scowl silenced her, and she followed the others. Raymond watched her go, his gaunt face forlorn.

Daisy was close enough to hear Smythe-Pike mutter to Harold Bretton, "After all, it's those Gillespies who've hooked the fish with the old man's death."

True, but the others might well believe they stood a better chance of changing Alistair McGowan's will with Albert out of the way. Harold Bretton was a gambler—Daisy recalled his talk of a win on the horses. And Smythe-Pike had an explosive temper.

Raymond set off walking very fast up the platform. The constable posted at the end stiffened as he approached. He turned on his heel and strode back towards the other end, past the huddled, shivering gentlemen and servants.

Leaving them, Daisy and Belinda penetrated the tiny, crowded waiting-room. Within, a dismal coal fire emitted more smoke than heat. Anne bemoaned Baby's wet nappy and snapped at Tabitha to stop whining. Enid Gillespie scolded Kitty for her hoydenish behaviour. Judith peered anxiously through the grimy window, muttering rebellion. Mattie wept.

Daisy turned back to the door, in two minds whether to shut it or to leave. Behind her stood the elegant Frenchwoman she had lunched with.

Why was she not on her way to Edinburgh on the Flying Scotsman? What on earth was she doing entering this madhouse? She stepped forward and Daisy moved aside.

"Mademoiselle." With a polite nod of acknowledgement, the woman passed Daisy, her high heels clicking on the stone floor. "Well, Amelia?" she said.

Mrs. Smythe-Pike ceased to pat Matilda Gillespie's

hand. She stared. Her mouth dropped open. "Geraldine?" she gasped.

"Golly!" Kitty swung round. "Never say you're Aunt-Geraldine-who-ran-away? How simply frightfully absolutely spiffing!"

At this interesting moment, a constable stuck his head around the door. "Miss Dalrymple? The Superintendent wad like a word wi' ye and the wee lassie, ma'am."

He led the way to the station-master's office, where Mr. Halliday sat behind the desk, talking on the telephone. He nodded as Daisy and Belinda came in, and waved them to chairs. Daisy chose to cross to the fireplace to warm her hands at the glowing fire. Belinda, still pale and quiet, stuck to her side.

"I have the young lady here, sir," said the Superintendent. "Do you want to speak to her? . . . No, sir, I haven't had a chance. . . . Yes, sir, Detective Chief Inspector Fletcher of the Met. He vouches for her—that is, he says if she claims it was murder she's very likely right. . . . Yes, sir, any of three counties, I'm afraid. We may be able to narrow it down after the postmortem. . . . Yes, sir, Dr. Redlow from Newcastle is on his way. Our Dr. Fraser doesn't. . . . No, sir, he is *not* more accustomed to doing autopsies on sheep, but. . . . Thank you, sir." He listened a moment longer, said good-bye, and replaced the receiver on its hook with a controlled precision as expressive of annoyance as any outburst.

"The Chief Constable?" Daisy enquired, moving to take a seat before politeness required him to rise. Belinda stood beside her, leaning against her shoulder. She felt the child trembling.

"The Chief Constable," Halliday confirmed. "In view of the rural nature of the general run of crimes committed in my district, the auld b . . . ahem. . . . has agreed to ask Scotland Yard for assistance. Your father, Miss Fletcher, is already on his way."

"Is he very angry?" Belinda asked with trepidation.

"He's not very pleased." The policeman cast a glance of quizzical amusement at Daisy. "In fact, I'd go so far as to say he's definitely hot under the collar."

Belinda missed the amusement. "Are you going to arrest me?" she whispered.

"Whyever would I do a foolish thing like that, young lady?"

"You don't think I did it?"

"Bless my soul, not for a minute. Why should I?"

"Because I was wicked today. I ran away from my granny, and stowed away on the train without paying, and . . ."

"Aha! Well, those are wicked deeds indeed, but not the sort we arrest little girls for, not out here in the wild and woolly North." He gave her a stern look. "Just don't do anything like that again."

"Oh I won't, honestly, I promise!"

"Very good. Now, Miss Dalrymple, you'll be making your explanations to the Chief Inspector when he arrives. I sincerely trust you are correct in your surmise, or I shall never hear the end of it. 'Credulous yokel' is the least of what I'll be called."

Daisy envisioned Alec's ire if she had called him out on a wild-goose chase as well as, in his view, enticing Belinda from home. She hadn't missed the hint that he was at least as angry with her as with his errant daughter. "Believe me, Mr. Halliday," she said, "you can't possibly hope I'm right any more fervently than I do."

With a noncommittal nod he stood up. "We should have somewhere arranged for you to stay shortly, ma'am."

"Thank you." Rising, Daisy offered her hand. He gave it a firm shake. "And thank you, Superintendent, for your kindness."

"Yes," Belinda said hurriedly, "thank you for sending for Daddy, sir." She too offered her hand, which he gravely shook.

"Mind you stay out of mischief now, young lady," he said.

"He's a nice man, isn't he?" Belinda said as the door closed behind them. "At first I thought he was awfully fierce, but his eyes twinkle like Sergeant Tring's."

She had perked up considerably. However, as they emerged onto the platform, she fell silent again and tucked her hand under Daisy's arm.

Smythe-Pike and Bretton sat on one bench, Peter and Jeremy Gillespie on another, all enveloped in overcoats, woollen scarves, and hats. Raymond was still marching up and down the outer edge of the platform, though more slowly now. As he approached the bench where his father and brother sat, Jeremy got up and accosted him.

"Come on, old chap, come and sit down. You'll exhaust yourself."

Raymond brushed him off with a violent gesture. "I'm all right. Leave me alone, I tell you."

His brother shrugged and sat down again.

Dr. Jagai came over to Daisy. "That young man is not well, I fear," he said. "Do you know what ails him, Miss Dalrymple?"

"That's Raymond Gillespie. He was in the trenches during the War and his nerves haven't recovered from the horror of it."

"Shell-shock? I wondered. I've seen cases before and been able to help them a little. Perhaps I should offer my assistance."

"I wouldn't," Daisy said frankly. "Not outright, anyway. He's very sensitive on the subject."

"Yes, many feel it's a weakness to be ashamed of. But I can't let him go on suffering unnecessarily. If I ask his advice, maybe he'll be willing to listen to mine."

"His advice?"

"On a matter of etiquette." The doctor grinned. "Here I am, stranded amidst his hostile family. He is the gentleman nearest to me in age. It will be quite reasonable for me, as a humble, uncivilized foreigner, to approach him to ask how best to ingratiate myself with the rest, won't it?"

Daisy smiled. "It might work. He's probably the least likely to snap your nose off."

"Apart from the charmingly outspoken Miss Kitty!"

"He's Kitty's favourite brother," said Belinda, "and he was nice to me. I could introduce you, just tell him your name and that you're my friend. Could I, Miss Dalrymple?"

Daisy hesitated. In the extraordinary circumstances, to insist on strict etiquette would be fatheaded. Yet, after all, Raymond Gillespie was one of the suspects.

Belinda would be in full view of everyone on the platform, though, including three police constables, and anyway the murderer had no reason to attack her. Raymond was given to irrational outbursts, admittedly, but Belinda would be safe with Dr. Jagai.

She obviously felt safe with him. Since he had come up, she had ceased to cling to Daisy. Glad to see the child regaining her confidence, Daisy said, "Right-oh. When he comes back this way. Don't try to stop him if he goes on walking, don't go near the edge of the platform, and come straight back to me." Gosh, she thought, what must it be like to be a mother?

Belinda and the doctor went to meet Raymond. He

stopped and politely lifted his Trilby hat to her. A moment later, he and Chandra Jagai shook hands. Daisy breathed a sigh of relief.

The two young men started talking. Belinda turned to come back, but at that moment the solicitor, Braeburn, advanced upon Daisy.

"I hope you'll excuse my speaking to you, madam," he said hoarsely, tipping his hat in a most perfunctory manner, and then jamming it down on his head again. He was swathed in an olive green muffler up to his chin, in spite of which a drip depended from the red, pointy tip of his nose. "I'm Braeburn, Mr. McGowan's—the elder Mr. McGowan's—solicitor."

He seemed more ill-at-ease than was called for by the indecorum of addressing an unknown lady. His eyes kept shifting, never quite meeting hers, and hands in black leather gloves twitched and fidgeted with the tortoiseshell head of his cane. Altogether an unprepossessing specimen.

It must be a shock to the system of a respectable solicitor accustomed to estates and conveyances to find himself involved in a murder, Daisy decided charitably. "What can I do for you, Mr. Braeburn?" she asked.

"You seem to be the only person with whom the police are communicating, and I wondered if you would mind informing me as to how long we are to be exposed to this abominable wind."

"I'm afraid I don't know. The police are doing their best to find lodgings for us, I understand."

"It's disgraceful! I am subject to sore throats at the least chill. Already I feel extremely unwell, and I fear the result may prove to be a quinsy. And all because I was so obliging as to remain to render what assistance I might to the police, though under no conceivable obligation to do so."

"It's everyone's duty to assist the police," Daisy said severely, then took pity on his obvious discomfort. "I expect you could squeeze into the ladies' waiting-room if you explain you're ill. And I'll ask Dr. Jagai to examine your throat once we're settled. He'll know what to prescribe."

"No, no, on no account!" the lawyer squawked.

Daisy gave him a withering look. "Dr. Jagai is as well qualified as anyone, but you can send for a local man if you prefer. The Superintendent mentioned a Dr. Fraser."

"Quite unnecessary. I . . . I've found medical men to do more harm than good. Dover's Powders, a hot mustard footbath, a hot poultice, and a gargle with bicarbonate of soda to ward off the quinsy, that's the ticket." His nervous agitation fading, he gave her a sickly smile. "And Friar's Balsam, of course. No doctors. I believe I shall take your advice and seek refuge in the waiting-room. Thank you, ma'am." Raising his hat, he bowed slightly and departed with his heron-like stride, his cane swinging in his left hand.

Dotty, Daisy thought, watching him go. But quite a lot of people were a bit dotty about doctors.

She jumped as someone clutched her arm.

"Oh, it's you, Belinda. You startled me."

Belinda stared after Braeburn. "What did he say?" she whispered. She looked pale and pinched again.

Daisy wondered if Jagai and Raymond had been asinine enough to discuss the murder in front of her. "He was telling me all about his sore throat," she said soothingly. "Very boring. He's fed up because the police are keeping us waiting while they find somewhere for us to stay."

"I wish they'd hurry."

"Are you frozen, darling? Let's go back to the waiting-room. I'm dying to find out all about Aunt-Geraldine-who-ran-away."

"Oh no, let's not." She shivered, but insisted, "I'm not really cold. I'd rather stay out here."

Remembering the atmosphere in the waiting-room, adding to it a disgruntled and possibly infectious solicitor, Daisy restrained her curiosity and agreed.

They had not much longer to wait. A police sergeant came to announce that vehicles were waiting to convey everyone to the Raven's Nest Hotel. Hurried along by Belinda, Daisy followed the sergeant to the station forecourt. Two touring cars, a char-a-banc, a pony-trap, and a motor-bicycle with sidecar stood there.

"Golly!" said Belinda. "I've never gone by motorbike."

"That's mine, miss," said the sergeant, "and strickly speaking not meant for the transporting of this here party."

"Oh." Belinda's face, momentarily animated, fell.

"But I reckon the Super would stretch a point, miss, if I was to run you over quick whiles the rest is sorting theirsel's out."

"Would you? Can we, Miss Dalrymple? Please?"

"The sidecar's only meant for one," Daisy pointed out. "You don't want to go alone, do you?"

"Gosh no!"

He eyed them. "Room enough for the two of you, ma'am," he said, opening the sidecar's door. "A great bruiser of a drunk and disorderly I had in there a week or two since. Quiet as a lamb he was sitting there, then what d'you know but soon as we got him in the cells he battered down the door with the bed!"

"Really?" said Belinda, squeezing over on the seat.

"Right enough. And what do you think the Super said when he come up afore the Bench?"

"I can't imagine," Daisy said truthfully.

" 'I think,' says he, 'I think the surroundings must not have suited him.' " The officer chortled as he started the motor, and Daisy smiled. She hoped the magistrates appreciated Mr. Halliday's dry humour as much as his sergeant did.

As the machine put-putted along, the policeman kept up a running commentary. They drove up Castlegate, past a huge pink marble drinking fountain with a green-patinaed crown on top, and under an arch in a high stone wall.

"Scotsgate," announced the sergeant, "and that's the Elizabethan city walls. There's older, from King Edward's time, they say, though I don't rightly know which Edward, but there's not much left of them. These here's dangerous in places, mind. Don't you go up there on your own, missy."

"I won't," Belinda promised.

Continuing down broad Marygate, they passed the Guildhall with its pillared portico and tall clock tower. Beside its open ground floor at the back, the Butter Market, they stopped to let a waggon heavy-laden with road-stone cross ahead.

Their guide pointed up the hill to the left. "See the Police Station, missy? You need anything, you just come by and ask for Sergeant Barclay. That's me. And down there"—he waved the other way as they started across—"there's the King's Arms, biggest hotel in Berwick and right busy now with the trout season just started. Lucky 'tis not the weekend. We had to move a few fishermen over there from the Raven's Nest to leave room for all of you in one place."

Daisy would have been happier housed apart from the murder suspects, but she assumed it would be easier for the police to have them all together. "Will Chief

Inspector Fletcher be staying there?" she called over Belinda's head as they drove along a narrow street called Woolmarket.

"Yes, ma'am, and there's a room for his detective officers, too."

"Is Mr. Tring coming with Daddy?" Belinda asked happily. "Goody!"

At the end of Woolmarket, on the opposite side of Ravensdowne, stood The Raven's Nest Hotel. Three stories high, uncompromisingly Georgian in style, it had two adjacent front doors onto the street, suggesting it was made up of two houses thrown into one. To the right, a narrow flight of stone steps led up between it and the next building.

"There's a path up onto the walls," said Sergeant Barclay. "Mind now, no exploring on your own." He drew up in front of the hotel and ushered them in.

With a sigh, Daisy realized she could no longer postpone telephoning Mrs. Fletcher.

The Newcastle police driver changed into low gear to cross the narrow bridge. "Nearly there, sir," he said.

With a sigh, Alec realized he could no longer postpone telling Sergeant Tring. "Tom," he said in a low voice, hoping the driver and Piper in the front seat could not hear him, "there's a reason besides our proximity why we've been called in."

"Ah?" said the sergeant in a ruminative way which somehow conveyed his awareness of information held back.

"The public-spirited citizen, *alias* meddlesome busybody, who insists the death's a murder is Miss Dalrymple."

The evening sun, low in the west, illuminated the

grin of sheer delight spreading across Tring's broad face. "Ah!" he said, in a quite different tone.

Alec scowled. "That's not the worst. How she's managed it I can't begin to guess, but she's entangled my daughter in the case."

"Miss Belinda?" Tom's relaxed bulk took on a sudden alertness. "She was on the train with Miss Dalrymple, Chief?"

"Yes, the devil knows why. I've a bone to pick with that young lady," he said through gritted teeth.

"With both of 'em, I shouldn't wonder. But don't go setting Miss Dalrymple's back up, Chief. If you ask me, the first thing we're going to need to tackle this business is her evidence!"

9

"Daddy!" Belinda scampered across the small room into Alec's arms.

"Sweetheart." Over her shoulder, he glowered at Daisy, fierce dark eyebrows meeting over his nose. His grey eyes, capable of icily piercing a malefactor through and through, were hotly angry. He looked about to explode. Daisy hastily shut the door of the landlord's small private parlour behind her.

"Everything'll be all right now you're here," sobbed Belinda.

"What I want to know is what brought *you* here, Bel," he said grimly. "I await an explanation, Miss Dalrymple."

"I think it's best if Belinda explains," Daisy said with a reasonably successful assumption of cool composure. She sat down on a hideous sofa upholstered in magenta plush. Thank heaven the bedroom and public rooms had been furnished with decent restraint, though the heating system left much to be desired.

Alec's glare was quite warming, though. She undid the top button of her long, cable-knit cardigan.

"I want to know how—and why—you persuaded my daughter to leave home with you," he snapped.

"Daddy, she didn't. It's all my fault. I'll never run away again, I promise."

"Run away! What's this?" Holding Belinda away from him, he studied her face. She developed a sudden interest in his Royal Flying Corps tie. "Come on, Bel, let's have it."

Out poured the story: the Indian school friend she wasn't allowed to see; his absence in the North, coinciding with Daisy's message about taking the Flying Scotsman; the platform ticket and stowing away on the train and Daisy's paying her fare so the ticket-inspector wouldn't arrest her. "And you will pay Miss Dalrymple back, won't you, Daddy? 'Cause she bought me lunch, too."

"Of course, sweetheart." Alec gave Daisy a distinctly sheepish look. He ran his hand through his crisp, dark hair in an unusual gesture of exasperation. "But honestly, Belinda, of all the daft things to do!"

"I *said* I won't do it again."

"I really don't think she will," said Daisy. "Any further punishment would be superfluous—she's had a nasty shock."

"Ah, yes. You'd better tell me all about it, Bel."

"It was *awful*, Daddy." Shuddering, Belinda buried her face in Alec's shoulder.

"I think it's best if I tell you first," Daisy proposed, "so that you'll know just how much you really need to ask her, rather than putting her through it unnecessarily."

Alec's disconcerted face made her lips twitch. The last thing he'd anticipated when he came roaring up to Berwick was to find *her* protecting his daughter from *him!*

He bit his lip. "Perhaps that will be best. Off you

go, then, sweetheart, and I'll talk to you in a little while."

Belinda looked dismayed. "I want to stay with you and Miss Dalrymple, Daddy."

"Grown-up talk, Bel."

"Go back to the lounge, darling, to Dr. Jagai."

The child's face cleared. "Oh yes, I'll stay with him." She kissed her father and left.

"Dr. Jagai?" said Alec.

"I'll get to him in due course. You know I like to present my evidence in the proper order, otherwise I get confused."

"Present your evidence! Daisy, how the deuce do you keep getting mixed up in these affairs?"

"For heaven's sake, don't you start ragging me! I've just had a frightfully uncomfortable—not to say unpleasant—bout on the 'phone with Mrs. Fletcher."

"Mother! Oh lord, I forgot. . . . She must have been biting her nails to the quick."

"I sent her a wire from York, then rang up as soon as we got here, to the hotel. Belinda spoke to her and apologised. But of course she blames me for Belinda's sins." Daisy noted Alec's flush, acknowledgement that he had jumped to the same conclusion. "I couldn't very well tell her it was her fuss over Deva made Belinda run away."

"No, I'm sorry." He looked tired and discouraged. "I'd better put through a call, though I haven't time for long explanations. Mother does her best, but she's old-fashioned in some ways and not young anymore. If only . . ." He stopped.

"If only your wife had not died?" Daisy said gently. She was on the verge of telling him about Michael, but this was no time for wallowing in vain regrets. "Your mother's attitude isn't actually so old-fashioned,

I'm afraid. You should have heard what some of the others were saying about Chandra Jagai. But let me begin at the beginning."

With an effort he smiled. "Yes, of course. We'd better get on with it if I'm to speak to everyone this evening. Halliday's managed to persuade all concerned to stay. He must have put it to them quite forcefully, which means you certainly persuaded him there's a case."

"He's a good egg. Did he show you the scene of the crime?"

"He tried. I was in too much of a hurry to see Belinda, but it's just as well. You'll be able to give me an idea of what I'm looking for, I presume. I'll just get Tring and Piper in here. They'll need to hear this, and I'll have Ernie take notes." He went out.

An official interview, then. Running over the course of events in her mind, Daisy shivered. She re-buttoned her cardigan and turned the cuffs down over her hands. The cold was partly internal, but the room, like the rest of the hotel, was decidedly chilly, hardly surprising as the radiators were all lukewarm. When she mentioned the matter to the landlord, Mr. Briggs, he had blandly explained that the boiler system was clogged with soot after the winter. The Raven's Nest's usual April customers were hardy anglers who never complained.

"But I'm complaining," said Daisy.

Mr. Briggs could shut down the boiler altogether, let it cool, and have it cleaned out, or he could leave things as they were. How long did Miss Dalrymple intend to stay?

Miss Dalrymple had retreated, defeated, to the residents' lounge, where a coal fire at least warmed half the room. It was balm to her soul to hear a blustering

Desmond Smythe-Pike routed in precisely the same fashion a few moments later.

She didn't like Smythe-Pike, but she must try not to let her likes and dislikes influence what she told Alec. Could the gouty squire have murdered old Albert McGowan?

Alec returned, followed by Detective Sergeant Tring and Detective Constable Piper. Despite his size, Tom Tring's tread was cat-soft, and Daisy noticed that Ernie Piper now walked less like a flatfoot on the beat. The sergeant was wearing his less appalling suit, the vivid blue and green checks not quite so offensive to the fastidious eye as his favourite yellow and tan. He winked at Daisy, his little eyes twinkling.

"Evening, Miss Dalrymple. Nice to see you again. What have you got for us this time?"

"Evening, miss," said Piper with a smile as he produced his notebook and two of his ever-ready pencils.

Tring lit the gas lamps as Daisy began the tale.

"It all started with Anne Bretton. I was at school with her, and she'd seen me at King's Cross and came looking for me in the train." Daisy saw Alec raise his eyes to heaven and guessed what he was thinking. She nearly told him she had no intention of taking Anne under her wing, but she didn't want Piper writing that down. "She told me she and all her relations were on their way to Scotland at the command of her dying grandfather. He . . ."

"His name, please, Daisy—Miss Dalrymple."

"Alistair McGowan, Laird of Dunston Castle. Anne and her husband had named their baby after him in an effort to persuade him to change his will in their favour. He'd left the huge family fortune and castle and everything to his brother, not a penny to his daughter—that's Anne's mother, Amelia Smythe-Pike. Do you want his reasons, Chief, or is that hearsay?"

"It is, but it might give us a hint as to motive and this is not formal evidence, only notes to work from. I'll have to get details of the will from his solicitor."

"Right-oh. In the first place, Alistair McGowan believes in inheritance through the male line. He had two daughters and Amelia Smythe-Pike had two daughters, so the baby is his first direct male descendent. In the meantime, his closest male relative was his twin brother Albert, the victim."

"Who was to inherit everything," said Alec. "So Amelia Smythe-Pike and Anne Bretton, or their husbands, had the best of motives to rid themselves of Albert McGowan."

"Wait, it's *much* more complicated than that. With Albert dying first, everything goes to their sister's son, Peter Gillespie. Not only is he a male—frightfully unfair, isn't it?—but his mother married a Scotsman and he was born in Scotland, as were all his family. Alistair's other prejudice is against the English. Amelia Smythe-Pike married an Englishman, her daughters were born in England, and Anne's husband is English."

"So it's the Gillespies who profit from Albert's death?"

"Unless the others persuade Alistair to change his will. They could have a better chance with Albert out of the way."

"Hmm." Alec pondered. "Possible, but not a very strong motive."

"That's what I thought, until I considered Harold Bretton's and Desmond Smythe-Pike's characters, not to mention Peter Gillespie's."

"Whoa! I must hear about all these characters, but in spite of your liking for chronological order you'd better tell me first what it was about Albert McGowan's death that aroused your suspicions."

"In case you decide I was wrong after all?" Daisy said indignantly. A muffled snort from D.C. Piper sounded suspiciously like a suppressed snicker. He bent his head over his notebook.

"It's always possible," Alec pointed out. "I've been known to be wrong myself. Once or twice."

"Hah! Just listen to this. Albert McGowan, having spent many years in India, liked it hot. In fact he had a morbid fear of draughts. Though the train was fearfully overheated, he kept his window closed and insisted that anyone entering his compartment shut the door quickly. Yet when he was found, the window was wide open."

"Since he wasn't stuffed through it, I fail to see . . ."

"You will. He suffered agonies from dyspepsia, for which he took bismuth. His valet, Weekes, put his medicine and a glass of water on a camp-stool by the window, yet he was found lying with his head towards the door, the medicine out of reach. The glass was empty but upright and there was a puddle on the floor."

"He knocked it over with his foot in his death throes . . . Ah, you're sure Belinda didn't set it upright? She's a tidy child."

"I didn't actually ask her, but even the tidiest child is unlikely to stop to right a fallen glass when confronted with a dead body!"

"True. Fingerprints, Tom, if Halliday hasn't done it already."

"Right, Chief," rumbled the sergeant. "McGowan could have taken his medicine and spilled the water before he lay down, though."

"True," Daisy conceded. "However, the valet and

Dr. Jagai agree he would never have lain down flat on his back, as he was found—it was Weekes pointing that out that first made me suspicious. He had his own pillow, which Weekes had taken down from the rack for him. Not only was he not using it—possible, I suppose, if he was having a seizure or something and felt too ill to arrange it under his shoulders—but it's missing."

"Missing?" Alec was suddenly alert.

"And Belinda found this on the floor." Daisy triumphantly produced the curly feather. "I think the murderer smothered the poor old man and then got in a panic and shoved the murder weapon out of the window, tearing it and knocking over the glass in the process."

"It might have been panic, or he might have had good reason. Tom, I want the railway line searched for that pillow, however many men it takes, from however many police forces. Let's hope the valet has some idea where the train was when he last saw it! And I think we'd better take a look at that compartment before we hear the rest. Piper, come with me. Join us, Tom, when you've arranged for the search."

"Right, Chief."

"Sorry, Daisy. I'll be back as soon as I can."

With that, the three men dashed off, leaving Daisy quite pleased with herself but frustrated. She went to find Belinda.

In the lounge, Mr. and Mrs. Smythe-Pike, Anne and Harold Bretton, and the mysterious Geraldine occupied a group of chairs near the fire. Smythe-Pike had one leg raised on a footstool. They had all changed for dinner, the ladies in black winter frocks with long sleeves and high necks, topped with warm stoles. The warm weather in the South had not left them unprepared for the chilly North, especially, Daisy guessed, for the miser's castle. The blacks, no doubt packed in case he died during their visit, served instead as mourning for Uncle Albert.

No sign of Belinda, nor of Chandra Jagai. Anne saw Daisy and gave a little wave.

"Daisy, can *you* tell us what's going on?" she said, coming over with her husband.

"Not much. Have you seen Belinda?"

"No. Perhaps she went up to her room. Mother says Mattie's taken to her bed with a hot water bottle. She's in a rotten state. I was never like that when I was pregnant."

"A rotten funk, if you ask me," Bretton put in. "It's my belief she knows something." He gave a significant nod.

"Poor Mattie," said Daisy with rather perfunctory sympathy. "Excuse me, I must find Belinda."

She went over to the Smythe-Pikes. Neither had seen the child. Nor was she in the bedroom she and Daisy shared.

Daisy started worrying. Where on earth had she got to?

Dismissed from the conference, Belinda trailed unhappily back to the lounge. She liked Dr. Jagai, but just now she wanted Daddy, or at least Miss Dalrymple.

She cheered up when she saw Kitty and Judith and Ray talking to the doctor. She'd be safe with all her friends. She joined them.

"Bel, have you got any sweets left?" Kitty greeted her. "Mine are all gone and they say it's going to be ages till they can serve dinner. They weren't expecting so many people."

"They're up in my room. I'll fetch them."

"Get your coat and hat, too. We're going out to explore the city walls and bastions. Hurry up, we've all brought our outdoor things down already."

"I don't know if I ought," said Belinda doubtfully. "Sergeant Barclay said the walls are dangerous."

"Don't be a baby."

"Don't be rude, Kit," her brother admonished. "Belinda doesn't have to come if she thinks she shouldn't."

"My father wants to see me soon, too."

"Oh well, never mind, then," Kitty said. "I'll find the best bits and show you in the morning. Come on, let's go."

By the time they had all muffled up and departed, Belinda was beginning to think better of her refusal. No one else was in the lounge. No one came to light the gas. It was dreary and even a bit scary. Sudden footsteps in the hall outside made her jump.

Daddy might go on talking to Miss Dalrymple for ages. Miss Dalrymple had told her to go to Dr. Jagai, and he was out on the walls. Sergeant Barclay had told her not to explore *alone,* but all the others would be there.

Belinda raced upstairs for her hat and coat and gloves.

She slipped out of the front door and round to the steps Sergeant Barclay had pointed out. There were just a few steps, then a path led upwards between stone walls. Soon she passed a gate on the left leading into the Raven's Nest Hotel's back garden.

Oh dear! she thought. If the others came that way, they might be far ahead. She hurried on.

The sun had set but the wind had blown away the clouds and it was still quite light outside, the sky above a clear blue. Lamps were lit, though, in the windows of the big house behind the hotel. Their friendly glow heartened Belinda. As the path levelled off and swung to the left around the front of the house, she glanced back at it, then stopped to look. On its gate-posts perched stone lions with long manes and lots of big teeth. They gazed out over Belinda's head, and she turned to see what they were staring at.

Ahead of her, the path met another running along the top of a steep, grassy bank, patched white and yellow with daisies and dandelions. The bank curved into the distance in both directions. Belinda guessed it must be the city wall, though it wasn't at all what she had expected.

One branch of her path led down to a narrow tunnel under the wall. As she took the other branch, she saw the sea beyond the wall, straight ahead. To both her left and her right, not too far away, high, square sort of mounds, grass covered, rose above the level of the bank. She couldn't see any of her friends.

Seagulls cried overhead. It was a lonely sound.

Reaching the wall path, Belinda stopped again. Nearby were steps going down to the tunnel. On the other side of the path, the grass sloped down a short, slippery way and then fell absolutely straight to the ground, an awfully long way below.

It did look dangerous. Perhaps she ought to go back to the hotel.

Then she heard Kitty's penetrating voice away to her right and saw a figure on top of the mound, silhouetted against the darkening sky. *That* was all right, then. She started off along the path, walking carefully.

As she approached the mound, she saw that it was actually a series of mounds and banks on top of a bit jutting out from the bank she was on. It must be a bastion, she decided, remembering Kitty's word. The base was a smooth stone wall as high as where she was walking, nearly as high as a three-storey house.

Just beside her, below her, was a sort of open room or courtyard with walls all around. One wall had barred windows. A dungeon? she wondered, stopping to look. Maybe there had once been a roof.

It was too dark way down at the bottom to see much. Peering down, Belinda stepped onto the grass beside the path, careful not to go beyond the narrow flat strip onto the sloping part. It would be a nasty fall, might even kill her, and if it didn't she didn't want to be stuck down there in the gloom with night coming on.

Dusk was falling fast, she realized. Maybe she shouldn't try to catch up with the others. She turned to look back at the town.

Close behind her loomed a muffled figure, dark, menacing, with arms outspread as if to herd her over the precipice. Silently it moved forward.

Belinda ducked under one arm and ran, screaming.

Her heart drummed in her chest. *Thump, thump, thump.* Her shoes thudded on the path. Was he following? She couldn't hear.

She risked a glance backwards. Her feet swerved, then slid out from under her. Suddenly she was slithering helplessly down.

10

Daisy stood in the lobby, wondering where one small girl might hide—and why. Should she knock on all the bedroom doors, question the hotel staff, or send for Alec right away?

Before she had made up her mind, footsteps and excited voices approached from the nether regions of the hotel. Kitty Gillespie appeared, dressed for outdoors, pink-cheeked and windblown. Raymond was visible behind her.

"Come on," cried Kitty. "She's right here, Bel."

A moment later, Belinda cannoned into Daisy's arms and raised a face streaked with mud and tears, a long scratch down one cheek. "I thought I was going to die," she wept.

"Die?" Daisy gasped. "What happened, darling? What on earth have you been up to?"

Kitty and Raymond burst into simultaneous explanations. Dr. Jagai's prosaic tones cut through. "I think it would be best, Miss Dalrymple, if we retired to somewhere rather more private."

"Undoubtedly," said Judith Smythe-Pike, her voice languid but the look she bent upon the doctor approving.

Her arm around Belinda's thin shoulders, Daisy led

them to the room set aside for police use. Judith raised delicate eyebrows at the magenta plush sofa. She was the only one in pristine condition. Belinda's coat was smeared with mud like her face, one black lisle stocking was laddered, one braid had lost its ribbon and the other was coming loose. The doctor, Kitty, and Raymond were almost as bedraggled.

"Dr. Jagai," said Daisy firmly as the brother and sister started gabbling again, "if you please."

Ray grinned and put his hand over Kitty's mouth.

"We decided," Chandra Jagai began, "we four, to inspect the Elizabethan wall before dark. Belinda turned up just before we left and was invited to go with us, but she refused because she expected her father to send for her shortly. So we went on, to the bastion known, I believe, as the King's Mount. We had been there for some time—a quarter of an hour, perhaps, I'm not sure—when we heard screams. Naturally, we ran."

"They ran," Judith put in dryly. "I walked fast."

"It takes more than a few screams to knock Judith off her dignity," said Raymond with an affectionate look. "We found Belinda stuck in a bramble bush at the bottom of the wall, luckily on the town side."

"Jolly lucky!" Kitty exclaimed. "That side's just a steepish slope, not too high. The other side's a sheer drop, miles high."

"About thirty feet," Dr. Jagai qualified this gross exaggeration. "Far enough to cause serious injuries, certainly."

"I thought I was falling on that side." Belinda's voice quavered. "When my feet slipped, I thought I was going to die."

Daisy hugged her and frowned at her all at once.

"You knew it was dangerous up there. The sergeant told you not to go alone."

"I wasn't alone, not really. I didn't realize how far ahead the others were. And I was being ever so careful, honestly, till . . . till . . ." A sob shook her.

"Shall I tell Miss Dalrymple what you told us?" Dr. Jagai asked gently. Belinda nodded and he went on, "Someone frightened her. In the dusk, she got the impression that he was trying to make her fall over the edge, the high edge. She was running away when she lost her footing."

"He *was* going to push me!"

"Did he touch you, Belinda?" Daisy asked.

"No, but he was right behind me, with his arms stretched out."

"You said you were standing quite near the edge," said Raymond. "I dare say he intended to pull you back to safety."

Belinda stubbornly shook her head.

"Did you see his face? Did he speak? Would you recognize him?"

"No, he was just a big black shape."

"She'd have seen him against the lighter western sky," Judith explained. "His face would have been shadowed, and it was already twilight."

"Didn't any of the rest of you see him? Not even a glimpse of his back disappearing into the distance?"

"It was a few moments before we were in sight of the path," said the doctor.

"You were out of sight?"

"The bastion has great mounds on it." Kitty's hands described a pyramid. "I was on the far side when Bel started screaming."

"Miss Smythe-Pike and I were sitting on a bench,"

Dr. Jagai said, "looking out over the river mouth to the pier and lighthouse, and the sea."

Judith nodded. "Just talking."

"Kitty was being an utter ass," said Raymond, frowning upon his sister, "racing up and down those slippery slopes. I was kept scrambling after to stop her breaking her neck, or at least to pick up the pieces."

"So if this man hurried," Dr. Jagai told Daisy, "perhaps for fear of being blamed for Belinda's fright, he could have reached the steps down to the tunnel under the wall before we appeared. We wouldn't have noticed him leaving once we reached her and started to extricate her from the briars." He examined his scratched hands. "No serious damage done."

"I don't know how to thank you all for rushing to the rescue," Daisy said with heartfelt gratitude.

They all made the embarrassed mutters proper to the occasion.

"I believe Belinda would be the better for a hot bath," said the doctor practically.

"Fortunately," Judith drawled, "the baths don't rely on the boiler. They have gas geysers. Kitty, we'd better go up and change for dinner."

"So had I." Raymond started after them, then looked back. "You'll dine with us, won't you, Doctor?"

"Thank you, but I haven't brought evening togs."

"Oh, righty-ho, then I shan't bother with the best bib and tucker either. Let's go and hoist a glass."

The two young men went out together.

"A bath sounds like a jolly good idea," said Daisy, "and then supper on a tray in bed, I should think. I expect one of the maids will clean up your things before morning."

"I didn't bring a nightie," Belinda said in a small voice, "or a toothbrush or anything."

"You'll just have to brush your teeth with your finger—I'll lend you toothpaste—and sleep in your combies, darling. Don't worry, we'll manage."

"I'm awfully glad I'm sleeping in your room." She rubbed her eyes, visibly wilting. "Daddy!"

Alec came in, followed by Tring and Piper. He fended off his grubby daughter. "Great Scott, Bel, where have you been?"

"Up on the city walls, Daddy. Someone . . ."

"The copper at the door didn't stop you?"

"I didn't see any policeman there."

"I 'spect Miss Belinda went out before we did, Chief," Piper suggested. "It was when we got back to the police station you asked for a guard on the front door."

"There's a back gate, too," said Belinda, "only I didn't know about it then. We came back that way."

"Ernie, check that there's a man on the gate, too. Who's 'we,' Belinda? Not Miss Dalrymple if you left before us."

"Tell your father the whole story," Daisy said, subsiding once more onto the magenta sofa and resignedly patting the place beside her. She and the sofa had already received a goodly dose of mud from Belinda, whereas Alec needed to stay professionally neat.

"Will you tell him? Please?" Just about dead on her feet, Belinda dropped beside Daisy. The men took chairs.

Daisy related Belinda's adventure as told to her, from the invitation to go with the others to the rescue from the brambles. Half-way through, Piper returned. By the time she finished, Belinda was slumped against her, fast asleep.

Alec was troubled. "I don't like it. It's just possible someone sees her as a threat, though the chances are it was a stranger trying to be helpful, as young Gillespie suggested. What about him? He was with his sister when this happened? Would she lie for him?"

"I haven't the foggiest. But I'll tell you about them, and the rest, when I've got her to bed."

"No. I don't want her left alone, without one of us four, until this business is cleared up." He crossed to the sofa and stood a moment looking down at Belinda with his heart in his face. Then with gentle hands he moved her to a more comfortable position, her feet up and her head on a cushion. She stirred and murmured something but didn't wake. "Besides," he said, returning to his seat, "I can't spare the time. Oh, by the way, we found a white thread snagged around the window catch."

"Aha!"

"And no dabs, either there or on the glass or his shoes, miss," said Tom. "Wiped clean."

"Aha!" said Daisy again.

"Precisely," Alec agreed with a smile. "Go ahead, please, Daisy."

"With the cast of characters? Right-oh, but you may wish for a family tree before I'm done."

"I already do, from what you said before. Can you make one out while you talk?"

"I'll try."

Piper presented her with a pencil and a sheet torn from his notebook, while Tom Tring moved a small table to her elbow.

"Thank you, gentlemen. Now where was I?"

"We got involved in what your school friend told you about her grandfather's will. Anne Bretton, was it? Let's have a thumbnail sketch of each suspect before we go into their movements."

"I'll start at the top of the family tree, then, not with

Anne. It'll make it easier to work out. First row, Alistair McGowan-the-will-maker, Laird of Dunston Castle; twin brother Albert-the-victim; and the unknown sister who married a Gillespie."

"Still living?"

"Presumed deceased." Daisy wrote them in. "Under Alistair there's his daughter Amelia Smythe-Pike. Kind, fussy, conventional. She wants the best for her family, of course, but I'd say she was upset more because her husband was raising a dust than because she was truly indignant. She caters to his every whim. I can't see her as a murderer. Besides, she's an elderly lady. I doubt she has the strength."

"The victim was her uncle, though, much older and in poor health."

"It don't take much strength to do in a frail old man," Tring agreed.

"On the other hand, she had no guarantee her father would change his will in her favour on Albert's death," Alec said.

"No. The same applies to her husband, Desmond, of course, but he's a fire-breather. I can see him simply losing his temper because Albert refused to change his mind about leaving the family fortune to a stranger. He's . . ."

"Hold on a minute, Daisy! Albert's heir isn't one of the family? That makes a considerable difference!"

"You didn't give me a chance to tell you before," Daisy pointed out.

"*Mea culpa.* I most humbly beg your pardon."

"How d'you spell that, Chief?" asked Piper.

" 'Pardon'? Oh, *mea culpa.* Never mind that, Ernie, we don't want all our trivial comments taken down in black and white."

"I wouldn't've put it in the report, Chief, but when I'm taking shorthand it just all flows through, like."

"Let's get back to Smythe-Pike," Alec said impatiently. "He had a temper and a reason for losing it."

"Yes," Daisy confirmed, "and a pressing need for filthy lucre—that's money, Mr. Piper—at least according to his son-in-law. Harold Bretton told me Smythe-Pike's only interest in the family estate is in the hunting, shooting, and fishing, and the place has gone to rack and ruin. He'll have to sell up if they don't get hold of pots of money pretty quickly."

"Ah," said Tom Tring, "but he hadn't got no guarantee of a single penny, and a bloke like that's more likely to hit someone over the head in hot blood than to hold a piller over his face."

Daisy nodded. "What's more, he's fearfully lame from gout. I don't know if he could have managed it. Whoever did it couldn't know when someone else might come along. They must have been desperate to get a move on, and they were lucky at that."

"I'll bear that in mind," Alec said. "Finished with him? Who's next on your little list?"

"Oh, she never would be missed, she never would be missed," Daisy carolled *à la Mikado.* "That's a beastly thing to say, or sing, but Anne Bretton, *née* Smythe-Pike is one of life's whiners. She moans that her husband has no interest in the children but sends them to their nurse as soon as they're any trouble."

"More than one child, then."

"Yes, there's Baby, *alias* Alistair McGowan Bretton, and Tabitha, who's five. Belinda was very good about looking after her, for quite some time. In fact, she was trying to amuse her just before she went and found Mr. McGowan dead. Anne took Baby back to his nurse and she was with me when Belinda came rushing in."

"How long was she gone?"

"Not very long, and she was quite calm when she returned. She's not the sort with nerves of steel who could murder someone one minute and scold Tabitha for dirtying her frock the next. In fact, I can't see Anne doing anything so positive as murdering someone. She prefers to complain."

Piper uttered one of his muffled snorts. Tring frankly grinned. "The chief was sure you'd taken Mrs. Bretton under your wing, miss," the sergeant revealed.

"Not I. And as for Harold Bretton—well, I wouldn't so much as pass the time of day if he weren't her husband. I believe he only married her for the money he thought she had. A wife from the landed gentry looks attractive to a would-be man-about-town. He's an out and out cad, rude where he sees no advantage to politeness, disloyal, abusing his father-in-law to a stranger but not willing to buckle down and try to get the farms in order."

"A bounder indeed," Alec said dryly, "but that doesn't make him a murderer. He doesn't benefit directly from Albert McGowan's demise."

"Not directly, no, but he's a gambler. He told me only an inheritance or a big win on the horses could save the Smythe-Pike estate. So I bet he'd be quite ready to gamble on Albert's death turning to his advantage."

"Hmm, it seems possible, though risking the loss of a stake, however large, is rather different from risking the hangman's noose."

Daisy didn't care for this reminder of the end result of the investigation. Studying her growing family tree, she hurried on brightly, "I don't imagine you'll put Tabitha or Baby on your little list, so Judith's next."

"Judith Smythe-Pike, who was out there with Belinda?"

"Yes, Anne's sister. Incidentally, Mr. and Mrs. Smythe-Pike and the Brettons are clear where Belinda's adventure is concerned. I saw them in the lounge just when it must have been happening. Judith's clear, too. She was with the doctor."

"We can't be sure that incident had any significance, or any connection with the murder."

Looking down at Belinda, deep in innocent sleep at her side, Daisy said, "Do you think she might have imagined the whole thing?"

"Alone, in the dusk, in a strange place, she might have, though on the whole she's not fanciful. More likely she misinterpreted a stranger's intentions. Yet who can tell?"

"She would have told me if she'd seen anything. In the train, I mean. If the murderer went after her because he—or she—*believed* Belinda had seen something, then Judith isn't the murderer. Which isn't to say I don't think she'd be capable of it, for Raymond's sake."

"Raymond Gillespie, her cousin if I'm not mistaken."

"Second cousin. They're unofficially engaged, and I'd say they're deeply devoted to each other, though on the whole Judith plays the part of a careless flapper most effectively."

"A bright young thing, is she?" Alec commented.

"Except when Raymond has one of his turns. He's badly shell-shocked; I'll tell you about him later. I gather Judith is the only one who can soothe him when he's in a rotten state of nerves."

"So she'd do anything for him, and he benefits directly."

"From Albert's death? His father does, at any rate." Daisy pulled a long face. "Oh dear, it does look black for Judith."

"You like her? There's plenty of others," Alec consoled her.

"All the Gillespies. Oh, I nearly forgot the mysterious Geraldine. She's old Alistair's younger daughter, Amelia Smythe-Pike's sister. All I know is that she ran away decades ago to avoid getting stuck looking after her father, and she's suddenly turned up looking frightfully *soignée* and prosperous."

"Swunyay, miss?" Piper asked.

"Chic. Smart. She and I met at lunch. No one recognized her. She's lived in France, but I don't know her surname."

"Mr. Halliday gave me a list." Sergeant Tring studied a sheet of paper. "That'd likely be Madam Pass-queer. That's P-a-s-q-u-i-e-r, lad," he told Piper.

Adding the surname to the family tree, Daisy said, "Geraldine Pasquier, *née* McGowan."

"Pas-key-ay, eh, miss?" said Tring. "If you ask me, that Frog lingo's passing queer." His mustache quivered with satisfaction at the quip.

"Well said, Sarge," Piper observed, surveying his notes with gloom.

Daisy smiled at the sergeant. "I can't tell you any more about Madame, so let's get on to the Gillespies. Peter Gillespie is Alistair and Albert's nephew. According to Harold Bretton, he inherited a flourishing boot factory but lost it during the War when he was prosecuted for selling the Army shoddy boots."

"Whew!" said Piper disapprovingly.

"Hard up?" Alec queried.

"Not on their beam-ends, I'd say, but income not coming up to expectations. Quite likely living beyond their means. And, as you will have noted, Peter Gillespie has no great respect for morality or the law." Daisy spoke with asperity. Gillespie's transgression had taken on a new ugliness since she'd come to know his son better. Had Raymond found himself in the trenches with his father's boots disintegrating on his feet?

"Noted," said Alec, "though you've only Bretton's word for it. What about his wife?"

"Enid Gillespie. I've not seen much of her, and when I did she was mostly scolding Kitty. It wouldn't surprise me if she frequently scolds her husband, too." She shrugged. "Can't say more. I can tell you even less about their daughter-in-law, Matilda. She's one of those women pregnancy doesn't suit, and she's far too pregnant to have murdered anyone."

"And her husband?"

"Jeremy, Peter's eldest. Fancies himself a womaniser, and deeply resents having to earn a living. I wouldn't put it past him to take drastic measures for the sake of money."

"Would you not! He's Raymond's brother, I take it."

"Yes. Poor Ray. He'd like nothing better than to earn a living so as to be able to marry Judith, but he can't keep a job because of his nervous attacks."

"Needs money to marry the girl he loves, eh?" said Tring. "That don't look too good."

"What form do his attacks take?" Alec asked.

"A blue funk, thinking he's back in Flanders. And anguish because he's not fit."

"Not violence, then."

"No. Oh, he did . . ." She hesitated.

"Come on, Daisy, out with it."

"It wasn't really anything. He was holding Judith's hand and she said he was hurting her, but he let go at once and was desperately sorry."

"Suppose something made him believe the old man was a Boche," Alec said slowly. "He might have killed him without realizing what he was doing."

Daisy was silent.

"The courts go easy on blokes like that," Tring said.

After a heavy pause, Alec said, "Is that the last, then?"

"There's Kitty Gillespie. Bother, I haven't left room on the page. I'll have to write her in sideways. Anyway, she's only fifteen and far too liable to blurt out whatever comes to mind to make a respectable murderer. She'd have told all and sundry by now. That's all the family."

"All right. Now for their movements. Where was your compartment in relation to Albert McGowan's?"

"We were next but one, with the lawyer between."

"You could see everyone passing along the corridor, then."

"As a matter of fact, for the relevant time, I saw nothing."

"Nothing! You didn't dog their every step and note down the exact times?" Alec teased.

"By that time I was fed up with their squabbling," Daisy said crossly. "They'd been arguing over lunch as to who was to tackle Albert first. I heard footsteps coming and going, but I buried my head in a magazine so they wouldn't come and talk to me."

"Belinda might have seen who passed in the corridor."

"She wasn't with me all the time. She went to see Kitty, and then to Dr. Jagai, in third class."

"Dr. Jagai!"

"She likes him, and I didn't see she could come to any harm."

"But I thought he was just a cooperative stranger, the first medical man to see the cor . . . the deceased."

"Gosh, no. Albert McGowan introduced him to us. Chandra Jagai was his protégé and his heir."

"His heir! Great Scott, Daisy, why didn't you tell me sooner? He has the best motive of all."

"Oh, bilge! Absolutely the opposite. He stood to inherit the whole family fortune if Albert survived Alistair."

"Unless the family succeeded in changing Albert's mind."

"Not much chance of that. He despised them. In fact, he was going to see the lawyer to ask advice about tying up the money for Dr. Jagai so that the family hadn't a hope of contesting his will."

"That's what Jagai told you? Hasn't it crossed your mind that he might have been lying? No, it was a perfect opportunity for him to bump off his benefactor while plenty of other people with motives were present to divert suspicion. Dr. Jagai goes high on my list."

Dismayed and disbelieving, all Daisy could think of to say was, "Don't tell Belinda."

11

Alec went over to the sofa and gazed down at his little girl. He loved her so much it made his heart hurt, from the skinny legs in muddy black stockings to the ginger hair just like Joan's. Curled in the total, trusting relaxation of innocent sleep, she was too young to learn about the beastliness abroad in the world!

What on earth had possessed her to run away from her grandmother, to run to Daisy? She needed a mother. Yet Daisy mustn't be led to think Alec only wanted to marry her for Belinda's sake.

This was no time for thoughts of marriage. Daisy was looking up at him questioningly.

"Thank you for taking care of Bel."

"It was a pleasure. She's a dear. I only wish we'd had a less eventful journey. She's had a frightening and exhausting time of it; must you question her tonight?"

"She might remember things now she'll have forgotten by the morning. And she'll probably rouse anyway if I pick her up to carry her upstairs." He gathered her in his arms and turned to sit down with her in his lap. As she stirred to wakefulness, he said over her head, "I did hear her say she's sharing your room, didn't I?"

"Yes, Mr. Halliday arranged it that way, and I'd have insisted if he hadn't. She needs a bath and supper and bed, Alec."

"Very soon. Belinda, sweetheart, I need your help."

"I'll try, Daddy." She wriggled. "Only let me sit up properly 'cause I can't *think* like this. Is Mr. Piper going to write down what I say?"

"If you don't mind."

She was sitting beside him now, between him and Daisy, and he had a poor view of her face. It was a pity, but he didn't want to deprive her of the comfort of his closeness. He took her hand in his.

"S'posing I don't remember right?" She sounded strained, and her hand was tense.

"It doesn't matter, sweetheart, it's only to help us, me and Mr. Tring and Mr. Piper, no one else. Just do the best you can."

"All right. Do you want to know about when I found him?"

"Yes, let's get the worst over first. All I need to know is whether you touched or moved anything."

"Just his hand." Now she spoke quite matter-of-factly. "You know how stiff Granny gets when she falls asleep in an awkward position? Well, Mr. McGowan's arm was hanging down and I thought he'd be more comfy if I put it across his chest. It didn't matter if he woke up, you see, 'cause he'd invited me to tea. Only he was dead. His hand felt sort of like a waxwork."

"Quite cold?"

Belinda considered this. "Not icy. Just like some people always have cold hands."

"You could have asked me that," said Daisy reprovingly, "or the doctor. I tried for a pulse just moments later, and he wasn't much after me."

"Sorry, Bel. I will ask the doctor. You didn't touch anything else?"

"No, I looked at his face and ran away. Oh, but before I moved his arm I picked up a feather off the floor. Just a little curly feather. It wasn't stealing."

"No, it's a very useful piece of evidence."

"Is it really, Daddy?" She beamed up at him. "Did I really help?"

"You did. Let's see if you can help some more. What did you do right after lunch?"

"We went back to our compartment, didn't we, Miss Dalrymple? The ticket-man came in to say he wouldn't forget to send your telegram to Gran when we got to York. Then there was York and we saw the big church, the Minister. Then I read the magazine Kitty lent me."

"You didn't look out into the corridor?"

"Not when I was reading. I stood out there for a while to look out the other side for a change—no, that was in the morning. When I got tired of reading I went to see Kitty. Tabitha was somewhere else with her nurse."

"Besides Kitty, who else did you see?"

"Oh, lots of people. They kept coming and going and talking about who was going to see Mr. McGowan first. The only thing they agreed was that Kitty wasn't to go because she'd only offend him. Kitty doesn't mean to be rude, Daddy, she just always says what she thinks without thinking first."

Daisy smiled, and Alec recalled her comment about Kitty's inability to curb her tongue, a definite handicap for a murderer.

"None of them spoke of having been to see him already?"

Belinda pondered, and shook her head. "Not that I heard. Mrs. Smythe-Pike said it'd be best to let his stomach settle for a while after his lunch, and I think she won. Anyway, I wasn't there all that long. I got tired of them arguing. So I went back to Miss Dalrymple and asked if I could go and see Dr. Jagai. He played draughts with me and told me about Durham. He's awfully nice, Daddy."

With Daisy's minatory eye upon him, Alec didn't disillusion his daughter. Time enough if they found evidence against the Indian. "Did you pass Mr. McGowan's compartment to reach Dr. Jagai?" he asked.

"Yes, but I couldn't see if anyone was there," Belinda said quickly, looking down. Her hand tensed again in his. "The blinds were down. He kept them down, and the door shut."

"You heard something, though, didn't you?" Daisy suggested.

"I didn't listen. I don't know what they were saying. I just hurried past."

"But someone was with Mr. McGowan?" Alec probed.

"Yes. No! I don't know. I don't know who it was," Belinda cried frantically.

Daisy's glare killed the next question on Alec's tongue. He substituted, "Well, that's enough for now. Shall I carry you up, Belinda?"

"No, thank you, Daddy," she said with a fragile composure. "I'm quite all right, honestly, and I know you're awfully busy. 'Night." Jumping up, she kissed him and hurried to the door.

" 'Night, sweetheart. Sleep well."

"Good-night, Miss Belinda," came Tom's rumble. "Night-night, miss," said Piper. "Sweet dreams." Under cover of her reply, Daisy said in a low voice, "I shan't leave her, not for a minute."

"Bless you." He pressed her hand in heartfelt gratitude. "I'll try to pop up for a word later. It's going to be a long evening."

Tom and Piper wished her good-night. As the door closed behind her, Tom said cogently, "Miss Belinda heard something."

"She's got the wind up," said Piper, "poor little duck."

Alec gave a grim nod. "The two are connected, I'd bet all Lombard Street to a China orange. Whatever it was, it's made too much of an impression for her to forget it. She'll be calmer in the morning. She'll tell me then. In the meantime, we can't sit still. I'll see the solicitor first, Ernie, to check Miss Dalrymple's information about the two wills."

"Mr. Braeburn? Right, Chief." The youthful D.C. hurried out.

"What d'you reckon, Tom?" said Alec.

Tom grinned. "I reckon it's the Indian doctor she's took under her wing, Chief."

"Dammit, man, that's not what I meant. No ideas about our villain?"

"From what Miss Dalrymple's told us? It's not Miss Kitty—nor yet the doctor."

"Oh, go to hell." Alec looked round as the door opened. "What is it, Ernie?"

"Seems Mr. Braeburn's took to his bed, Chief. He's got a sore throat from waiting around on the station in the cold. Been ordering mustard baths and hot poultices right and left, Mr. Briggs says."

"Indeed! Well, I can't insist on his coming down, so I'll tackle him in his room. Let's hope he's not asleep. Ernie, come with me. Tom, have a word with the victim's manservant, Weekes, wasn't it?"

"Right, Chief. How's about summat to eat?"

"You gotta be prepared to starve in a good cause, Sarge."

"Ernie may be prepared to starve," said Alec, "but order some sandwiches for you and me, Tom, and we'll snatch a bite whenever we can."

"Blimey, Chief, have a heart!" Piper protested.

"That'll learn you to cheek your elders and betters," said Tom, grinning.

Alec and Piper went upstairs. Though the hotel was not large, the first floor boasted a bewilderment of corridors and corners, with flights of two or three steps here and there to add to the confusion. The numbers on the room doors seemed to present no logical order. However, having already asked the way, Piper threaded through the maze with unerring accuracy.

"This is it, Chief."

Alec knocked. The grunt in response could have been "Who is it?" but he chose to interpret it as "Come in."

Piper slipped in behind him and noiselessly closed the door.

"About time, too." The pettish, slightly hoarse voice issued from the green wing chair, its back to the door, pulled up close to the grate where a small, sulky coal fire smouldered. Only the tip of an old-fashioned nightcap was visible. "The water's nearly stone cold," the voice continued.

Nodding to Piper to stay where he was, Alec advanced, saying, "I'm afraid I'm not the chambermaid, sir."

The nightcap jerked. "What . . . ?" The word was a squawk of alarm, and the long, narrow face which appeared around the side of the chair twitched nervously, as if the man feared he was to be the next victim. "Who the deuce are you, sir?"

"Police," said Alec soothingly. "Detective Chief Inspector Fletcher, Scotland Yard. You're Mr. Braeburn, the solicitor?"

The lawyer gave a grudging nod, and pulled his muffler closer around his neck. Below the knitted scarf one end of a black silk cravat stuck out incongruously. He wore a warm but expensive dressing gown, brown woollen cloth with darker brown velvet collar, lapels, and piping. Green silk pyjama-legs protruded below, and sheepskin bedroom slippers. The once-hot mustard foot-bath had been pushed aside. The air was redolent of Friar's Balsam.

"What do you want?" he croaked. "I'm ill." He looked ill, his face pallid, thin lips bloodless. Behind the gold-rimmed glasses, dark pouches sagged beneath his eyes.

"I'm very sorry to disturb you, sir," Alec apologised. "It was good of you to agree to stay and lend the police your assistance. The thing is, I shan't be sure how to tackle this business until I have certain information about the McGowan brothers' wills."

"I was never Albert McGowan's solicitor, though Alistair McGowan has employed my firm since before I became a partner."

"But Mr. Albert consulted you, on the train?" Alec remained standing, since there was no second chair in the room and he couldn't very well perch on the bed without an invitation.

"I suppose his man told you. Yes, Mr. Albert sent his servant to beg the favour of a word of advice whenever convenient."

"And you spoke to him?"

"Yes, yes, though I made it plain the usual fee was expected despite the unconventional circumstances."

"What time did you go to his compartment, sir?"

"I've no idea, no idea at all," Braeburn said irritably. "Some time after the train left York."

"Was Mr. Albert lying down when you arrived? Did you happen to notice a pillow?"

"Really, Inspector, I cannot be expected to recall such details. My only concern was his queries about changing his will, which I understood to be your interest, also."

"Yes, sir. He *was* intending to change his will, then?"

"It is scarcely proper for a solicitor to discuss a client's affairs. However, in the circumstances I dare say it is permissible, especially as he was not a regular client. Yes, he wished to change his will, but *not* in favour of his relatives."

"Not?"

"In fact, his purpose was to make it less likely that they should be able to overturn his wishes."

"Which were?"

"I understand, though I have not seen his will, that apart from a small legacy to his manservant he left everything to a young doctor. A foreigner, I believe, and in no way related. It is scarcely surprising that the family wishes to challenge it. Nonetheless, a suit is most unlikely to be successful as I had already informed Mr. Smythe-Pike and Mr. Gillespie. However, Mr. Albert persisted in his desire to ensure his will's standing."

"How did he—or you—propose to do that?"

"Quite sensibly." Braeburn's tone was indicative of a lawyer's reluctance to credit a layman with sense in legal matters. "He proposed to set up a charitable trust. Its director was to be the person in question, and its purpose to found and support a medical clinic in India."

"Admirable," said Alec. His approval stemmed not from any legal consideration, nor even from the benevolent intent, but from relief that Belinda's friend and Daisy's protégé was off at least that particular hook.

"Unfortunately," said Braeburn, "I was forced to advise him that the sum he might expect from his brother's estate was quite inadequate for the grandiose enterprise he envisioned. Dunston Castle has been allowed to become thoroughly dilapidated, and the demesne is mostly moorland, fit only for shooting and fishing. More seriously, of late years Mr. Alistair has speculated most unwisely on the Stock Exchange, as well as giving considerable sums to charity. Extreme age takes some people that way."

"You mean the family fortune's gone?" Alec exclaimed.

"A few thousand left at most. A very few thousand."

"Have you told Mr. Gillespie?"

"Certainly not!"

"Peter Gillespie *is* Alistair McGowan's heir, is he not?"

"He was not then."

"Then you confirm that Albert McGowan's death made him heir?"

"I do. However, I should consider it highly improper to inform him of the condition of the estate before it becomes his."

"Why is that, sir?"

"In the first place, I doubt he and his wife and son would hesitate to reproach Mr. McGowan for the losses, even on his deathbed. In the second, I anticipate that Mr. McGowan may change his will in favour of his own offspring. In the third—a felon cannot profit by his crime, and you must agree, Inspector, that whether as principal or accessory Mr. Peter Gillespie is by far your most likely suspect."

"That's as may be, sir." Alec swiftly reviewed in his

mind what he had learned. Daisy had been right about the wills on every count.

Braeburn had been surprisingly forthcoming. His voice, though husky, was holding up quite well. In Alec's experience, solicitors, though notoriously close-mouthed, tended to be unstoppable once set in motion. He didn't want to be responsible for any further damage to the man's sore throat.

"Just one more question, sir," he said. "Did you see anyone else go into or come out of Albert McGowan's compartment?"

"I did not," the lawyer snapped. "I brought important papers with me to study and I had no interest in his visitors, nor reason to expect to suffer an inquisition on the subject."

"Just so, sir. Thank you for your cooperation. It's a pity more members of the public don't see it as their duty to assist the police."

Braeburn essayed a feeble smile. "Ah well, we're both on the same side of the law, eh, Inspector? By the way, I trust you will not disclose information given you in confidence?"

"I see no reason to do so, sir," Alec assured him, with the usual mental reservation. If it seemed likely to help him find a murderer, he'd use his knowledge like a shot.

The lawyer must be sicker than he appeared, or he'd have made sure before he gave away any secrets that they would be treated in confidence.

Alec and Piper returned downstairs. In the parlour they found Tom and a small man in stiffly correct black, who stood up as Alec entered.

"This here's Mr. Weekes, Chief, as was gentleman's gentleman to the deceased. We've been having a bit of a chin-wag over a pint."

"I'll be getting along, now, sir, if there's nothing more I can do for you."

Behind his back, Tom gave a slight nod.

"Thank you for your help, Mr. Weekes," said Alec. "I hope the loss of your employer hasn't left you in too bad a hole."

"Not too bad, sir, which isn't to say I'm not sorry to see the last of the poor old chap. Treated me very handsome, he did, like I told Miss Dalrymple. Now there's a real lady! Well, I hope you get the villain that did it, that's all. Good-night, sir, and good-night to you, Mr. Tring." With a condescending nod to Piper, the valet left.

"That's put you properly in your place, young 'un," Tring observed.

"Is that food I see beside you?" said Alec, suddenly ravenous.

"Cor, Sarge, you didn't scoff the lot while we was gone?"

"Mr. Weekes having already eaten, not so much as a nibble's passed my lips. What d'you think, Chief, can we spare Ernie half a sandwich?"

"If he runs to the bar first. You'll have the same again, Tom?" He gave Piper a half-crown and the lad hurried off.

While he was gone, Alec told Tom what the lawyer had said. "So the huge family fortune the old man was killed for turns out to be no more than a few thousand," he concluded.

"Ah," Tom ruminated. "There's been murder done afore now for a few hundred, or less."

"In any case, it seems they weren't aware the riches had vanished. Miss Dalrymple certainly wasn't."

"No, but she got all the rest right, Chief, didn't she? As usual!"

12

"What about the valet?" Alec said as Piper returned with two brimming tankards in one hand and one in the other. "Miss Dalrymple didn't mention, or didn't know, that he gets a legacy from Albert. It may not be much, but as you so rightly say, murder has been done for very little."

Tom shook his head. Taking a deep draught of bitter, he wiped the suds off his mustache and reached for a sandwich. "I'd count him out, Chief. He wasn't even on Miss Dalrymple's list of suspects."

"That's no reason for not putting him on mine!" Noting too late the twinkle in the sergeant's eyes, Alec realized he'd been had. "All right," he said resignedly. "Explain."

"Weekes knows about the legacy, and it's just a couple of hundred and a gold watch. McGowan paid him a hundred and fifty a year, all found, of course."

"Blimey," said Piper, "I'm in the wrong business."

"Ah, but you got a future, lad. Weekes is out of a job. He's sorry the old man's gone, though more peeved than grieved, I'd say. The other thing is, he reminded me what Miss Dalrymple told us: He was the one first drew attention to suspicious circs."

"That's right, I'd forgotten. He confirmed the rest

of Miss Dalrymple's statement, about McGowan's illness and the window and so on?"

"Every word, Chief."

Alec chewed on a mouthful of ham-and-tongue sandwich while he considered. "All right, he can go to the bottom of the list."

"Who's next, then, Chief?" Piper asked.

"Efficient of Halliday to collect everyone in one place so we don't have to race around town. We'd better see this Indian doctor chap. No apparent motive, rather the reverse, but you never can tell. And he may have some medical information for us." Not to mention the fact that Alec was all agog to meet the fellow who had so quickly wormed his way into both Daisy's and Belinda's good graces.

Piper swallowed a final bite, emptied the last drop of his abstemious half of mild, and went off to find the doctor. As he opened the door, the sound of a wireless or gramophone wafted down the hall from the residents' lounge, playing "K-K-K-Katy." So much for mourning Albert McGowan.

"I'll be waiting at the k-k-k-kitchen door," warbled a hearty tenor.

"Turn the blasted thing down!" bellowed an irate voice.

The wireless was silent when Piper ushered in Dr. Jagai. His youth took Alec by surprise; for no good reason he had expected a man of forty or so, older than himself. Chandra Jagai was nearer Daisy's age than Alec's.

"Detective Sergeant Tring." Alec waved at Tom. "And I'm Detective Chief Inspector Fletcher, Scotland Yard."

The Indian's round, rather serious face broke into a white smile and he held out his hand. "How do you do, Chief Inspector. So you're Miss Belinda's father. A delightful child." His English was perfect.

Alec shook his hand, warming to him. "Thank you, Doctor. I think so, too. Do sit down." He must not let the praise of his daughter influence his attitude to this man. "We're hoping you can help us."

The smile vanished. With a sigh, Jagai said earnestly, "I only wish I could. Mr. McGowan was a father to me from the day my parents died, when I was a small boy. I shall miss him, and it would be some satisfaction to think I had assisted in apprehending his murderer. He was old and not well, but he should have died peacefully in his bed."

"My condolences." So Albert McGowan had at least one sincere mourner. Alec paused for a respectful moment, then asked, "You are satisfied that it was murder, sir?"

"From a medical point of view, I can give you no assurance. The observable symptoms were constant with a heart attack or, I believe, with asphyxiation—but I am no forensic expert, merely a general practitioner."

"Don't worry about that. We have a forensic pathologist coming up from Newcastle. Did you happen to notice the temperature of the body, Dr. Jagai?"

"His wrist was cold to the touch, but he had poor circulation and his hands generally felt slightly clammy."

"He had a weak heart, did he? And what about the dyspepsia?"

"I was not his personal physician, but any man of eighty or so is lucky not to have a weak heart. As for the dyspepsia, he most certainly suffered acutely. He would have been in great discomfort flat on his back, and I never knew him not to have his bismuth within easy reach. Miss Dalrymple's arguments are most convincing."

"Including the open window?"

Jagai gave a faint smile. "He used to tease me that my blood had adjusted to Scottish conditions as his had to the climate of India. He preferred it hot enough to be uncomfortable to the average Englishman in jacket and waistcoat and necktie. In fact, he never failed to invite me to strip to my shirt-sleeves if no one else was present. He'd put up with the cold when he went out, but indoors draughts were anathema."

The doctor surely would not have been so eager to confirm Daisy's points had he had a hand in the old man's death. With some relief, Alec decided his daughter's new friend was probably just as nice as she thought him.

"You were in the third class, I understand?" he said.

"Yes. Mr. McGowan gave me a more than adequate allowance, but I didn't choose to blow it on traveling first."

"Very wise, but that's not what I meant, sir. I was thinking that you were too far off to see who visited him in his compartment."

"Alas, yes. Now I wish I had sprung for a first-class ticket and insisted on staying with him. The first I knew of trouble was when Belinda came to fetch me."

"She did?" Alec exclaimed. "Dai . . . Miss Dalrymple sent her off alone when she'd just discovered a dead body?"

"I gathered Belinda had offered. At that time she was quite calm and composed, though naturally somewhat excited. After the first shock, children are often remarkably resilient. It was later, when she'd overheard talk of murder, that she became frightened."

"Of being attacked."

"No, surprisingly not." The dark forehead wrinkled. "Her first fear was of being accused of the crime. Miss Dalrymple managed to reassure her on that head, and then she and I did our best to distract her."

"Thank you," Alec said absently, wondering why such an odd notion should so much as cross his daughter's mind.

Into the brief silence, Tom dropped a question. "Did Mr. McGowan ever mention being afraid of any of his relations, sir, or being threatened?"

"On the contrary, Sergeant, I'm afraid he rather despised them. You see, he had gone to India with nothing and made a fortune. They had started with every advantage and ended up . . . er . . . financially embarrassed, and none of them with the gumption to do anything about it."

"That's pretty much what Weekes said, sir," Tom told Alec.

"One of them appears to have found the gumption," Alec said grimly. "Thank you, Doctor, that will be all for now, though I may want to speak to you again. We're a bit rushed for time this evening if we're not to keep everyone up into the small hours."

"I am at your disposal, Mr. Fletcher. I've taken a few days off from St. Thomas's to visit friends in Edinburgh, but needless to say it's far more important to me to see Albert McGowan's murderer brought to book."

They shook hands again. As Jagai turned to leave, Alec said, "Oh, by the way, Doctor, Belinda has taken a great liking to you. If she should happen to tell you anything that has the remotest bearing on this case . . ."

"I shall come to you at once."

The wireless was playing again, though softer than before. *"Ev'*rybody has *got* somebody to *tell* their troubles to," it announced dolefully, then was cut off as the door closed behind Dr. Jagai.

"Cor," said Piper, "if it wasn't for his skin, you'd never guess he was a wog!"

"An Indian gentleman, Ernie. Not a murderer, I'd say. Let's see if we can eliminate a few more of the less likely suspects, and find out about the movements of the more likely. We'll have Mrs. Smythe-Pike next. She'll be able to enlighten us about her mysterious sister, too, before we tackle her. Do try to get her without her peppery husband!"

Pink-cheeked from her bath, Belinda sat up in bed in her woollie combinations and Liberty bodice, the sleeves of Daisy's russet jumper rolled up to her elbows. She regarded without much interest the plate of cold meat, bread and butter, and pickled beetroot on the tray on her lap.

"I'm not very hungry."

"Have you been eating sweets?" asked Daisy, who was absolutely starving. She, too, had a tray, much of its contents already gone.

"Not since after lunch."

"We missed our tea. You really must eat something, darling."

"I had some bread. I don't like beetroot when it's all vinegary like this."

"Then leave it. It's a pretty asinine thing to give anyone to eat in bed, I must say, the way it stains. Have another bit of bread—it's cut very thin—and a slice of ham. Shall I cut it up for you? It's difficult in bed."

"Yes, please. I've drunk all my cocoa."

"Good."

Sitting on the edge of the bed, Daisy cut the ham into bite-sized pieces. Belinda listlessly ate a little more, then pushed the tray away.

"I'm too tired."

"All right, darling, we'll call it a day. Do you want to keep the pullover on, or will you be warm enough without it."

"I'll take it off, and my bodice. I'll be warm enough with the hot water bottle."

Daisy helped her take off the extra garments. Kissing her good-night, she turned off the gaslight above the bed.

"You won't go away, will you?" Belinda asked in a quavery voice.

"No, I'll be right here."

"Even when I'm asleep?"

"Even when you're asleep. Darling, won't you tell me what it is you're frightened of?"

"The m-murderer."

"But even murderers don't kill people for no reason, and he has no reason to kill you . . . has he?"

"N-no."

"You think he might have, don't you? Tell me why."

"No, I can't!" cried Belinda, panic-stricken. "Don't ask me. I don't know anything."

"Hush, love, hush." Daisy held her tight, stroking back from her forehead the tendrils of carroty hair still damp from the steam of the bath. "I shan't ask you anymore. Are you ready to sleep now?"

"Yes. Only could you please not turn the light off?"

"I'll turn it down till you're asleep, then leave it on low when I go to bed. Good-night, darling, sweet dreams."

When Daisy turned round after lowering the gas over her bed, Belinda was already sunk in exhausted sleep. Thankfully she brightened the light again. After setting the two trays outside the door, she sat down with a book she had picked up in the lounge downstairs. It was a detective story, *The Mark of Cain*, an old one by Carolyn Wells but Daisy hadn't read it.

Nor did she read it now. With a real murder mystery on her hands, she simply could not concentrate on an imaginary one.

She wished she was downstairs with Alec, listening to his interviews with the suspects. But even if he let her, which was highly unlikely, she couldn't leave Belinda. Suppose the child's fears had some basis in fact? Daisy didn't dare slip out even for a minute.

Not even to go to the lavatory, as she wanted to with more and more desperation as time passed. Alec *had* said he'd pop up to see her, hadn't he?

"If young Kitty confirms Mrs. Smythe-Pike's story," Alec said, "then those two can go to the bottom of the list."

"And Mrs. Jeremy Gillespie," Tom agreed, "without disturbing the poor lady."

"If she's half as pregnant as she sounds, she's out anyway. I'm surprised Alistair McGowan expected her to travel so far."

"More like he just said 'all' and they was afraid of offending . . ." He stopped as the door opened.

"Oh *do* go away, Jeremy," said a clear young voice, its owner invisible. "I don't need you to hold my hand, any more than I need Mummy or Daddy. And if I did need someone, I'd choose Ray. Come on, Detective Constable Piper."

Detective Constable Piper came on, looking rather harassed, hustled in by a chubby, sandy-haired schoolgirl. "Miss Gillespie, sir."

"You're Belinda's father?" Kitty Gillespie advanced upon Alec with her hand out, her hazel eyes frankly appraising. "How do you do, Detective Chief Inspector Fletcher. You're really from Scotland Yard? Golly, this is simply ripping. They'll never believe it at school."

Shaking her hand, Alec did his best not to smile. "How do you do, Miss Gillespie."

"Oh, call me Kitty. 'Miss Gillespie' sounds like when I'm in trouble at school. I say, Detective Chief Inspector Fletcher is an awful mouthful. Can I call you something shorter?"

"Mr. Fletcher will do nicely. This is Detective Sergeant Tring, my right-hand man."

"How do you do, Mr. Tring." Kitty shook hands with him, too. He beamed at her. "Golly," she said again, plumping down on the sofa with a satisfied sigh. "What do you want to know?"

"Let's start with your whereabouts from York until the train stopped near Holy Island."

"That's easy. I was stuck in the compartment with Aunt Amelia and Anne and Mattie. It was a rotten do. Mummy made me stay there because they were all afraid I would go and see Gruncle Albert and upset him. As though they weren't going to upset him anyway!"

"Those three were with you all the time?"

"No, Mattie was but Anne and Aunt Amelia went out just after Belinda came along to see me. Uncle Desmond and Horrible Harold decided it was best for the ladies to try their charms on Gruncle Albert first." In effect, if not in choice of words, that agreed with Mrs. Bretton's and Mrs. Smythe-Pike's statements. "They weren't gone long," Kitty continued, "because it didn't work. Then Mummy came and kicked up a dust because they'd stolen a march on Daddy and

Jeremy. That was when Belinda got fed up and left, and I wished I could have."

"You wanted to see your great-uncle?"

"I wanted to ask him to leave some money to Ray—my brother Raymond. You see," she said earnestly, "Daddy and Mummy and Jeremy don't really need it, not *really*, but Ray does. It's not his fault he can't keep a job. I thought if he knew he'd get some money, he'd marry Judith and she could take care of him all the time, and maybe he'd get better. Anyway, now Daddy'll get it all, and he can give Ray a share."

"What about you, don't you want your share?" Alec asked with real curiosity.

"Not me. I'm going to be a writer, like Miss Dalrymple. Isn't she absolutely topping?"

This innocent query left Alec groping for an answer. Piper muffled a snicker. Tom was up to the occasion. "Absolutely," he said with apparent gravity. Alec didn't dare glance at him, sure he'd meet a wickedly teasing look.

"Your father may not get it all," he pointed out hurriedly. "Your great-uncle Alistair may change his will."

"I hope he will. I don't see why we Gillespies should get it all when there's plenty for everyone."

"It's a large fortune, is it?"

"Well, he inherited simply pots of money from my great-grandfather, and being a miser he never spent any, so it must be even more now, with interest and things, mustn't it? Aunt Geraldine says she doesn't need any, but it would be rotten if Uncle Desmond's house had to be sold. They've got horses! Gosh, I've got a spiffing idea. I'll ask Aunt Amelia to invite Belinda next time I go to stay, and we can ride together. You'd let her, wouldn't you, Mr. Fletcher?"

"I'll have to think about it," Alec said diplomatically.

"Let's get back to business. Do you know which of your relatives actually spoke to Albert McGowan, and when?"

"Pretty much all of them, I think, but I haven't the faintest when. People kept coming and going and telling us things. I can't remember who said what when, except they all said Gruncle Albert said no. I think Anne went out again. Mattie didn't, but Aunt Amelia might have without me seeing. I didn't know there was going to be a murder, so I was reading and didn't take much notice," Kitty explained with deep regret.

"A pity. If anything comes back to you overnight, you can tell me in the morning. Just one more thing. When you were out on the city wall and heard Belinda scream, could you see anyone?"

"No. Actually, I was behind a tower thing, sort of hiding from Ray. He kept telling me to be careful, as if I was a baby. But Belinda imagined that man, didn't she? I don't blame her, it was pretty eerie out there when it started getting dark. It was easy to imagine the Scots or the Spanish Armada or someone creeping up on you. Belinda's all right, isn't she? She wasn't at dinner."

"Miss Dalrymple thought it best she should go straight to bed. She hasn't told you about seeing anything, has she? Other than the man on the walls, I mean."

Kitty shook her head. "No. Give her this with my love, will you?" From a pocket she produced a lint-adorned liquorice bootlace. "It's my last one, but Daddy said I can buy some Berwick cockles in the morning. They're peppermints."

"Thank you, Kitty." Touched, Alec wrapped the sweet in his handkerchief and pocketed it. "That's all for now, then. I'll see you in the morning, I expect."

"I hope so. Good-night, Mr. Fletcher." With a punctilious "Good-night" to Tom and Piper, Kitty departed.

"A nice young lady," said Piper, poring over his shorthand notes, "but she didn't half rattle on."

"You can start transcribing into longhand, Ernie," said Alec. "Leave out the bit about the Berwick cockles! Tom, I want you to put a call through to the Yard; have them get on to the Sûreté and find out if Madame Pasquier's really as affluent as she's made out to her long lost family. What did Mrs. Smythe-Pike say her husband's name is?"

"Jewel," said Piper promptly. "Funny name for a man."

"Jules—J-u-l-e-s, Tom. I'm going to see if Belinda's told Miss Dalrymple anything useful. Shan't be long."

He went upstairs and, after one false start down the wrong passage, knocked on Daisy's door. Opening it, she gasped, "Thank heaven you've come.

Thoroughly alarmed, he started to ask what was the matter, but she pushed past him, took a pair of steps in a single bound, and disappeared around a corner.

No hell-fiend followed on her heels. Alec looked into the room. No one there but Belinda, in bed, sound asleep. He crossed to the bed and stooped to kiss her cheek very softly, then returned to the door, puzzled.

The muffled rattle of a chain and whoosh of water enlightened him. When Daisy returned, he was leaning against the door-post, shaking with silent laughter.

Rather pink, she said indignantly, "I promised not to leave her alone for a single minute."

"Bless you, my dear." What would she do if he kissed her? No, this was neither the time nor the place, in the middle of a case and on the threshold of her bedroom. "I wondered whether Belinda's said anything of significance."

Daisy frowned. Glancing both ways along the passage, she said, "Come in, just for a minute."

He stepped in and closed the door, fighting a well-nigh irresistible urge to take her in his arms. Her back to the light, her hair was a halo of honey brown curls. Her blue eyes, always so beguiling in their open cheerfulness, were pools of mystery. Between her brows were two little lines of worry—worry for his daughter. He put out a finger to smooth them away.

She smiled, but he thought the pink in her cheeks deepened.

"Belinda's frightened," she said quickly, "which is only natural after today. I'm quite sure she believes the murderer has some reason to come after her, but she absolutely denies it, denies she knows anything."

"It is the murderer she's afraid of, not—heaven forbid—of the police? Dr. Jagai said she feared being accused."

"She did ask if they—you—would think she'd done it. I suspect that was because she had been in a lot of mischief, what with running away and stowing away. I made the mistake of saying she had been 'wicked' to run away from her grandmother rather than just naughty. And then the ticket-inspector threatened, in quite a joking way, to arrest her for being on the train without a proper ticket. I should have made sure she understood it was a joke."

"Don't blame yourself, Daisy. You couldn't have guessed it would matter, and if it stops her running off again it's all to the good."

"I hope so. But, you see, she had a general sense of being in serious trouble already which explains her initial worry about being accused of murder. I don't think that's what's disturbing her now. I have the strangest feeling, Alec, that Belinda holds an essential piece of the jigsaw puzzle. Perhaps she doesn't recognize its place, but if we got hold of it, it would give us the whole picture."

"That," said Alec sombrely, "is exactly how I feel."

13

Failing Belinda's piece of the puzzle, Alec could only do his best to collect as many other pieces as possible. "Madame Pasquier," he said to Piper.

Piper returned to report that Madame had retired to bed. "Plumb wore out, she was, having come all the way from gay Paree."

"Mrs. Gillespie, then. Mrs. Peter Gillespie."

Enid Gillespie brought her husband with her. Not, as Alec momentarily assumed, because she felt in need of his protection. Her grip on his arm was the grip of a dog-owner on a collar, and he hung back like a reluctant dog hauled towards an unwanted bath. "Hangdog" was the word. His heavy lower jaw and bristling red mustache failed utterly to give him an aggressive air.

It was otherwise with his wife. Short, spare, and erect, she looked the martinet from rigidly waved grey hair via thin-lipped mouth and stiff back to the sharp rap of her heels on the tile in the hallway.

"Don't be silly, Peter," she chided as they followed Piper into the parlour, "you'll only make a fool of yourself if you see them on your own. Remember, the police cannot force us to give statements. We are doing our duty."

"Yes, Enid."

He appeared to be altogether under her thumb. However, she had signally failed to stifle her daughter's spirit, Alec thought, biting back a smile at the memory of Kitty's exuberance. He introduced himself and deliberately invited them to sit down before Mrs. Gillespie decided for herself to do so. His only hope with her was to gain and keep the upper hand.

He'd start by ignoring her. "It must be a great relief to you, Mr. Gillespie, that Albert McGowan is dead?"

"Yes . . . No . . . I mean . . ." stammered the unhappy man.

"You asked to see *me*, Chief Inspector," his wife interrupted.

"True, madam," Alec said coldly, "but since you chose to bring Mr. Gillespie with you, you can scarcely protest when I choose to ask him a few questions first. You are free to leave and return later, if you prefer."

"I shall stay. My husband is naturally distraught at his uncle's untimely demise."

"You are distraught, sir? Or relieved? It must be a relief to know that you will soon inherit a large fortune, since your circumstances are somewhat straitened. Are they not?"

"Not to say straitened!" Gillespie's protest was feeble.

"But you can no longer afford to keep up the style to which you were accustomed."

"Everything is so expensive these days."

"My husband understands little of money matters," Enid Gillespie snapped. "That's how he came to . . . to lose money," she ended lamely. A determined woman, but not clever.

"To be prosecuted for fraud, you were going to say?"

"He wasn't convicted!"

"Found innocent? Or, there's a verdict in Scotland:

Not Proven." Alec knew at once he had hit the mark. Peter Gillespie stared miserably at his shoes and his wife's tight mouth became still tighter. "Not the same as innocent," Alec said.

So Harold Bretton's disclosure to Daisy was the truth, not mere spite. Peter Gillespie had run afoul of the law, and was in financial difficulties. Whether the fraud was deliberate or the result of genuine incompetence was immaterial. He needed Alistair's fortune, and he believed it to be large.

With Enid Gillespie off balance, Alec changed his tack. "Mr. Gillespie, what time did you go to Albert McGowan's compartment to try to persuade him to change his will?"

"I . . . What time did we talk to Uncle Albert, dear?"

She gave him a furious look and Alec guessed she had intended to deny seeing the old man. "I didn't look at the time."

"But it was after Mrs. Smythe-Pike and Mrs. Bretton," Alec stated.

"*And* after Desmond Smythe-Pike and Harold Bretton." Her resentment burst forth. "They've always thought themselves superior because he's a landowner, and since our troubles they've been quite unbearable. It'll serve them right if the place has to be sold."

"You don't think Alistair McGowan is likely to change his will in their favour, then? In favour of his great-grandson?"

"He's more likely to change it in Geraldine's favour," Peter Gillespie said gloomily, "even though she doesn't need the money. She has two sons who are his grandsons."

"They are French," his wife spat out.

"The Scots have always preferred the French to the English."

No matter who the Scots preferred, Alec reflected, the identity of the heir to Alistair McGowan's largely mythical fortune was still problematical. Albert's death had not guaranteed the inheritance to either side of the family. Even before his death, they all had hoped his elder twin intended to disinherit him.

Which left none of them with a strong motive for murder. Whoever killed Albert McGowan had gambled on a change in his favour—or had lost his temper.

Harold Bretton was a gambler, according to Daisy. Desmond Smythe-Pike had a nasty temper, and Raymond Gillespie was emotionally unstable. Peter Gillespie was no longer the prime suspect.

"So the Smythe-Pikes and Brettons had already seen Albert McGowan when you found him alive and well."

"Yes," said Mrs. Gillespie regretfully, "but I'm certain one of them went back later. Harold Bretton wanted to try a calm, reasonable discussion, which wasn't possible with his father-in-law present. Desmond's notion of persuasion is to shout louder."

"You *know* Mr. Bretton returned?"

"Ye . . ." She wavered under Alec's hard gaze. "No, not to say *know,* but he was talking about it, wasn't he, Peter?"

"Yes, oh yes, seemed dashed determined to try again."

"What about your sons? When did they try their powers of persuasion?"

"They didn't," said Enid Gillespie at once, but her husband said at the same moment, "Oh, Ray went before us, too. Judith dragged him along. Judith Smythe-Pike, that is. Nice girl, and good for him."

"Judith Smythe-Pike is one of these dreadful modern young women who think it clever to smoke and drink and swear. Amelia has no control over her whatsoever. Raymond is putty in her hands."

"You mean Raymond would kill if Miss Smythe-Pike told him to?" Alec shot at her.

"Certainly not," she said, but uneasily. "In any case, we spoke to Uncle Albert after Raymond saw him."

"And Jeremy?"

"Jeremy declared nothing would make him approach his great-uncle. He said he considered it both useless and tasteless, but it's just that he always prefers the easy way out." She threw a glance of contempt at her husband. "Like his father."

Once started, Mrs. Gillespie was showing a disposition to be as outspoken as her daughter. Alec doubted she could lie convincingly.

"Albert McGowan was alive and well when you found him," he said. "And when you left?"

She glowered at him. "Alive and as well as he ever was. He had ruined his constitution with overindulgence. No one could have guessed he would outlive his brother!"

"Are you sure he didn't just drop dead, Chief Inspector?" Peter Gillespie enquired plaintively. "He was very old and not at all well."

"So I gather." Alec ignored the question. "Was he sitting up or lying down when you saw him?"

"Sitting up," said Enid Gillespie, "and complaining bitterly that he was being kept from his after-lunch nap. We didn't stay long. It was impossible to talk sense into the old . . . gentleman. He preferred that wretched black interloper to his own family!"

Not without reason, thought Alec.

From the corner of his eye, he saw Tom ostentatiously take out his watch and consult it. Time was passing and they still had several suspects to interview.

"That will be all," he said, "for now. I shall want to speak to you again in the morning. Thank you for your cooperation."

"Cooperating is all very well," Mrs. Gillespie snapped, "but we are expected at Dunston Castle."

"Haven't you telephoned?"

"Sent a cable," said Peter Gillespie. "Uncle Alistair refuses to put in a telephone. We haven't had a reply so we don't know what he thinks of the delay."

"I shall endeavour to see that you are all delayed as brief a time as possible," Alec said, adding dryly, "and all the same length of time, so that no one gains an unfair advantage. Allow me to offer my somewhat belated condolences on the loss of your uncle."

Mrs. Gillespie snorted, but her husband had the grace to look a trifle shamefaced as they departed.

"Judith Smythe-Pike, please, Ernie. Well, what do you think, Tom?"

"He might do it if she told him to, Chief, but I don't think she'd trust the poor worm to do it right, and I don't think she'd dirty her own hands. She wasn't sure of Raymond."

"No, I noticed that. It's a devilish thing, shell-shock."

Tom nodded sober agreement. "And he's not accounted for on the city walls, neither. If his sister'd spotted him, he'd only to say he'd tried to save Miss Belinda."

"If that was him," Alec said savagely, "I'll nail him come hell or high water, shell-shock or no." He forced himself to calm. "He seems to have spent most of his time on the train with Miss Smythe-Pike. We'll see what she has to say."

He looked round at the sound of footsteps in the hall. Instead of the expected Piper, a tall, thin young man in a well-cut but slightly shabby lounge suit appeared in the doorway.

"If you want Judith," he announced belligerently, "you'll have to put up with me, too."

"Really, darling, don't be tiresome," came a drawl from behind him. Miss Smythe-Pike hooked her arm into her fiancé's and he moved aside a little. Her shingled hair was so fair it was almost silvery by gaslight. Her black evening frock, long-sleeved and high-necked like the other ladies', was unmistakably chic, with elaborate beading. "I'm sure the Chief Inspector won't object. He let Uncle Peter stay with Aunt Enid."

Her ironic glance met Alec's and he guessed she was very much aware that Peter Gillespie had not been there for his wife's protection. There was a hint of a plea in her eyes, too. *I don't need protection either,* it said, *but let him think I do.*

Or so Alec imagined. "Certainly you may stay," he told the young man, though he'd rather have seen them separately. He waved them to the magenta sofa, where they sat holding hands. Piper came into the room after them and took up his pad and pencil. "Miss Smythe-Pike—and Mr. Raymond Gillespie, is it not?"

"Yes." His point won, Raymond recovered his manners. "How do you do, Mr. Fletcher," he said with a charming smile. His gaze flickered across Alec's Royal Flying Corps tie but he didn't mention it. His own tie was plain blue, not regimental. "I know your daughter, of course. A nice kid, and a great friend of my brat sister."

"I understand I have you to thank for liberating Belinda from a bramble bush."

"Oh, that was quite as much Kitty's and Jagai's doing."

"How is Belinda, Chief Inspector?" Miss Smythe-

Pike asked. Her fashionably languid voice made it difficult to tell if she was concerned or merely polite. "The poor child had quite a fright."

"A few bruises and the odd scratch. She was lucky. Does either of you have any idea whether she was really approached by a man, hostile or would-be helpful, or whether it was her imagination?"

They looked at each other and both shrugged. "We've been talking about it," said Raymond. "At first we assumed it was imagination, at least that she'd mistaken his intent. But suppose she saw something on the train which made someone want to put her away?"

Surely he would not make such a suggestion if he were responsible—unless it was a bluff?

"I expect Mr. Fletcher's considered the possibility, darling." Again her eyes met Alec's, and he was sure she knew what he was thinking. "I can't see how we'll ever know, failing a confession. You'll want to hear about our movements on the train, Chief Inspector. We were together all the time. Ray didn't want to pester Uncle Albert, but Daddy made me go, so he went with me. You see, Daddy and Uncle Albert had a row and he hoped I might be able to soothe the savage breast."

"And did you?"

"A bit, but only by not mentioning money or wills."

"You don't want your share of the family fortune?"

"Oh I do, but Ray doesn't. Or at least he refuses to beg for it." She gave Raymond an affectionate, if slightly mocking smile.

"Even for your sake, Miss Smythe-Pike, so that you can get married?" Alec felt like an utter cad, but it had to be said. "I understand your fiancé is unable to earn a living, because of his . . . disability."

Raymond paled.

"He'd never plead that!" the girl said angrily. "He won't even let *me* ask for a penny, on any grounds. We'll manage somehow."

"Calm down, old dear." Raymond's voice was a little shaky. "Mr. Fletcher has a job to do."

"I beg your pardon," Alec apologized. "I've no intention of offending, but as you say, I've a murder to investigate. The two of you saw Albert McGowan after Mr. Smythe-Pike and Mr. Bretton, but before Mr. and Mrs. Gillespie?"

Miss Smythe-Pike answered, the bored, cynical drawl already back in place. "Yes, and wasn't Aunt Enid mad!"

"Can you put a time to it?"

"I can't. Can you, Ray? No, I'm afraid not. We didn't stay long. It was ghastly hot in there, and he was out of humour and seemed tired."

"You didn't see him lie down when you left?"

"No, though he had a pillow on the seat beside him, so he may have. We went for a walk along the train—Ray gets fed up with sitting. Oh, just after we started out, the train went through Durham; you should get a time from that. The corridor we were in happened to be on the right side of the train and there's a marvellous view of the castle and cathedral. Then we stopped for a bit to amuse Tabitha, my sister's little girl, who was with her nurse in third."

Alec glanced at Tom, who nodded. He'd check with the nurse tomorrow. He already had to ask the woman about the timing of Anne Bretton's movements.

"Superintendent Halliday had his men take the names and addresses of all the passengers, Chief," the sergeant reminded him. "We can always get hold of 'em if need be."

"Did you talk to anyone else?" Alec asked Miss Smythe-Pike.

"Did we, darling?"

"I had a word with the guard and a chap who was visiting his dog in the guard's van. A very fine setter. That was while you . . . er . . ."

"While I powdered my nose. A minute or two, no more. Then we strolled back to the others, not in any hurry—in fact we stopped to watch the sights of Newcastle passing the corridor window. The next thing we knew the train was braking."

"You've forgotten, Ju, I didn't stay with you. I went on to . . ."

"To powder your nose?" she said lightly, but Alec saw her hand tighten on Raymond's in a warning grip.

He ignored or failed to recognize the warning. "No, to speak to Uncle Albert."

"You decided you could do with some funds after all?" Alec asked casually, every sense alert.

"Not a bit of it. I suddenly remembered I'd meant to ask him to do something for Aunt Julia. She's kept house for Uncle Alistair forever, and all *he's* left her is a measly hundred a year. I didn't say anything the first time because Uncle Desmond and Harold between 'em had put the old chap in such a taking I was sure he'd refuse."

"Was he more amenable the second time?"

"I don't know if he would have been. I didn't find out because when I opened the door he was lying down, asleep I assumed. Was he dead already?"

Alec fixed on him the gaze that made crooks cringe and subordinates shiver. "If he wasn't dead already, he died very shortly after you opened that door. Very shortly."

Raymond neither shivered nor cringed. Instead he looked sick. "I didn't kill him, that helpless old man. It was bad enough having to do it, over there, when they were trying to do it to you. You were all right, you bird-men up above our heads. You couldn't see, you can't imagine. . . ." He buried his face in his hands.

"It's all right, darling." His fiancée put her arm around his shoulders. "Take a deep breath, that's it. Hold it; now let it out slowly. Better? We really must ask Dr. Jagai to explain a bit more. Now tell Mr. Fletcher just what you saw."

"Not much." He looked up with a self-deprecating grimace. "Not enough to give me nightmares. In fact, nothing but his feet, up on the seat."

"At which end of the seat?"

"The far end. I couldn't have seen them at the near end, I only opened the door an inch or two and it opened the opposite side to where he was lying. The seat facing the engine, where he was sitting, Ju, remember? He sat over by the window, Chief Inspector, that's why I looked that way."

"You would have seen if anyone had been with him?"

"Oh yes, I think so, unless they had climbed into the rack."

"Did you notice a glass, a drinking tumbler?"

"No. Why? He was poisoned?"

Alec did not answer. "Did he have shoes on?"

"Shoes?" Raymond pondered, brow wrinkled. "I honestly don't remember. I have a vague impression that he had a rug over his legs, one of those tartan traveling rugs."

"He had one earlier, when he was sitting up," said Miss Smythe-Pike. "You could be remembering that."

"Possibly. Sorry, can't be sure."

"Was the window open?"

"No, he'd never have stood for that. Thin-blooded

he was after a life in the tropics, poor old chap, and terrified of draughts."

"Darling, are you certain the window was closed, or are you just presuming it must have been?"

Slower than his fiancée, Raymond caught on. "It was found open? Is that what made Miss Dalrymple suspect something amiss? I couldn't swear to it either way. Now I come to think of it, I didn't notice a blast of heat wafting in my face like the first time. But then, the whole train was frightfully overheated and I only opened the door an inch, because of his fear of draughts."

"And through that gap you saw his feet," said Alec. "What did you do next?"

"I assumed he was sleeping. Since Aunt Julia's plight is hardly urgent, I had no reason to disturb him. I closed the door sharpish and went to find Judith."

"Which of the others did you join?"

She winced. "No one. We'd bagged four compartments at King's Cross, between the lot of us, and everyone kept moving around. At that moment one was empty, so I went in there. But honestly, he wasn't gone more than two minutes, Mr. Fletcher, if that long."

Her assertion was worthless, seeing she had already lied for him. The question was, had she lied because she knew or suspected he had killed the old man, or simply to protect him from police harassment?

Raymond himself was very convincing. Alec saw three possibilities: He was telling the truth; or he was a brilliant actor; or he had murdered his great-uncle in one of his fits and honestly did not remember.

Sighing, Alec studied the young couple, who gazed anxiously back, holding hands again. He liked them; he wished them well; but he could not take them off his list.

14

"Don't look too good for young Raymond, Chief," said Tom forebodingly.

"No, but we've others to see yet." Alec consulted his watch. "Eleven-thirty, dammit. I hate to skimp on the initial interviews, but I do want to see them all and I can't very well keep them up after midnight."

"Nor me, Chief." The sergeant failed to stifle an enormous yawn. Beneath the hairless dome, his broad face was lined with weariness.

The week in Newcastle had been no picnic, and the sergeant wasn't getting any younger. Mrs. Tring wouldn't hesitate to give Alec what-for if he returned her husband to her in less than apple-pie order.

As for Alec himself, energized by the hint of a threat to his daughter, he would have been prepared to work all night if it served any purpose.

"Only three to go," he said.

"You're leaving the two young chaps to stew, eh? Jeremy Gillespie and Harold Bretton?"

"Partly, and partly I've a feeling Smythe-Pike would take it amiss if he was left till last. If his temper is as uncertain as . . ."

A bellow from the residents' lounge cut him short.

"Demme if I'm struggling to my feet for any demned whippersnapper of a flatfoot. Let him come here!"

"It is," said Tom, grinning.

"If Mahomet will not come to the mountain," Alec said philosophically, standing up as Piper reappeared, "then the mountain must needs go to Mahomet. All right, Ernie, we heard. We're coming."

"He's got the gout, Chief, and if you ask me, he's been at the port all evening."

"Squiffy, is he?"

"Plastered," said Piper. "Though the old fella don't show it as bad as the other two. Mr. Gillespie's been swigging whisky and Mr. Bretton's on brandy and soda. Not much soda, neether."

"Oh hell! And they'll have heads in the morning, I suppose. I can only hope it's loosened their tongues. The rest have gone to bed?"

"Yes, Chief."

"That's something." Pushing open the door, he entered the lounge. "Good-evening, gentlemen. Detective Chief Inspector Fletcher, Scotland Yard."

"You a Scot, too?" asked the sandy-haired, bleary-eyed man slouched in a chair by the fire. Presumably Jeremy Gillespie—in fact he looked more like his sister Kitty than Raymond, his brother. "These chaps are Sass . . . Sass . . . English. We Scots have to stick together."

"Scotland Yard, sir. The Metropolitan Police."

"Bloody Shcots," said the man leaning against the mantelpiece. Thinning, pomaded hair, beautifully tailored evening dress, he must be Harold Bretton, the would-be man-about-town. Taking a step forward, he waved his glass. "What'sh yours, Chief Inshpector?" His drink sloshed over his hand and he prudently retreated to prop himself up again.

"Not on duty, thank you, sir." He had no desire for a drink, but the ash-tray on the mantel shelf, full of cigarette ends, made him wish he could light up his pipe.

"Stop drivelling!" No question of the identity of the purple-faced, stentorian gentleman with his leg raised on a footstool. Desmond Smythe-Pike looked every inch the hard-riding, hard-drinking squire. On the table at his elbow, beside a silver headed cane, stood an almost empty decanter. Between white hair, slightly disordered, and white cavalry mustache, his eyes were glazed, but his enunciation was unaffected. "You there, if you have the demned impertinence to insist on questioning me, at least get on with it."

Alec decided against asking the two younger men to wait elsewhere. They would only go and pass out. Leaning on the back of a chair opposite the squire, he said, "Tell me about your interview with Albert McGowan, sir."

"The man was a demned traitor to his family and his race," trumpeted Smythe-Pike. "My wife's own uncle leaving the family fortune to a native!"

"You remonstrated with him?"

"I lost my temper." He had the grace to look a bit sheepish. "Not quite the thing to shout at the old fella like that, I dare say, but it made my blood boil, him sitting there saying he'd do what he liked with his own, calm as you please."

"Didn't shtay calm," Bretton put in sardonically. "Gave as good as he got, though going by volume my dear papa-in-law won by a nose."

Alec turned to face him. "But Mr. Smythe-Pike failed to win his point, didn't he, sir, so you went back later to try again."

"Who the devil told you that?" Straightening, Bretton glared at Jeremy Gillespie.

"Not me, ol' man. Haven' had my turn to blab to the coppers yet."

"I suppose when you do, you'll admit *you* went to see him, after all that talk about not pestering a sick old man? I saw you coming out of his compartment."

Gillespie sat up. "Now wait a bit! I don' care for your insin . . . insinu . . . your damn sly hints. I wasn' coming out 'cause I didn' go in 'cause I c'd see fr'm the door he was asleep."

"Or dead," said Bretton unpleasantly. "Turning to look back at your handiwork, were you?"

"Asleep, 'ntil you came along 'n' bumped him off in his sleep."

"Horsewhip both of you," roared Smythe-Pike.

"Let's have some facts here," Alec said sharply. "Mr. Gillespie, you went to speak to your great-uncle as soon as your parents left him?"

"No, not at once." Gillespie stared at him with shocked though still befuddled concentration. "The mater said Uncle Albert was on the boil after the set-to with Uncle Desmond, so I waited a bit to let him cool down."

"How long?"

"How long?" His eyes ceased to focus on the present. Alec hoped they were focussed on the past, but after his brief moment of lucidity the whisky took charge again. "How long? How long what?"

"How long did you wait before going to see Albert McGowan."

Gillespie waved vaguely. "Oh, that. A while. 'What's the use of worrying?' " he sang, " 'It never was worth while, so pack up your troubles in your ol' kit bag an' smile, smile, smile.' "

Alec gave up on him. "What about you, Mr. Bretton? You went to Mr. McGowan's compartment after seeing Mr. Gillespie at the door?"

"More or less." Leaving the support of the mantelpiece, he came over to Alec, his steps unsteady. "Actually, my dear chap," he said confidentially, breathing brandy fumes into Alec's face as he clutched the back of the nearest chair to steady himself, "actually, my dear old chap, what does it really matter? He's got something there, you know. What's the use of worrying? Albert was an old man, a very old man, not in good health. He was going to die soon anyway. Give the old bastard a helping hand, what?"

"Did you?" Alec asked, through teeth gritted in disgust.

"Me?" Bretton asked with owlish dismay. "Me? Not me! My best bet was to change the miser's mind. Grandfather, y'know. Wife's grandfather, baby's great-grandfather. Named the squalling brat for him, bound to turn the trick."

"Then why did you . . ."

An ear-shattering snore interrupted him. Desmond Smythe-Pike had nodded off unnoticed. Now, having woken himself, he blinked, said thickly, "Bed," and fumbled for his cane.

Resigned, Alec gestured at him. "Tom."

The big sergeant supported the big squire's stumbling limp from the room. Alec surveyed the other two. Jeremy Gillespie was dozing more quietly, obeying his own injunction to "smile, smile, smile." After all, why shouldn't he? As things stood, his father was heir to the McGowan fortune.

"Ernie, can you manage him?"

"Reckon so, Chief."

Harold Bretton was still upright. More or less. Alec

was about to invite him to sit down and answer a few more questions when he said with querulous dignity, "Make it under my own steam!" Groping his way from chair to chair, he headed for the door.

As Bretton left, the landlord, Briggs, came through from the bar-parlour next door, long since closed to the public. "If you're all done in here, sir," he said, "I'll be closing up."

"Have you been listening in there?" Alec asked, annoyed, as he moved towards the fireplace rubbing his cold hands. The remains of a coal fire flickered sullenly.

"Not to say listening, sir. Couldn't help overhearing the odd word. Didn't get much out of those three, did you? Sozzled, the lot of 'em."

"How much did they actually drink?"

"Plenty. They weren't faking it, believe you me. Nerves, it'd be, being suspected of murder. Was it one of them did it?"

"I can't discuss the case with you, Mr. Briggs, and you're to hold your tongue about anything you overheard. I'm not quite ready to close up shop, but we'll go back to your parlour if it's more convenient."

"Might as well stay here, sir. You'll turn off the lights when you go up?"

"Yes. Before you go, bring three hot toddies, please, and take mugs of cocoa to the bobbies on the front door and back gate."

The landlord heaved a martyred sigh. "Right, sir," he said and stumped off.

Tom arrived at the same time as the hot toddy. Sinking into a chair by the fire, he took a deep swig. "Aah! Ta, Chief, that hits the spot. Smythe-Pike'd forgotten his room number, but young Ernie's memorized the lot, even their servants', so I fetched his man to him."

"And had a word with the fellow, I hope?"

" 'Course, Chief. The squire's gout's real all right. He'd be strong enough but likely not agile enough, and more likely to hit the old chap over the head with his cane in a temper than hold a pillow over his face. The vally saw Miss Smythe-Pike and Raymond Gillespie with the nurse and the children, but he doesn't know what time."

"We may have to get onto the guard and the ticket-inspector about times," Alec said. "At least we'll need a train timetable, and to ask everyone whether they noticed passing through Durham and Newcastle. Let's hope it doesn't come to tracking down all the other passengers in search of alibis."

Ernie came back and, with him referring to his notes of the interviews, they discussed the other suspects. Finishing his toddy, Alec decided this exercise could not usefully proceed further without proper statements from Smythe-Pike, Bretton, and Jeremy Gillespie. Something someone had said niggled at his mind, but he could not pin it down. It would probably come to him at three o'clock in the morning.

He was about to say it was time to turn in when they heard the front door opening and the constable on duty saying, "There's a light on in the lounge still, Sarge."

Heavy footsteps in the hall, then a uniformed officer tapped on the open lounge door and came in, carrying a bundle wrapped in brown paper.

"Sergeant Middlemiss, sir. Superintendent Halliday's compliments, and here's the missing pillow. Leastways, it looks like whit's left o' yon. The Gateshead police found it, right by the railway track, and it doesna look like anyone's washing blown off a line."

"Gateshead? If he'd waited just a couple of minutes, it would have landed in the Tyne!"

"Aye, sir."

As Alec, Tom, and Piper crowded round, Middlemiss unwrapped the bundle. It contained a grubby, torn pillow-case with the limp remains of a pillow inside—striped ticking, also ripped, with a couple of handfuls of feathers.

"What's this?" Alec grabbed the bottom of the pillow-case and lifted it so the dirty white cloth was spread out between him and Middlemiss.

Amid the black smuts and general grime, to be expected of anything which had spent several hours close to the railway, were four long, brownish smears.

"Ah!" said Tom.

"Turn it inside out."

Piper reached in for the pillow and Middlemiss turned the case inside out. Alec noted a laundry mark which would make the ownership easy to prove. Against the still-white inside of the pillow-case, the brown smears stood out clearly. Four of them, starting out roughly parallel, closing together as they grew fainter. The first and third started level with one another. The second was slightly longer, the fourth shorter and narrower.

Alec curled the fingers of his left hand into a claw and held his hand just above the marks.

"Blood!" Piper exclaimed. "Good old Albert marked him, Chief. We've got 'im."

"I hope so. If it's what it looks like, our chummy's got scratches on him it's going to be very difficult to explain away. Dr. Redlow will tell us if it's human blood. With luck he might be able to check the blood group."

"What's a blood group, sir?" asked Sergeant Middlemiss, an interested observer of their speculations.

"Everyone has one of four different types of blood, Sergeant, some rarer than others. It's quite a new discovery, which came in handy during the War as it makes blood transfusions safer. If we find a man—or woman—with scratches whose blood group matches this on the pillow-case, then it's another bit of evidence, not conclusive but useful."

"Only thing is, Chief," rumbled Tom, "we've seen the lot of 'em 'cepting Madame Passkeyay and I haven't seen a scratched face yet."

"Would you have noticed scratched hands? I don't think I would."

"Raymond Gillespie and Dr. Jagai got scratched getting Miss Belinda out of the brambles," Piper reminded him. "Maybe that was the whole point of that business, scaring Miss Belinda into the bushes so's he'd have an excuse for the scratches."

Alec's mind boggled at the thought of taking such a risk for such a chancy outcome. What was the likelihood of being able to direct the steps of a terrified, fleeing child into a thorny thicket, especially in an unknown place? He couldn't be sure without going up on the walls to study the situation, but it seemed a long shot.

He didn't want to discourage young Piper by pointing out the flaws in his theory before a stranger. "It's a good point, Ernie," he said, "but I should think we, or the doctor, can tell the difference between thorn scratches and fingernail scratches if it comes to that. Well, we'll just have to check everyone's hands tomorrow, but in the meantime I'd like to make sure it's a tenable theory. Ernie, you play the victim."

"Right, Chicf!" said Piper enthusiastically.

"Sergeant Middlemiss, if you wouldn't mind, take that cushion and smother him while Sergeant Tring and I watch. Go easy, now. I'd hate to have to explain a dead detective constable to the Assistant Commissioner."

Middlemiss gingerly placed the cushion over Piper's face. He held it there while Ernie thrashed around a bit like a beached fish then reached up to scrabble at his attacker. His fingernails scraped down the blue uniform sleeves, then he plucked at the cushion, trying to pull it away from his face.

"That'll do!" said Alec.

Piper emerged, red-faced and breathless. "Cor, you didn't have to be so realistic!" he panted at Middlemiss. "Was that all right, Chief?"

"You oughta be in the pictures," said Tom.

"Not bad, except you stopped scratching before you reached his hands."

"Didn't want to do the sergeant an injury, did I, Chief, or he might've done me in for good and all!"

Alec smiled at him. "You showed our scenario is possible, even probable." He turned to the Berwick officer. "Sergeant Middlemiss, do you know if Dr. Redlow's still working on the autopsy? I'd expected him to telephone by now."

"Still at it, I think, sir. He didna leave Newcastle till he'd etten his dinner."

"Then will you please take the pillow-case to him. I'll ring up right away and explain what I want."

Somehow Piper had the appropriate telephone number on the tip of his tongue. Going out to the lobby with Middlemiss, Alec wondered what happened to all the numbers no longer needed. Did they lurk there in the young man's head, strings of figures just waiting for the proper stimulus to pop out of his mouth?

The fancy faded as he took the earpiece off its hook and spoke to the telephone girl. For once it wouldn't matter if she listened in to the conversation. This was no local murder; his investigation could not be disrupted by a gossiping switchboard operator.

The bell rang several times. "I'm sorry, caller, there's no answer," said the girl, but just then the bell cut off in mid-ring.

"This is Dr. Fraser," said an impatient voice. "Who is it?"

"Detective Chief Inspector Fletcher, sir. I'd hoped to speak to Dr. Redlow."

"Dr. Redlow cannot come to the telephone just now, Chief Inspector," Fraser said dryly. "If you saw his hands you'd know why. I'm assisting him."

Alec explained about the pillow-case. "I'm assuming it was in fact murder," he said then. "Has Dr. Redlow come to any conclusion?"

"Just a moment, Chief Inspector." Footsteps and a murmur of voices; Fraser came back. "I'm authorized to tell you that Dr. Redlow is prepared to swear in court that Albert McGowan died of suffocation due to the pressure of some soft object over his mouth and nose."

Alec's breath came out on a long sigh—he hadn't realized he was holding it. He listened to the technical details with half his mind. Medical evidence he followed better on paper. When Dr. Fraser finished, he asked, "What about time of death, sir?"

"Dr. Redlow concurs with my original estimate, Chief Inspector, since I saw the body much earlier. McGowan died between three and four this afternoon, with a half-hour margin of error either way. Sorry I can't be more exact."

"That's better than most, sir." But no help whatsoever.

"We'll get onto the pillow-case as soon as it arrives," Fraser promised. "Do you want the results tonight?"

"First thing in the morning'll do, sir. Thank you." He rang off. About to return to the lounge, he had a sudden thought. Jogging the hook until the operator answered, he asked for the local police station. "This is Chief Inspector Fletcher. Is Superintendent Halliday still there?"

"Yes, sir. Just a moment, please."

Halliday came onto the line. "Mr. Fletcher?"

"I thought you'd like to know, sir, that Dr. Redlow confirms murder."

A windy sigh whistled down the wire. "Thank you, Mr. Fletcher. Then I can sleep in peace."

Alec chuckled, glad to have set the man's mind at rest. He must have been on tenterhooks wondering if he'd made a complete ass of himself.

Back in the lounge, he announced the news to Tom Tring and Ernie Piper. "Murder it is," he said. "Albert McGowan was smothered to death."

"Well of course, Chief," said Piper. "Miss Dalrymple said so, and she's always right."

15

Where on earth was she? Daisy lay trying to think why she was uncomfortably stretched out on a sagging mattress, a faint light shining through her eyelids though surely it couldn't be daybreak yet! She'd only just fallen asleep.

Her eyes resisted her unenthusiastic effort to open them. What had roused her in the depths of the night? Where . . . ?

Oh, the Raven's Nest Hotel, in Berwick. Yesterday flooded back, making her even more reluctant to wake fully. She turned over and buried her face in the lumpy pillow.

"No!"

The childish wail brought Daisy instantly upright. Belinda, caught in a nightmare by the sound of it; that was what had woken her. She slid out from under the covers, shivering as she reached for her dressing gown, and crossed to the other bed.

Belinda was curled on her side, her eyelids flickering though she seemed fast asleep. "Don't," she whimpered, "please don't. I didn't mean to."

"Wake up, darling." Daisy gently shook her shoulder. "You're all right, it's just a dream. Wake up now and it'll go away. Come on, Belinda, you're quite safe now."

"No-o-o!" Her eyes opened, bright with fear as she looked up at Daisy.

"It was a dream. Don't be afraid, it was just a nightmare."

Belinda burst into tears. "It wasn't," she sobbed, "or I'd be at home. It's all real. I don't want to go to prison!"

"Darling, they don't put little girls in prison." Daisy pulled the unheeding child into her arms.

"I didn't mean to be wicked. I wasn't really listening, honestly. I wasn't eavesdropping. I couldn't help hearing, 'cause they were shouting."

"Of course you couldn't. Who . . ."

"And I haven't told anyone. I mostly didn't understand anyway."

"Belinda, *who* was shouting, and what didn't you understand?"

"I can't tell you or I'll have to go to prison."

"What makes you think that? Listen. Listen to me. *They don't put little girls in prison!*"

Belinda stopped soaking Daisy's bosom with her tears and twisted to peek up at her face. "Really? Are you sure?" She hiccuped a last sob. "Quite, quite absolutely sure? Cross your heart?"

"Quite, quite absolutely sure, cross my heart and hope to die," Daisy said solemnly. "Now, when you happened to pass, who did you overhear?"

"I heard lots of people talking," Belinda evaded. "Most of the doors were open 'cause it was so hot."

"Let's stick to Mr. McGowan's compartment for the moment. I remember you told me you heard him shout. Who was with him?"

"The first time it was Mr. Smythe-Pike—he was

shouting, not Mr. McGowan. All he said was something about no loyalty to the family. I understood that." Belinda's bowed head and twisting fingers revealed her continued fearfulness despite Daisy's reassurances.

Daisy tried to speak patiently. "And the second time, what was it you didn't understand? What Mr. McGowan shouted? Or whoever was with him? Who was that?"

"I don't know. I didn't hear him say anything."

"Bel, darling, you *must* tell me what you did hear. Your daddy needs to know everything you can remember. You know he won't let any harm come to you. Let's see, didn't you tell me about some name he mentioned?"

"Miss Probation. But you said it was probably 'disapprobation,' meaning disapproval. I didn't *tell* you, I *asked* you who it was."

"So you did." If the difference mattered to her, Daisy was quite prepared to go along. "Why don't you *ask* me about the other words you didn't understand?"

Belinda heaved a shuddering sigh. "All right, if I can remember. I already asked about 'orbit' and you said it means the earth going round the sun."

"Oh yes, I'd forgotten. An odd sort of word to shout!"

"What about 'arsony'?"

" 'Arson' is setting buildings on fire on purpose. I don't know where the 'y' comes from. How extraordinary!" Far from enlightenment, Daisy found herself more bewildered than ever. "What else?"

"A word that sounded like 'puzzlement,' only it wasn't quite. I know what 'puzzlement' means."

" 'Puzzlement' means what I feel! What on earth was he on about?"

"There was something that reminded me of sheep,

too. I can't 'member exactly, just that it made me think of sheep."

"Sheep. 'Puzzlement.' 'Orbit.' 'Arson.' And Miss Probation."

"You're really absolutely sure? About prison?"

"Absolutely. Your father will say exactly the same, I promise. You know, darling, I think we'd better go and tell him right away. I dare say he'll be mad as fire at being woken up, but then he might be equally shirty if we don't."

Daisy helped Belinda pull the woolly jumper on over her combies. In the corridor a light was burning, gas turned low. As kindly arranged by Mr. Halliday, Alec's room was opposite theirs, no twists and turns and steps to negotiate. They crossed and Daisy tapped on the door.

No response. She knocked louder.

"Who's there?" came Alec's drowsy voice.

Without waiting, Belinda opened the door and rushed in. By the light from the passage, Daisy saw her vault onto her father's bed as he sat up, looking adorably rumpled. His arms wrapped around his daughter, he blinked owlishly over her head at Daisy, hesitating on the threshold.

Suddenly self-conscious, she felt herself blushing in the frightfully Victorian way she so despised. After all, she was in her nightclothes in a man's bedroom, with him in bed in his blue-and-white striped flannel pyjamas, too. At least they had both been fully dressed when he came to her room. He couldn't see her blush, thank heaven—she must be just a silhouette to him.

She couldn't stay hovering in the doorway, though. Which was worse, to light the gas and let him see her red cheeks, or to talk to him in the dark, their little chaperon invisible?

"I'd better turn on a light," she said.

"Here's matches." He reached out to take a box from the bedside table and toss it to her. "What's going on?"

She missed the catch, of course. She'd always been rotten at sports. Luckily the matches didn't spill so she didn't have to grovel after them.

"I had a bad dream, Daddy." Cradled safe in Alec's arms, Belinda already sounded sleepy again.

"I thought you ought to hear right away." Daisy lit the sconce over the fireplace, turning the gas just high enough not to go out. Shutting the door, she turned, noting his clothes neatly folded on a chair. Her gaze firmly fixed on Belinda's bare feet, she went on, "Belinda overheard Albert McGowan in the train. She's told me what she heard, but I can't make head or tail of it."

"I didn't *tell,* I asked."

"I take it you think this is significant," Alec said dryly, "or you wouldn't have woken me."

Daisy looked at him and was relieved to see his smile. "I'm not sure, but I didn't want to be accused in the morning of keeping something from you!"

"Fair enough. Sit down, Daisy; I can't do the polite." He waved at the foot of his bed. "What did you hear, Bel?"

"Daddy, do they put little girls in prison?"

"Great Scott, no!"

"Miss Dalrymple said not." Belinda yawned. "Mr. McGowan was shouting about houses on fire, and sheep, and puzzlement, and the sun and the world." Another yawn overtook her. "Oh, and someone called Miss Probation. Miss Anne Probation, but Miss Dalrymple says it was 'disapprobation.' "

"I'm not too sure about that." Perched on the very

end of his bed, the alternative being to move his clothes from the chair, Daisy elaborated. " 'Disapprobation' was my original guess, but now I've heard the rest. . . . It wasn't 'puzzlement' and 'sheep' she heard, Alec, but something like 'puzzlement' and something she connected with sheep."

"What about the burning houses, and the sun? Are you sure this isn't just part of her nightmare?"

"I'm sure about Miss Probation and the sun business—the word she remembered was 'orbit'—because she asked me about them right after hearing them. The rest I can't be certain. It was nothing to do with houses, either, that was just my attempted explanation of 'arson.' "

" 'Arson'! Well, it may all make sense in the morning."

"I'm sorry to have woken you for nothing."

He reached out one hand, and without thinking she put hers in it. "Never mind," he said. "Better safe than sorry, unless you can think of a more appropriate cliché."

With a tingling glow running up her arm from their clasped hands, Daisy couldn't have come up with an appropriate cliché to save her life. It was a jolly good job Belinda was there, or she might have jumped in between the sheets with Alec like a flash. He was looking at her oddly, making her feel quite breathless. She didn't quite like to pull her hand away in case he guessed how she was feeling.

"D-did you learn anything useful this evening?" she managed to stammer.

"We've got the pillow, and there's what appears to be blood on the pillow-case. It looks as if McGowan scratched his murderer. You haven't noticed scrapes or scratches on anyone's face or hands, have you?

Apart from the briar scratches on Jagai's and Raymond's hands?"

"No, nothing." But there was something she ought to tell him, if she could only think straight! She sighed. "The miser of Dunston Castle certainly is responsible for a lot of trouble."

"The *what?*"

"Old Alistair McGowan."

"What did you call him?"

"The miser of Dunston Castle. Why?"

"That's what I've been trying to remember," Alec said triumphantly. "That's what Bretton called him, and someone else—Kitty, was it? Alistair McGowan is a renowned miser?"

"I'm surprised no one else mentioned it. They never seemed to tire of the subject, except when they started raving about Albert leaving his all to an Indian. Does it matter?"

"It may." Alec being cautious. It gave her the excuse she needed to withdraw her hand from his warm, disturbing clasp.

"Well, if you're not going to tell me," she said indignantly, "we'd better get back to bed. Come on, Belinda . . . Oh, blast, she's fast asleep again!"

"I'll carry her. Will you go ahead and open the doors?"

Daisy complied, and turned back Belinda's bedclothes. Alec carried her in, set her down gently, and tucked her in. He dropped a kiss on her forehead.

"I hope she'll sleep soundly now," he said, turning to Daisy. "I'm sorry she disturbed your sleep."

"I'm sorry to have disturbed yours."

"It's part of the job—both being a policeman and being a father." He stood for a moment looking down at her, then suddenly, unexpectedly, he put his hands on her shoulders and kissed her on the lips.

Then he bolted.

Daisy stared blankly at the door as it clicked shut behind him. Her lips burned.

Gosh, she thought, it was *frightfully* lucky Belinda had been between them if that was how he felt, too. Dreamily she slipped off her dressing gown and wriggled back under the bedclothes. They still held a trace of her body-heat. What would it be like to climb into bed beside a man, beside Alec, to let herself sink into the warmth of . . .

Sternly she reined in her imagination. Emancipated she might be, immoral she was not, she reminded herself. But she had a new appreciation of how easy it would be to kiss one's proper upbringing good-bye.

Kiss. She touched her lips.

Stop it!

Concentrate on something else, on the puzzle of puzzlement, Miss Anne Probation, "orbit," sheep, and "arson." Arson—the flame Alec's touch had lit within her. Alec the Arsonist.

No, Miss Anne Probation. Who was Miss Anne Probation? Why had Albert McGowan flung her name in a fury at the person with him, and who was that person? Was it a name Belinda had heard, or was it in fact something else, something closer to "disapprobation"?

"Orbit," "arson," "sheep." Flaming sheep in orbit. Aries the Ram? Michael had loved star-gazing and had taught her some of the constellations. Michael, dearest Michael, dear, dead Michael who would wish her happy, wish her every happiness, a long and fruitful life with the man she was beginning to love as much as she had loved him.

No! "Orbit," "arson," "sheep." Orson, arbit, sleep. It was hopeless. At this rate she'd never get to sleep. Better count sheep. She pictured them, popping one by one over a low wooden fence, beautiful sheep, each with a black face and a thick, white fleece shining in the sun—"fleece"?

All at once Daisy was wide awake.

"Fleece"? Was that what Belinda had heard to remind her of sheep? Daisy looked longingly over at the other bed, but the little girl was sleeping peacefully. It would have to wait for morning.

All right, suppose it was "fleece." Suppose Albert McGowan had accused someone of fleecing or trying to fleece him. What could the other words be? Miss Anne Probation was obvious: "misappropriation"—of funds. "Puzzlement" must be "embezzlement," of course. "Orbit?" "Orbit, orbit, orbit," Daisy muttered to herself. An "orbit," or a "norbit." No, when she suggested "orbit" Belinda had agreed, had thought she recognized the word. Try substituting consonants. Orbit, orcit, ordit, orfit, orgit . . . Ordit! Or rather, "audit."

Which left "arson." Had someone burned something down and cheated the insurance company? It sounded like the sort of thing Peter Gillespie might try, given his previous record. Yet if Albert McGowan knew about it, surely Harold Bretton must, too, and he'd never have kept his mouth shut.

Perhaps he hadn't. Perhaps Alec knew all about it and had only pretended to be stumped. He had told her about the scratches, though.

Well, she wasn't going back to his bedroom to have it out with him!

Apart from "arson," the rest applied to Peter Gillespie's boot factory misdeeds, more or less. He had fleeced the public, but that was no secret to be covered up, no new cause for murder. In fact, there was no proof the row Belinda overheard had any direct bearing on the murder.

So why was Daisy racking her brains about it in the wee small hours of the morning? Anyway, she might have been misled by the coincidence of sheep and the apparently meaningful fleece. Try counting sheep again.

Sheep, lamb, ram, ewe, wool, mutton, lamb, spring; Spring, the sweet Spring is the year's pleasant king; Sweet lovers love the spring . . . Daisy slept.

16

Waking, still drowsy, Alec tried to sort reality from his dreams. Had Daisy come to him in the night? Had she set him a puzzle, like the quests in fairy tales, which he had to solve to win her? Had he solved it, and kissed her, and had she shared and warmed his cold, lonely bed?

No, only the puzzle was real, the rest sheer wishful fantasy. She had come, but she had brought Belinda with her. The puzzle was Belinda's, and if he had found a solution in his dreams he had forgotten it.

In fact, he had forgotten the puzzle. One word remained: arson, and that only because the heat of Daisy's hand in his had lit a fire those dreams had only partly quenched.

A cold bath, he advised himself.

Half an hour later he joined Tom and Ernie in the dining room. Tom was half-way through a large bowl of porridge.

" 'Oats,' " quoted Alec, " 'a grain which in England is generally given to horses, but in Scotland supports the people.' "

"Porridge makes a good starter to breakfast," Tom grunted, "if it's done right. Would you believe it, Chief, the Scots eat it with nowt but a bit of salt? Lyle's

Golden Syrup, that's what I like on it, though I'll make do with brown sugar at a pinch. This here Demerara hasn't got the flavour." Nonetheless he helped himself to another lavish teaspoonful of the golden crystals.

Piper laughed. "You should have heard the fuss, Chief. The waiter thought he wanted syrup 'stead of marmalade for his toast. Want a cuppa?" He reached for the tea-pot.

"No, thanks. I'll wait for coffee."

The waiter brought Piper's bacon and eggs and fried bread, and took Alec's order. "No, no porridge, thanks, and no fried bread." He was ten years older than Daisy, ten years nearer to middle-age spread. He'd better start watching what he ate. Perhaps he should take up Swedish exercises?

With an effort, he brought his mind back to business. "Either of you have any bright ideas overnight?"

Ernie Piper consulted Tom with a glance.

"Go ahead, young 'un." The sergeant continued to plough through his syrupless porridge.

"It's nothing much, Chief, may have nothing to do with the murder, only it seems a bit fishy. We was thinking, Miss Kitty and Mr. Bretton both saying Alistair McGowan's a miser, what's he doing gambling on stocks and shares and giving away his brass to charity?"

"That very question struck me," Alec said, "in the middle of the night. I've come up with three possible answers. First, as Braeburn pointed out, some people do go dotty in old age and do utterly unexpected things. Second, possibly Kitty misunderstood and Bretton exaggerated his parsimony." Except that Daisy said the others also described him as a miser—though he couldn't tell Tom and Ernie so without revealing her midnight visit.

"We can ask the others if it's true," Tom pointed

out, wiping his mustache after the last spoonful of porridge. "What's third, Chief?"

"That it really is fishy. Perhaps someone has been forging the old man's name on checques, or on instructions to his stockbroker or Braeburn."

"Peter Gillespie," said Tom. "Fraud's his line."

"Mr. Bretton," said Ernie. "Forging signatures is kind of like gambling."

"Gillespie's more likely," said Alec. "He expected to inherit and could have covered up the . . . *Bonjour, madame.*"

The three detectives rose as Madame Pasquier came into the dining room and approached their table. She was impeccably dressed in a smart black costume and white silk blouse with a sardonyx cameo on a gold chain, and impeccably made-up despite the early hour.

"*Bonjour,* Chief Inspector, gentlemen," she responded with a smile. "May I join you? You wish to speak to me, I expect. I regret that I was overcome with fatigue yesterday evening."

Piper gallantly sprang to hold a chair for her. "It's a long journey from Paree, madarm," he ventured.

"It is indeed. Don't let me interrupt your meal," she said as the waiter reappeared with plates of food for Tom and Alec, racks of toast, and a pot of coffee. "Oh dear." She eyed the bacon and eggs with distaste. "I've grown unused to the English notions of breakfast. I don't suppose you have *croissants,* or any kind of hot rolls?"

"Just toast, madam, besides the porridge and . . ."

"Porridge! It must be thirty years since I ate porridge. I'll have some, for the sake of auld lang syne. A *small* bowl."

"We haven't got syrup, madam," said the waiter mistrustfully.

"Syrup? *Mon dieu,* what sacrilege! Salt and milk are all that I require."

"Spoken like a true Scot," Alec said with a grin, "but too French to drink tea for breakfast, I dare say. May I pour you a cup of coffee?"

"Eat, eat! And while you eat, I shall explain myself. You have heard, no doubt, that I ran away from home not long after my sister Amelia's marriage. I had many friends in France, having been sent to a French finishing school. To my great good fortune, I soon met and married *mon cher* Jules. I wrote to my father on that occasion. The only response was a letter from my cousin Julia Gillespie, who had taken on the thankless task of catering to Papa's crotchets, destined for me. Papa refused to communicate, but I continued to write to Julia every Christmas."

"Miss Gillespie notified you of your father's illness, I presume," Alec said. "I wondered how you happened to turn up just at this moment."

"Yes, Julia wrote to announce the gathering of the clans." Mme. Pasquier sighed. "Perhaps it was foolish after so many years, but I felt a filial impulse to see Papa one last time, to tell him about his grandsons. You must not suppose we have any need of the family fortune. Jules is a wealthy *homme d'affaires,* even since the War and our two sons are doing well in the family business."

"We're checking that, madam," said Tom, having apparently failed to succumb to the lady's undoubted charm.

Alec produced the usual bromide. "A matter of routine.

"But naturally. However," she continued with a slightly malicious smile, "I believe I can set your suspicions at rest without difficulty. When the Flying Scotsman reached Berwick, I had not yet revealed myself to my family. I might easily have passed as a total stranger, but I chose to disclose my connection with poor Uncle Albert to the local police. You may ask Superintendent Halliday or that nice sergeant of his if this is not so."

"Fair enough. May I ask why you chose to reveal yourself to the police but not, earlier, to your family?"

Her shrug was Gallicly expressive. "You may ask. Whether I can answer is another matter. Perhaps at first I wanted to leave myself a chance to turn tail and run at the last minute, yet I preferred not to lie to the police. I am a respectable woman, Chief Inspector. And perhaps, though it is quite easy to ignore one's family from a distance, I did not care to stand aside when they were so close and in trouble."

Alec nodded. "Serious trouble, madame. Did you see or hear anything on the train which might conceivably help us to find your uncle's murderer?"

"Nothing. Being lucky enough to find a compartment to myself, I closed the door and pulled down the blinds. There I stayed except for venturing to the dining-car for lunch, where I sat with the charming Miss Dalrymple. No doubt she knows better than I whether anything transpiring there might be of interest to you."

Her bright, enquiring eyes fixed on Alec's face and he felt a slow heat rising in his cheeks. "Just one more question for the present," he said hastily. "Your father has been described as . . . er, frugal in his habits. Would you agree?"

"Frugal?" Her laugh pealed out. "Papa is, and always was, a niggardly skinflint. If he paid for his daughters to attend a finishing school, it was only in order to get us off his hands the sooner. Not until Amelia married and went away did he realize that if I found a husband he'd lose his unpaid housekeeper."

"So you took French leave."

"Precisely. I'm not at all sorry I ran away, only that poor Julia has borne the brunt of my defection. Jules agrees that I shall ask her to come and live with us in Paris when Papa goes. She is owed a little gaiety, *hein?* Ah, here is my porridge." She stared at the greyish brown mush with distaste. "*Quelle horreur!* I believe I shall stick to toast and coffee, after all. Please, Chief Inspector, don't let me keep you from your business."

Alec and Tom had availed themselves of her permission to eat while she talked. They made their excuses, thanked her for her cooperation, and repaired to the landlord's parlour. Alec took out his pipe and tobacco, while Piper lit up a Woodbine.

Tom, who preferred a rare good cigar to any more frequent but lesser indulgence, said broodingly, "More Frog than Scot, if you ask me, Chief. All right if I go and ring up Sergeant Barclay?"

"Go ahead, and while you're at it, ask whether there's any further news from Dr. Renfrew. If we've guessed right, those scratches may be all we need." He struck a match as Tom padded out.

Alec was huffing and puffing at his pipe when Daisy knocked on the door and entered the parlour, Belinda at her heels.

"Good . . ." puff ". . . morning," he said around the stem clenched between his teeth.

"Good-morning, Daddy. Good-morning, Mr. Piper. It's no good trying to talk to Daddy when he's lighting his pipe, Miss Dalrymple. Let's go and have breakfast first. I'm *starving.*"

Daisy chuckled. "That's all right, he won't be able to interrupt me. Perhaps Mr. Piper would go with you to the dining room and help you choose your breakfast." She looked at Ernie Piper, avoiding Alec's eyes, hoping he'd realize her aim was to spare Belinda, not to catch him on his own.

"If you don't mind, Ernie," said Alec.

" 'Course not, Chief," Piper said gamely. "Come on, Miss Belinda."

"You can have some of my toast," she promised, slipping her hand into his. They went off.

Crossing to the fireplace to warm her hands—the hotel was no warmer today—Daisy said apologetically over her shoulder, "She's so bright this morning, I didn't want to talk about the murder in front of her. Have you thought about what she overheard?"

"To tell the truth"—puff, puff—"I forgot the words, all except arson. I'm afraid something distracted me. Dash it, it's going out."

She looked at him suspiciously. He was poking at the bowl of his pipe, his face hidden in clouds of fragrant blue smoke. Did he mean that *she* had distracted him? Did he even remember having kissed her? "You don't think it's important?" she asked.

"I don't see how I can tell, not without some idea of what she actually heard."

"I have some idea. Alec, do put that blasted thing down and listen. It's only guesswork, of course, but if I'm right it all fits together, sort of. All except arson."

"Arson is what I'm trying in vain to commit. Sit down, Daisy, and tell me. I can listen and light my pipe at the same time, no matter what Bel says."

Daisy sat down on the magenta plush sofa. Alec took a step towards her, cast a glance at the nearest arm chair, then, with an air of resolution, joined her on the sofa. She bit back a small smile. He did remember, though whether he regretted that kiss she couldn't be sure.

"It was the sheep that gave me the clue," she said as he took out his tobacco pouch and stuffed a few more shreds into the bowl. Unburnt tobacco smelled so good, Daisy could never understand why anyone wanted to burn it. She hated cigarette smoke, and even worse cigar smoke, but she had never minded pipe smoke; she was actually coming quite to like it, since she'd known Alec.

"Sheep?" he queried between fierce sucks on the mouthpiece. The ashtray was filling with spent matches.

"Something to do with sheep, Belinda said, and I came up with fleece." She explained where that had led her. "So, fleece, misappropriation, embezzlement, audit—it all adds up to financial shenanigans, unless I'm completely on the wrong track."

"Hmm." The pipe had gone out again, but he didn't seem to notice. Frowning, he spoke around it. "It sounds good, but it would be more convincing if we could fit in the arson."

"Belinda didn't actually say arson, she said arsony."

"Hell! Arsony? Sorry, Daisy."

She scarcely heard his apology. "Alec, that's it! Larceny! I bet he said something like . . . oh, 'It's plain, simple larceny,' or 'that's foul larceny.' "

"Could be," Alec said slowly. "It fits with the rest, which is rather stretching coincidence. And with what Braeburn told us. . . . Daisy, this is strictly in confidence. Braeburn says Alistair McGowan's vast fortune is largely mythical, or at least historical. The past few years, he's been speculating on the Stock Exchange and giving away large sums to charity. There's only a few thousand left."

"The miser giving away large sums? Not likely! I

can't see him speculating, either. Much more probable that someone's been cheating him."

"It is, isn't it? Even without Belinda's clues, we'd considered that possibility. But how did Brother Albert find out?"

Daisy pondered. "Braeburn told you about the vanished riches? In confidence? You mean he hadn't told any of the family?"

"Only Albert, as Alistair's heir, when Albert consulted him on the train."

"But Albert knew perfectly well that his twin brother is a penny-pinching skinflint. I distinctly remember his saying something of the sort. He wouldn't have believed for a moment in donations to charity." She and Alec stared at each other, comprehension dawning. "So when he was told . . . by the man who'd have found it easiest . . ."

"Now hold on, Daisy," Alec begged, "don't go off half-cocked!"

"He accused Braeburn of larceny and threatened an audit."

"Hold on! This is a flight of sheer fancy, a house of cards. All we have to go on are a few words misheard by a child, addressed to we know not whom. Even if you've guessed every one right, it doesn't prove the person spoken to killed Albert. It's not evidence."

"What's not evidence, Chief?" Sergeant Tring came in. "Morning, Miss Dalrymple."

"Good-morning, Mr. Tring. I've just made some simply brilliant deductions and the chief says they're not evidence."

Alec briefly explained. Not for the first time, Daisy admired his ability to render a convoluted tale concisely and clearly. He was a wizard at it. In fact, he was altogether wizard, even if he had punctured her balloon.

Tring listened, then shook his head. "Sorry, Miss Dalrymple, but you could've got it all right and it still doesn't mean anything. Who's to say old Albert wasn't shouting at Braeburn about someone else's swindle?"

"Hold on, Tom," said Alec. "If that was the case, surely Braeburn would have mentioned Albert's suspicions to us. He was quick enough to point to Peter Gillespie as the most likely murderer."

"And we already agreed Mr. Gillespie's the most likely swindler, Chief."

"True. It's all pretty thin, but all the same, I think I'll 'phone up the Yard and have someone from the Fraud Squad go and speak to Braeburn's partners. Inspector Fielding, I think. He owes me one, and he's tactful but persistent."

"He'll need to be, trying to pump a bunch of lawyers about one of their own!" said Tring.

"With any luck it won't matter. You spoke to Sergeant Barclay?"

"Yes, and it looks like Madame Paskeyay's in the clear. They'd never've guessed she was connected if she hadn't spoke up."

"Any news from Dr. Redlow?" Alec asked impatiently.

"I talked to Dr. Fraser." Tring's mustache twitched as he grinned. "It's blood on the pillow-case, Chief. And what's more, they found blood and skin under the old man's fingernails."

"The same type of blood?"

"The very same, Chief. Group three, he says, which is not too common. Seems it's different from Albert McGowan's, and he's got no scratches on him, anyways."

"Then our chummy has four scratches on one hand." Alec curled his fingers into a claw. "Albert's left hand—no, the pillowcase was inside out. Albert's right, chummy's left hand. I doubt he attacked from behind, though we'll check both."

"There should be marks on the other hand, too, Chief. He scratched with his left hand as well, just didn't draw enough blood to stain the pillow-case. Leastways, not enough to soak through or to see under all that dirt. The doc says it should be easy to tell fingernail scratches from bramble scratches, but to call him in if there's any problem."

"Excellent. All we have to do now is examine everyone's hands. I'll. . . . Oh, Daisy, I'd forgotten you were here. I need Piper. Could you go back to Belinda?"

So much for the kiss, Daisy thought gloomily. "All right," she said with a sigh. "But there's one thing you need to take into account."

"What's that?"

"I told you the train was fearfully overheated, and the wireless had forecast a summery day. The younger ladies were in short-sleeved dresses, and Raymond had abandoned his jacket and rolled up his shirt-sleeves. Mr. McGowan's compartment was even hotter. I heard him invite Dr. Jagai to take off his jacket when he went in there. The other men may have followed suit. You'd better check people's arms as well as their hands."

"Oh lord!" Alec groaned. "Asking people to show their hands is one thing. They're bound to kick up a dust when I ask them to start stripping!"

17

"Have any of the rest come down yet, Ernie?" Alec asked as the young D.C. hurried into the parlour.

"Most of 'em, Chief. Mr. Smythe-Pike's laid up with a bad attack of the gout—and Mr. Bretton and Mr. Jeremy Gillespie look like they wish they had half as good an excuse to stay in bed. Mrs. Jeremy's come down. If you ask me, Chief, she's *much* too big to murder anyone. Wouldn't be surprised if it popped out any minute."

"Let's hope not! Things are going to be difficult enough as it is. It seems we're right about those scratches."

Piper looked puzzled. "Don't that make it easy, Chief? All we have to do is check their hands and we've got chummy by the short hairs."

"We're going to have to look at their arms, too." Alec explained Daisy's reasoning. "It's easy enough for the gentlemen to take off their jackets and roll up their sleeves," he went on, "though some of them will undoubtedly squeal. The difficulty's with the women. If they're wearing tight sleeves they'll have to change, and then they'll have every right to object to our scrutinizing their arms. I suppose I'll have to get hold of a police matron. I hope Halliday can produce one."

"Why not ask Miss Dalrymple to do it, Chief?"

"Because. . . ." Why not? Because he hated to see Daisy involved in the sordid business of murder any more than she herself made absolutely necessary?

"Do what?" Tom returned from the telephone.

"You got through already?" Alec asked. "That was quick."

"Told the girl urgent police priority, Chief. Don't want to be stuck up here longer'n we must, do we? The missus'll be getting in a pucker. She's always afraid I'll fade away without good home-cooked meals."

"No fear of that, Sarge," said Piper.

"Cheeky cub," the vast sergeant said tolerantly. "Inspector Fielding's on his way, Chief. What are we asking Miss Dalrymple to do?"

"Check the women's arms. But we're not." He had come up with a reasonable reason. "I don't want Belinda either mixed up in it or left alone, and I need you two."

"She likes the Indian doctor, Chief," said Piper. "He's already out of it, pretty much. Check his arms first, then ask him to look after Miss Belinda."

Alec considered. There was nothing against it but his own reluctance to ask for Daisy's help. And if the Berwick force had no matron, it might take hours to bring one in from elsewhere.

"All right, assuming Dr. Jagai is cleared, I'll see if Miss Dalrymple is willing." Fat chance she'd refuse. "We could take them in two groups, men and women, but I think we'll do it one by one in case chummy gets excited. I don't think it's any of the women, but Ernie, you'll stand at the door of whatever room Miss Dalrymple's in and get in there fast if you hear the slightest squeak."

"Don't worry, Chief," said Ernie importantly, "I'll

take care of her. Shall I go and ask her to come here so's you can explain?"

"Not yet. We'd better let her—and everyone else—eat their breakfasts in peace. Then I'll see Dr. Jagai first to make sure he's willing to keep an eye on Belinda. In fact, go and tell him I'd like to consult him as soon as he's finished. Discreetly, Ernie. I don't want the others wondering."

"Easy, Chief, he's sitting with Miss Dalrymple and Miss Belinda."

Piper popped out again. Alec discussed with Tom the best order in which to call in the gentlemen. Bretton and Jeremy Gillespie first, they decided, as their statements were sketchy in the extreme.

"Then Peter Gillespie, while Miss Dalrymple keeps his missus out of the way," Tom suggested.

"Good point! In fact, we'll see him first to make sure of coordinating with his wife's absence. Then Bretton and Jeremy, then we'll tackle Smythe-Pike, in bed or out of it. Any further details we can get out of them may help our case. I'd say the scratches will be damning evidence, but you know what lawyers are like."

"Slippery as jellied eels," Tom agreed. He looked round as Piper came back once more. "Hooked our fish, young 'un?"

"Dr. Jagai'll be here in a coupla minutes, Chief. He eats his porridge the Scotch way, Sarge, and he don't follow it up with a ton and a half of bacon and eggs. Nor curry, neether," Piper added regretfully, as if such proof of foreign eccentricity would have pleased him.

The doctor didn't keep them waiting long. "A medical consultation, Mr. Fletcher?" he asked. "I have my black bag upstairs."

"No, Doctor. I have a favour to ask of you. But first, would you mind letting me look at your hands?"

Jagai raised his eyebrows, but he promptly held out his hands, brown-skinned, blunt-fingered, competent, with well-trimmed, spotless nails. The scratches he had received while helping Belinda now formed a network of rows of tiny scabs. Fingernail scratches would be in roughly parallel lines, Alec thought, and wider, therefore slower to start to heal.

The Indian turned his hands, revealing pink palms, one stained with iodine where a thorn had stabbed more deeply. "Nothing vital pierced," he said quizzically. "Cat scratches are worse. They tend to fester."

"What about human?" Alec queried. "I'm afraid I must ask you to take off your jacket and roll up your sleeves."

Jagai shrugged out of his jacket and unfastened his cufflinks. "So Mr. McGowan branded his assailant," he said, baring arms unmarked but for a small white scar near one elbow. "Good for the old boy! Human scratches can be nasty, partly because of the width, partly because they are usually inflicted by dirty nails, though not, of course, in this case."

Alec held his jacket for him to put back on. "By the way, did you in fact take this off in Mr. McGowan's compartment?" he asked.

"Yes. It was too hot in there for comfort."

"He invited you to do so? Would he have done the same for his other visitors?"

"I rather doubt it," Jagai said dryly. "He disliked them and wouldn't have cared for their discomfort. But it's possible, certainly."

"I'm sorry to have had to check you. You weren't really still under suspicion but I had to be quite sure, partly just for the sake of thoroughness, partly because of the favour I spoke of."

"What can I do for you?"

"You're free to leave, but would you be kind enough to take charge of my daughter for a while this morning? I need Miss Dalrymple's help, I need both my men, but I dare not leave Belinda alone after what may have happened out on the walls yesterday. She likes and trusts you."

"It will be a pleasure, Mr. Fletcher," Jagai said, smiling.

"You realize she must not be left for so much as a minute?"

"You truly think she is in danger?" he asked gravely. "Believe me, I had no idea or I'd not have left her yesterday."

"We didn't know then. She's no threat to the murderer now, if she ever was—she's told us what she knows, whether it turns out to be useful or not, and in any case we now have the scratches to go by—but he or she isn't aware of that."

"Better safe than sorry. I'll keep my eye on her. It might do her good to get away from the hotel for a while. May I take her for a walk, in the town, not on the walls?"

"That sounds like a good idea, for an hour or so. Thank you, Doctor." Alec shook his hand. "Don't mention the scratches to anyone, please. I'd rather they didn't know exactly what we're looking for. Piper, go with Dr. Jagai; explain to Belinda and tell Miss Dalrymple I request the pleasure of her company."

Daisy was rather disappointed to find Alec intended to share the pleasure of her company with both Piper and Tring. However, she cheered up when she discovered she was actually being invited to lend a hand in the investigation.

"Gosh, need you ask, of *course* I'll help," she said.

"If anyone decides to be difficult, I'll tell them the alternative is a grim old police matron. Do you want me to ask them questions, too?"

"No, Daisy, absolutely not!" Alec looked appalled. "Don't you dare. In fact, if you should find suspicious scratches, which I don't expect, you're not to comment, let alone ask for explanations or make accusations. Just tell Piper. He'll be right outside your door."

Daisy had not considered that there might be a threat to her own safety. She still didn't really, not when she'd only be seeing the ladies, but it would be comforting to have help at hand in case someone went for her with a poker. "Good," she said, with a warm smile for the young detective, who blushed and beamed.

They decided her bedroom was the best place for her to operate. She went up, and a few minutes later Piper ushered in Enid Gillespie.

"Really, Miss Dalrymple," she snapped, "I can scarcely believe *you* are lending yourself to this sordid business."

"If you prefer to go to the police station and see a police matron, I'm sure Chief Inspector Fletcher will oblige," Daisy assured her.

"Certainly not!"

"Then I rest my case. May I look at your hands, please, Mrs. Gillespie?"

"My hands? Good gracious, is that what all this fuss is about? The police must be quite baffled if they are taking up palmistry," Enid Gillespie said sarcastically, holding out her hands palms up. At Daisy's request, she turned them over to display several singularly ugly rings, ornate Victorian settings of not very valuable stones. No scratches.

"Now I must see your arms."

"This is going too far!" Mrs. Gillespie spluttered.

"Shall I ask Detective Constable Piper to escort you to the police station?" Daisy prayed the obstreperous woman would give in. Whether Piper, or even Alec, had the authority to do anything of the kind she had no idea. She should have found out.

In grim silence, Mrs. Gillespie removed the fitted jacket of her black costume, unbuttoned the cuffs of her white blouse, and rolled the sleeves up to her elbows. Daisy was quite disappointed not to discover any evidence blazoned upon that loose, pallid, blotchy skin.

After her, the rest were easy. Mrs. Smythe-Pike, though bewildered, was willing. Madame Pasquier was quick and businesslike. Anne was so busy complaining about the hotel's lack of facilities for small children that she was hardly aware of baring her arms for Daisy's inspection. Judith seemed distinctly uneasy, worried even, but she complied without demur. As for Kitty, she considered the whole thing a terrific lark. All were unmarked.

As Kitty bounced out, Piper stuck his head into the room. "There's just Mrs. Jeremy Gillespie left, miss," he said, "and I don't think she oughta be running up and down more'n she need 'case she has her baby on the stairs."

"Is she crying?" Daisy asked apprehensively.

"No, miss, not at the moment, but the chief's decided to see her right after her husband, and he's in there now."

"Let's hurry, then." Daisy headed for the stairs, Piper on her heels. "If everyone's finished in the dining room, I'll see her in there. Not that I believe for a moment she could possibly have attacked anyone."

"Don't seem likely, do it, miss?" Piper agreed.

Mattie Gillespie was scratchless—and tearless until, lumbering from the dining room with Daisy, she met Piper with a request to proceed to the Chief Inspector's lair. Eyes swimming, she clutched Daisy's arm.

"Come with me," she begged.

Suppressing with ease a noble impulse to suggest Jeremy as a preferable escort, Daisy went. Alec couldn't very well object after asking for her help. In fact, he looked resigned but made no protest.

His questioning was of the gentlest, without the least hint of suspecting Matilda. Nonetheless all he got out of her, through floods of tears, was that Jeremy didn't do it and she didn't care about the money, all she wanted was to go home.

Alec sighed and let her go. Daisy supported her tottering steps from the room, though obviously dying to stay and find out what progress he had made.

She wasn't missing anything. He was, as Tom said, "No forrader." Peter Gillespie without his wife was no more informative than with her. Jeremy Gillespie and Harold Bretton sober remembered no more than they had drunk—less if anything. Not a scratch on any of them.

"None of the women scratched, I take it, Ernie?" Alec said. Piper shook his head. "We'll go up to Smythe-Pike then. I want to leave Raymond till last. It won't hurt to give him time to get the wind up."

"Poor chap," Tom murmured.

"Poor chap indeed," Alec soberly agreed, "but it's for the lawyers to argue over diminished responsibility. Our job's to find Albert McGowan's killer."

From the fuss Smythe-Pike kicked up when asked to bare his arms, anyone might have guessed him to be the murderer. Sitting up in bed in his crimson-striped flannel pyjamas, he roared curses at the presumptuous peelers who dared disturb a sick man's rest. However, the Chief Constable with whom he claimed intimate friendship was hundreds of miles away. At last he grudgingly pushed up his pyjama sleeves, revealing sinewy arms without a sign of a scratch.

That was his only concession. When Alec tried to ask a few questions, Smythe-Pike brandished his fist and gobbled like a turkey, his face turning as crimson as the stripes on his pyjamas. Afraid of causing an apoplectic fit, Alec desisted.

"Crikey," breathed Piper as the door closed behind them, "I'm glad we don't have to try and arrest *him!*"

"What about the lawyer, Chief?" Tom asked.

"If he done it, why'd he stick around?" said Piper. "He didn't have to. You'd think he'd be off like a shot."

"He'd've wanted to keep tabs on things," Tom informed him, "see if we was looking his way. They often do. Not that I think it was him."

"Nor do I," Alec agreed, "but I suppose we'd better check him. The more I think about it, the more Miss Dalrymple's theory seems like a far-fetched farrago, but I don't want to have to tell her I didn't even look. You take a dekko at McGowan's valet, Tom, while Ernie and I pay a call on Braeburn. See you downstairs."

The solicitor was up and dressed, but once again huddled in the chair by the fire. He still looked thoroughly miserable, red-eyed and hollow cheeked, his black silk scarf wound close about his throat.

"I'm very sorry to disturb you again, sir," Alec said. "Your throat's still bad, is it? Well, I shan't be asking you to do much talking, unless you have recalled anything new?"

"Nothing," said Braeburn gruffly. "What do you want?"

"We're just asking everyone who entered Mr. McGowan's compartment to show us their hands and arms, sir. If you wouldn't mind . . ."

"Mind? Of course I mind! You can't do that without a warrant."

Alec raised his eyebrows with a cold stare. "I can't insist without a warrant, sir. I'm just requesting. None of the others has refused."

"They all have a motive for wanting Albert McGowan dead. No doubt they're anxious to clear themselves."

"We don't have to prove motive, sir, though it helps. I'd be remiss in my duty if I didn't check everyone who had means and opportunity."

"Well, I don't practise criminal law," Braeburn reluctantly conceded. "I am not conversant with the ins and outs of it. Very well." He stood up, took off his jacket, and rolled up his sleeves.

His bony arms were clean as a whistle. So much for Daisy's wild conjectures, Alec thought, solicitously helping him on with his jacket. Young Ernie must be disappointed at this proof of her fallibility.

18

Daisy hadn't minded helping Alec by examining the women, but now she found it slightly embarrassing to face them. Unwilling to skulk in her room, she retreated to a corner of the lounge and hid behind last week's *Berwick Journal*.

Still snow on the Cheviots, she noted. No wonder it was so cold. She had just missed Wanda Hawley in *Miss Hobbs* at the Playhouse, and a film of the eruption of Vesuvius, with music by the Playhouse Orchestra. A motor-car speeding at over twenty miles per hour had hit a perambulator on the bridge. No one badly hurt, she gathered. The motorist's defense was that the pram was being pushed in the roadway, but as Superintendent Halliday pointed out in court: "We have hardly come to that stage yet when the public has no right to be on the highway. In a recent decision, a learned judge has laid it down that even if a person is sitting in the middle of the road they have no right to run over him."

An advertisement offering farmers tenpence ha'penny each for moleskins caught Daisy's eye, then her mind wandered. Alec hadn't placed much faith in her interpretation of Belinda's mystery words. What else could they mean? "Arsony"—"arsenic"? Had Albert McGowan somehow got wind of a poisoning? Had someone been poisoning him? She rather thought an upset stomach was a symptom of arsenic poisoning.

She should have asked Belinda about the bits of shouting she *had* understood, which might well give a clue to the rest. Nor had the child ever answered the question about what made her believe she would be sent to prison.

Surely she ought to be back from her walk by now. Oh lord, Daisy thought in a sudden panic, were she and Alec both quite wrong to trust Chandra Jagai?

Jumping up, she dropped the newspaper on her chair and hurried out to the lobby.

"Miss Dalrymple!" Belinda, rosy-cheeked, was just taking off her hat. Behind her the doctor, smiling, unbuttoned his coat. "We had ever such a nice walk, on the walls by the river. It's perfectly safe there. We saw fishing boats and swans and all sorts of things."

"And we talked, didn't we, Belinda?"

"Dr. Jagai says I have to tell you or Daddy absolutely everything."

"Thank you, Doctor, I was just thinking we hadn't quite got to the bottom of things." Daisy noticed Briggs pausing on his way through the hall and pricking up his ears. "Come into the dining room, Belinda. There shouldn't be anyone in there."

"I'll be in the lounge if you need me," said Jagai.

The tables in the dining room were already set for lunch. Daisy pulled out a chair and sat down. Belinda stood before her, hands tightly clasped, looking guilty.

"I didn't *mean* not to tell you."

Daisy took her hands. "It's all right, darling. I know you were frightened. But what exactly was it that frightened you? Why did you think you'd be sent to prison?"

"He said so. It was in the corridor, after I fetched Dr. Jagai, 'member? He went in with you and I waited outside, and then the guard came to see why the train stopped, and everyone came out. Someone whispered in my ear about wicked little girls listening at doors and they'd get put in prison if they told what they heard."

Leaning forward, Daisy asked urgently, "Who?"

"I can't be quite absolutely sure. There were lots of people crowding around and talking. But I thought it was that lawyer."

"Mr. Braeburn! Now I remember you asked me if lawyers could put people in prison. It's a pity you're not sure, but I think we'd better tell your father right away. Come on."

They went to the landlord's parlour but no one was there. As they came out, Tom Tring came down the stairs. "Looking for the chief, ladies?" he asked. "He's upstairs, with Mr. Braeburn."

"I don't want to go!" cried Belinda.

"Mr. Tring, could you take Belinda to Dr. Jagai?"

"O' course, miss. Come along, Miss Belinda." He engulfed her small hand in his vast one. "Room nine, miss."

Daisy sped upstairs. After a false start she found the room just round the corner from hers, and was raising her hand to knock when she heard Alec's voice thanking Braeburn for his cooperation.

It must mean the solicitor was not scratched. Confused, Daisy let her hand drop. The door opened and Alec stared down at her in surprise.

"What is it?"

In a low voice she told him, "Belinda says Braeburn threatened her with prison if she repeated what she'd overheard."

She was about to add that Belinda wasn't quite sure, but Alec didn't wait. He flung back into the room.

"You threatened my daughter?" he roared in a voice worthy of Desmond Smythe-Pike, standing arms akimbo glaring down at the chair by the fireside. Unfortunately it hid the lawyer from Daisy and she couldn't very well just barge in.

"Threatened?" he squeaked. "Good lord, no."

Suspicion joined the fury in Alec's face as he stared down. His dark, heavy brows met over his nose in a formidable scowl. "Take off that scarf," he demanded, his tone deceptively calm.

"I really must protest, Chief Inspector," Braeburn said shakily. "I'm an ill man. I shall take a dangerous quinsy if I expose my throat to the cold. You yourself admit that you have no legal right to insist on . . ."

He spluttered to a halt as Alec leaned forward and grabbed. His hand returned to Daisy's view with a black cravat dangling. Piper, standing just inside the door, moved towards them.

Now Alec's voice was as soft as a panther's footfall, and as dangerous. "Just how did you come by those scratches on your neck, Mr. Braeburn?"

"I must have done it when half asleep," Braeburn squawked.

"You claim they are self-inflicted?" Alec asked sceptically.

"It has happened before," he gabbled. "I am subject to acutely painful quinsies. One instinctively reaches for an itch or a source of pain, and in a half waking state one is not aware of clawing oneself until too late. It is most embarrassing. You will understand why I didn't care to reveal such a ridiculous plight."

"Hardly ridiculous. They look nasty. You ought to ask Dr. Jagai to wash them with boracic and apply iodine." Was Alec backing down? Daisy wondered in dismay. But he continued, "We are losing sight of my original query: What's this about your threatening Belinda?"

"Not threatening, Chief Inspector, warning." Braeburn had regained his composure. "I had seen Miss Fletcher in the corridor when Mr. Smythe-Pike and Mr. Gillespie were consulting me. When I saw her again lurking, as I supposed, outside Mr. McGowan's compartment, I merely warned her in a fatherly way that eavesdropping is wrong."

Nonplussed, Alec glanced back at Daisy. She mouthed "prison" at him.

"My daughter understood you to threaten her with prison."

"Prison, ha ha! I know enough of criminal law to know little girls are not sent to prison. I said something about telling tales; perhaps she misheard it as gaols. There was a good deal of noise in the corridor by then."

"Perhaps," Alec said noncommittally. "Well, I'm glad that's cleared up. Thank you." He started towards the door, then stopped halfway and returned. "You won't object, I trust, to the local police surgeon taking a sample of blood to test."

"Blood?" said Braeburn faintly. "I don't care for doctors."

"Just a pinprick in the finger, I understand, sir. It's amazing what they can tell from a few spots of blood these days. They'll prove in no time that yours doesn't match what we found."

"Yes. Yes, of course. If you really consider it necessary, Chief Inspector."

"I do. I'll ask Dr. Fraser to step round, and in the

meantime, I must request that you do not leave the hotel. Thank you, sir."

The moment Piper closed the door behind the three of them, Daisy said, "I didn't realize they could tell exactly whose blood was on the pillow-case."

Following her down a step and along the passage, Alec said in a low voice, "They can't. The most they can prove is that his blood is or is not in the same group. It can't convict him, though it could clear him. But few people know that, any more than you did."

"You hoped he'd give himself away?"

"Yes, or at least refuse the test."

"That would have been a reasonable reaction, innocent or guilty," Daisy pointed out, "as reasonable as his explanations of the scratches and what he said to Belinda."

"In fact," said Alec, "he was altogether *too* reasonable. He ought to have threatened to have *my* blood for harassing him."

"You still think he did it?" She started down the stairs.

"We haven't found scratches on anyone else. Tom's checking the manservant. Otherwise there's no one left but Raymond Gillespie. Ernie, find him, will you, and bring him to the back parlour."

At the foot of the stairs, he turned towards the rear of the house while Daisy and Piper went on to the lounge.

"The chief's worried, isn't he?" Daisy said.

"Mr. Braeburn agreeing to the blood test, meek as a lamb—well, it don't look like he done it, miss. And the chief was counting on them scratches to give the game away."

Daisy nodded.

As they entered the lounge, Belinda bounced up to

her. "Miss Dalrymple, Dr. Jagai says he'll buy me a ginger beer now the bar's opened, but only if you say I may. It won't spoil my lunch, honestly."

"I don't suppose it will. Tell him you may, and don't forget to thank him."

"I won't. He said he'd buy some for Kitty, too, and I went to ask her, but she's not allowed to sit with us."

"What a shame. Perhaps now I'm here her mother will let her." Daisy paused, biting back a sigh as Anne approached, wearing a peevish pout.

"Daisy, will you speak to that policeman of yours for me? He really must let us go. It's not at all good for the children being cooped up in a tiny room with Nurse for so long."

"Bring them down here for a while."

"Oh, I couldn't, not with a murderer about. Besides, Harold says they'd disturb everyone. Do come and see, and you'll be able to explain to Mr. Fletcher how impossible it is"

"All right." This time the sigh escaped. "Just a minute."

Daisy went to meet Dr. Jagai, who was coming towards her. "May I offer you a sherry?" he asked.

"Thanks, but not just now. Doctor, would you mind keeping an eye on Belinda just a little longer? Mrs. Bretton wants me to go up to the children with her."

"Not at all. She's lively company."

As Daisy and Anne went out to the lobby, Piper and Raymond came from the bar-parlour, Ray with a tankard of beer in his hand. A tremor made the surface of the dark liquid shimmer. He was pale—whether paler than usual Daisy couldn't be sure—and one corner of his mouth twitched. She gave him what she hoped was an encouraging smile. He didn't seem to notice.

Alec had better be gentle with him, or he'd have her as well as Judith to reckon with.

Alec didn't like the look of Raymond Gillespie. Nor, judging by his wary expression, did Tom Tring. Perhaps it had been a mistake to let the young man stew. If he had one of his nervous attacks, Alec had no idea what to do.

Inviting him to sit down on the magenta sofa, he went over to Piper and murmured, "If he cracks, run for Miss Smythe-Pike."

"Right, Chief."

Alec sat opposite Raymond. "Have you recalled anything which might be useful?" he asked, trying to put him at ease. "For instance, anyone you saw in the corridor near Mr. McGowan's compartment, either before or after you looked in?"

"There wasn't a soul. I've been thinking and thinking. I'm pretty sure he was dead by then. There's a sort of . . . a sort of horrible absence. . . . Haven't you ever felt it?"

"I know what you mean." Though he had indeed experienced the emptiness of death, Alec had always ascribed it to his own mind, not to an exterior force, or absence thereof. He certainly didn't believe it could be sensed through a slit an inch or two wide in the absence of definite knowledge. Raymond's oversensitive imagination was running riot after the event—or he was prevaricating.

Not much point in delaying the moment of truth, he decided. "May I see your hands?" he requested.

Raymond held them out. They shook. "They're a bit of a mess," he said, a quaver in his voice.

They were considerably worse than the doctor's hands, perhaps reflecting the vigour with which Raymond had striven to release Belinda from the briars. Alec noted one reddish, irritated swelling with a black spot at the centre, as if a thorn had broken off in it. However, none of the scratches appeared to have been caused by fingernails.

"You ought to get them seen to," he said. "Ask Dr. Jagai to extract that splinter for you and disinfect the wound."

"You're as bad as Judith, Chief Inspector. She keeps fussing." His wobbly attempt at a smile failing, he bit his lip. "You want to see my arms, too, don't you? The others said that's what you've been doing."

"Please."

Rising, he took off his jacket and fumbled with shaking hands at his cufflinks. Alec had to help him. Clumsily he pushed up his sleeves, not troubling to roll them. His right forearm, thin but muscular, bore two faintly visible abraded streaks. The left had four parallel grooves, red and sore-looking, running nearly from elbow to wrist.

"Not brambles," said Alec grimly. "Do you mind telling me how you came by these scratches?"

"No, I won't!" Raymond's voice rose. "I know what you think. You looked at everyone's arms, it's obvious the old man marked his murderer. But I didn't kill him, I tell you. I didn't do it!"

"Now calm down! Did I accuse you? All the same, if you could just explain . . ."

"I won't!"

"You must admit it looks bad," Alec pointed out in a reasonable tone. "I should tell you that a voluntary statement is looked upon with a good deal more sympathy than one made by a man answering a charge. Besides, there's a lot of sympathy for those who suffer from . . . their war service."

"You think I'd plead shell-shock? Never! I didn't kill him. I had enough of killing over there, don't you understand?"

"I understand that shell-shock victims are liable to periods when they are unaware of their own actions."

Raymond slumped back onto the sofa. "I don't believe it," he said dully. "I always know when there's a bit missing, and there wasn't. There just wasn't." He shook his head. "I swear there wasn't"

"Then you won't mind letting the police surgeon test your blood."

He looked up, his thin face eager. "A blood test? Of course not. That'll prove I didn't kill that poor old man." Then he sagged again and buried his face in his hands. "Or that I did. If I did, I deserve to hang. I shan't plead shell-shock, never!"

Alec's heart bled for him, and for his fiancée. If he didn't hang, he'd probably be confined to Broadmoor for life.

Piper had slipped out unnoticed, and now returned with Judith Smythe-Pike. "Come on, darling," she said gently to Raymond. "Let's get your coat on."

Child-like, he obeyed. "Judith, I can't believe I did it."

She threw a glance of venomous hatred at Alec. "Of course you didn't, darling. Dr. Jagai says it takes at least four minutes to die of suffocation, and you simply weren't gone that long. We'll prove it somehow. Are you arresting him, Chief Inspector?"

"Not immediately, ma'am." After all, except for Raymond's refusal to explain, he had as much cause to arrest Braeburn. "Mr. Gillespie has agreed to a blood test. While I make arrangements, he is not to leave the hotel."

"But he's not confined to this room? Come on, Ray, you'll feel better elsewhere."

Alec followed them out and went to the telephone cubby under the stairs. Though Redlow had already started back to Newcastle, the local man was perfectly competent to draw and test a couple of blood samples. Sergeant Barclay, answering the 'phone at the police station, said that Dr. Frascr had gonc to opcn his surgery for his regular patients.

"But I'll ring him up, sir, and he'll come over to the Raven's Nest right away, I'm sure. Police business comes first, short of an emergency."

Returning to the back parlour, Alec found Tom and Ernie far from happy, showing none of the usual satisfaction at a crime's approaching solution.

"Looks like him, Chief, don't it?" said Ernie glumly.

"Can't help feeling sorry for a young chap like that," Tom rumbled. "He's got a fine young woman there as'd turn him around given time."

"It doesn't look good," Alec admitted. "Raymond Gillespie has the obvious motive, but there's still an outside chance Braeburn's our man. I suppose it's too soon to expect results from Inspector Fielding."

"Them Fraud Squad lads don't know the meaning of hurry," Tom agreed. "Could take weeks."

"We're lucky the blood on the pillow-case isn't from a common group. With luck the tests will eliminate one or the other of our suspects. Well, while we're waiting for Dr. Fraser, we might as well run over everyone's statements and see if we can pick out anything of interest. Ernie?"

Piper flipped back to the front of his notebook. He started reading fast from his shorthand, proud of the skill which had helped earn him a place in the C.I.D.

"Slow down, laddy," said Tom. "Mebbe we won't get

as far, but at least we'll notice any landmarks on the way."

However, none of them noticed any landmarks which tended to implicate either Raymond Gillespie or Braeburn. They had just finished the interview with Peter and Enid Gillespie, and Alec was beginning to wonder where Dr. Fraser had got to, when there came a knock on the door.

"Come in, Doctor," Alec called, rising.

But it was Briggs the landlord's head which appeared around the door. "Telephone for you, Chief Inspector."

"Damn, I hope Fraser hasn't been delayed." He went out to the cubby and picked up the apparatus. "Fletcher here."

"Chief Inspector, everyone here wants to know how the deuce you do it!"

"Fielding?"

"Yes, sir. As per your instructions, I called on Messrs Braeburn, Braeburn, Tiddle and Plunkett. Would you believe it, they've already got the auditors in? They'd suspected for some time that all was not according to Cocker in your Mr. Donald Braeburn's accounts. They had just been waiting for him to go out of town for long enough to check up."

"And?"

"He's been cooking the books all right, making free with more than one client's funds, naughty boy. It'll take days, or weeks, to sort out the details, I'm afraid, sir."

"No great rush, but ask them to concentrate on Alistair McGowan's losses first, please."

"Sergeant Tring mentioned a possible motive for murder?"

"Possible," Alec stressed. "Thanks, Fielding, a good job."

"My pleasure, Chief Inspector. We'll bag Braeburn if you don't, never fear."

Alec hung up the ear-piece. So Daisy was right! At least, she was pretty certainly right about the quarrel Belinda had overheard, and without her interpretation they would never have suspected the lawyer. The quarrel might or might not have led to murder. The case against Raymond was still equally strong, or stronger, because of his lack of an alternative explanation for those damned scratches.

Where was Fraser?

The police surgeon had arrived in the landlord's parlour while Alec was talking over the wire. A prosperous-looking gentleman, he had opened his black bag on the table by the window and was taking out the necessary equipment for drawing and testing blood samples.

"I can do it all right here, Mr. Fletcher," he explained cheerfully. "Where are my victims?"

"Piper, fetch Raymond Gillespie, please. He'll want to know the worst as soon as possible, I imagine." Alec told Fraser about Raymond's unfortunate condition.

Piper was gone an unexpectedly long time. At last he returned, breathless. "Can't find him, sir. He wasn't in the lounge or the bar-parlour, nor Miss Smythe-Pike, so I went up to his room, and he's not there neether. So not wanting to keep the doctor waiting, I thought I'd bring Mr. Braeburn down first instead, afore searching any further, but he's not in his room eether."

"Did you speak to the constable at the front door?" Alec asked sharply.

"Crombie? Yes, sir. He hasn't let nor one nor t'other of 'em out that way, only a couple of local blokes he knows personal who came in for a quick nip in the bar-parlour. I didn't take the time to go out to the back gate."

"Both in the lavatories, no doubt," Fraser suggested. "Nervous anticipation takes a lot of people that way."

"Could be. Sergeant Tring, check, please. Piper, try the chap on the back gate."

Tring returned first. "All lavatories and bathrooms vacant," he reported, "and I took a quick dekko round their rooms again, sir—no one there."

"You'd better try the bar-parlour and lounge again. It's just possible both you and D.C. Piper missed them in transit in that maze of passages upstairs."

Again Tom came back before Piper and with him came Daisy.

"Alec, have you seen Belinda? I can't find her or Dr. Jagai."

Alec's heart jumped up and got stuck in his throat. Before he was able to speak, Ernie Piper dashed in.

"Chief," he panted, formality in the presence of strangers forgotten, "the constable on the back gate's lying there unconscious. Summun's been and gone and hit him on the head."

19

The stranger in the parlour, the man Daisy didn't know, sprang to his feet and reached for the black bag on the table. Clicking shut the catch, he snapped at Piper, "Show me!" They hurried out.

"Tom, try the dining room, kitchens, servants' quarters, cellars—anywhere you can think of. Ask Briggs. I'll 'phone Halliday, get a proper search organized." Alec, grey-faced, turned to Daisy, reaching for her hand. "Both our two suspects are missing. When did you last see Belinda?"

"Just after I saw you, when we came downstairs together from Mr. Braeburn's room." She held onto his hand, ignoring his painfully tight clasp. "Anne insisted on dragging me up to see her children, so I left Belinda with Dr. Jagai. He was taking her to get a ginger beer in the bar-parlour. Alec, he's not one of your suspects?"

"No, not him. Braeburn and Raymond Gillespie, and *both* of them gone. I don't understand it."

"I can't believe they're accomplices," Daisy agreed.

"If either's harmed Belinda, I'll kill him and bedamned to the Law!" He closed his eyes and took a deep breath. "I must get on to Halliday."

Going with him to the telephone, she listened while

he explained the situation to the Superintendent. "So you see, sir," he finished up, "I'd like every man you can spare. . . . Yes, sir. . . . Thank you, sir." Hanging up, he ran his hand through his hair. "Halliday's calling in every man on his force, on or off duty. Thank God he's not one of those who resents the Met operating on his manor."

"He seemed pretty efficient, as well as being nice. I'm sure he'll do all he can."

"Yes, he's coming right over himself, to see the poor chap who's injured and to help organize the search and question everyone."

"He'll be here in no time. The police station's just around the corner, isn't it? Sergeant Barclay pointed it out."

"Three minutes, he said. I feel so helpless, Daisy, having to stay here giving orders when I'd rather be out scouring the town. I wish I knew the place, knew where to start looking for her. I have a dreadful vision of her lying out on the walls somewhere, injured . . . or dead."

So did Daisy, but she put all the optimistic pragmatism she could muster into her voice. "I can't see how either Ray or Braeburn could have overcome Dr. Jagai, hidden him, and spirited Belinda away without creating a frightful hullabaloo."

"Unless they asked him to treat their scratches, which I advised both to do, knowing Jagai had his black bag with him," Alec said despairingly. "He knew Belinda wasn't to be left alone, he'd have taken her upstairs with him."

"More likely he's taken her for another walk." Though it seemed highly unlikely he would do so without consulting her or Alec. "The bobby at the front door knows they're allowed to go out."

"And Piper wouldn't have asked about those two!" As he spoke, Alec headed down the hall at a purposeful stride, Daisy at his heels. He opened the front door and asked, "Crombie, have the Indian doctor and my daughter gone out again?"

"Not sin' they cam' back, sir, not unless they went by the back gate. Ye'd best ask Constable Spiers."

Alec's shoulders slumped. "I'm afraid Spiers has been hurt." Taking in the constable's shocked face, he assured him, "Dr. Fraser is with him now, and Superintendent Halliday is on his way. For heaven's sake, don't let anyone leave." He shut the door, saying wryly, "Talk about locking the stable door after the horse has been stolen!"

"I could go and start searching on the walls," Daisy offered.

"No, please stay. I want you here if . . . if they bring her back. Tom! Any sign?"

Sergeant Tring shook his head as he came down the last few stairs. Daisy had never seen him look so grim. "Not that I can find, Chief. I haven't spoke to Briggs yet."

"Go and find him now. I'm going to check Jagai's room."

Daisy knew Alec was considering the possibility that the doctor and Belinda had been ambushed when he went to fetch his black bag. She followed him as he took the stairs two at a time, catching up as he banged on the bedroom door next to hers. No answer. Reaching for the handle, Alec said savagely, "I'll break it down if I have to."

But the door was not locked, and no one was there.

The doctor's black bag was not in evidence either. Daisy went to the wardrobe. His overcoat hung there, but still no sign of the black bag, not at the bottom with his bedroom slippers, neatly placed side by side, nor on the shelf above with his hat.

"That's odd," she said, turning round. Alec was gone, to see if Mr. Halliday had arrived, she assumed.

She glanced under the bed, though Alec had looked there for a body or bodies. A man who tidied away his slippers into the wardrobe was not likely to shove his medical paraphernalia under his bed, but one never could tell.

Nothing. A minor mystery to add to the inexplicable disappearance of four people. Daisy plumped down on the edge of the bed to think.

She found difficult to believe Raymond or Braeburn, or even the two acting in concert, could have biffed the unfortunate Spiers on the nob while abducting both Dr. Jagai and Belinda. One or both must still be in the hotel.

Assume Dr. Jagai took his bag to treat Raymond's or Braeburn's scratches. Where? Piper had checked both their rooms. Sooner or later Alec would undoubtedly go through every bedroom with a fine-tooth comb, but he was fully occupied with Mr. Halliday for the moment. Besides, he might have to get a search warrant, she wasn't sure—not that he'd let that requirement delay him if he suspected his daughter was in one of them.

Which might land him in frightful trouble, whereas Daisy could pop in and out in no time, risking no more than a bit of a row if she were caught.

Her own room was next door, so she went there first. Before, hunting for Belinda, she had merely glanced in. Now she checked inside the wardrobe and under the beds, uncertain whether she was praying to find or not to find one or two bodies bound and gagged, unconscious even, surely not dead!

No bodies, alive or dead.

After a moment's hesitation, she crossed the passage to Alec's room. It was close to Dr. Jagai's and the villain would not expect a busy police officer to go up to his bedroom anytime soon. Quickly she searched it, forcing herself not to dwell on her midnight visit, the visit which had ended in a kiss.

Then to Tring and Piper's shared room, next door. Here she began to feel like a horrible Nosey Parker. It didn't stop her peeking under the beds, opening the wardrobe door. There was the sergeant's "second-best" blue and green chequered suit—he was wearing the ghastly yellow and tan today—but no body.

Daisy hurried down the two steps and round the corner. Lavatory, bathroom, one step up, the next door was Room 9, Braeburn's, where Piper had already been. But he was looking for Braeburn; he had probably just glanced around, as Daisy had in her own room. Holding her breath, she knocked, softly, then louder. To her relief there was no response. She let out her breath, turned the handle, and peeped in.

The solicitor was not lying in wait to savage her. Nor had he carelessly left any victims lying around. Thirty seconds later, Daisy was knocking at the next door.

She scurried from room to room, two more on this corridor then back to the other wing, down three steps this time. All were empty of both their lawful inhabitants and extraneous bodies. Growing quite blasé, she already had her hand on the door-knob of the fifth room when her knock was answered with a bellow.

"Who the devil is that? Can't a man get any rest in this godforsaken hole?"

Unmistakably Desmond Smythe-Pike. Anyone trying any funny business in his presence would have quickly learned the error of his ways.

"Verra sorry, sir," Daisy squeaked, hoping she sounded like a Scottish chambermaid, "wrang room." Did the Scots say wrang? She swallowed a giggle, reminding herself of the dreadful reason for her search.

Crossing the passage, she raised her hand to knock. A strange humming sound came from beyond the door. The sound of someone trying to yell through a gag? Surely not, but she had never heard anyone trying to yell through a gag, so perhaps it was. And she rather thought this must be the room shared by Judith and Kitty—Judith who'd do anything for Raymond, Kitty who adored her older brother.

Daisy looked back to make sure the Scottish chambermaid she had impersonated was not creeping up on her. Then she put her ear to the door, blatantly eavesdropping. Mmmmmmmmmmmmmmm. It sounded like a thousand bees having a wonderful time on a heather-covered moor.

She raised her hand to knock again, then changed her mind. With infinite caution she turned the doorknob. Inching the door open, she peered through the slit.

Someone was sitting on the floor. All she could see was a thin strip of the back of a man's jacket from the shoulder down. She pushed the door wider—a knee in grey flannels, and resting on it, palm upturned, a dark hand. Dr. Jagai's hand.

The bees continued to buzz uninterrupted. Emboldened, Daisy opened the door far enough to peer around it. The scene that met her eyes left her utterly baffled.

On one bed, Judith sat cross-legged, her hands palm up on her knees, eyes closed. On the other perched Kitty and—thank God—Belinda, and on the floor

Chandra Jagai and Raymond Gillespie, all in the same posture, eyes closed, humming.

"Good gracious heavens above!" said Daisy blankly. "What on earth are you doing?"

The hum abruptly cut off. Five pairs of startled eyes stared at her. Then they all started babbling at once.

Judith raised her voice. "Hush a minute," she said calmly. "Let Chandra explain."

"It's a form of an ancient Hindu discipline." The doctor rose smoothly to his feet, Ray following suit less elegantly. "A very minor, elementary exercise which . . ."

"Never mind now," Daisy broke in, "it'll have to wait. Belinda, your father's in a fearful pucker. He's afraid you've been kidnapped, possibly by you, Raymond. You'd better both come down at once."

Belinda slid down from the bed and ran to take Daisy's hand. "Why does Daddy think I'm kidnapped?" she asked anxiously.

"Because you couldn't be found and the constable guarding the back gate has been knocked out."

"Oh my sainted aunt!" Raymond exclaimed, horrified. "Not by me!"

"No, not by you, since you're still here. Come on."

Judith, Kitty, and Dr. Jagai followed them downstairs. Halfway down, Daisy stopped. The front hall was aswarm with blue uniforms, their occupants chattering excitedly. Kidnappings and man-hunts were not exactly common fare in Berwick.

Among them, Daisy spotted a face she recognized. "Sergeant Barclay," she called.

Silence fell as he came over to the foot of the stairs. "Yes, miss, what can I do for you?"

"I've found some of the missing people. Most of them, in fact. Is Mr. Fletcher in the back parlour?"

"Yes, miss, and I don't s'pose him and the Super'll mind being interrupted! Good for you, miss. And hallo to you, missy. Glad to see you're safe and sound."

"Hallo, Sergeant Barclay," Belinda replied shyly.

He led the way, opened the door, and ushered in the small procession.

Alec and Mr. Halliday were bending over a map spread out on the table by the window. They glanced round at the sound of the door opening and Alec frowned.

"Miss Dalrymple, not now, we. . . ."

Belinda dashed past Daisy and flung herself at her father. "Daddy, I'm all right! I wasn't kidnapped, I was upstairs in Kitty's room. I stayed with Dr. Jagai all the time, every single minute. I'm all right, honestly."

Crushing her to his chest, he looked over her head at Daisy. His grey eyes glimmered with unshed tears. He smiled at her and she smiled back in pure joy at having restored his beloved daughter to him.

Then he saw Raymond. At once he was all business.

"So you're here, Mr. Gillespie. Have you left the hotel since I last saw you?"

"Eek, Daddy, you're squashing me. He's been with us all the time, with me and Dr. Jagai and Kitty and Judith."

"Then it's yon lawyer we're looking for," said Superintendent Halliday.

"He won't have gone far," Raymond observed with a grin.

"Why not?" Alec demanded.

"Darling, let Chandra tell the story," Judith put in. "It's all his doing."

They were all crowded into the small room by then. Dr. Jagai closed the door, but immediately it opened again behind him. Dr. Fraser and Piper squeezed in.

"Doctor, how is Spiers?" Mr. Halliday asked at once.

"Concussed, but not badly, Superintendent. I'll keep him under observation in the Infirmary for a day or two. Mr. Fletcher, Detective Constable Piper has been of the greatest assistance."

"Good," Alec grunted impatiently. "Now let's get on with catching the man who put Spiers in the Infirmary. Dr. Jagai, what's this about Braeburn not going far?"

"I took the liberty of slipping quite a largish dose of bromide into his whisky," Chandra Jagai said diffidently. With a half-penitent glance at Dr. Fraser, he went on, "Not enough to harm him, sir. But I very much doubt that he's more than a few hundred yards away, Chief Inspector, and he'll be sound asleep by now. I believe he was heading for the King's Arms Garage on Hide Hill."

"Great Scott," said Alec, "well done, Doctor!"

"Wasn't it clever of him, Daddy?"

"Not exactly correct medical practice," Dr. Fraser said, his lips quirking, "but forgivable in the circumstances."

"What were the circumstances?" Alec asked. "What made you believe he was about to take to his heels?"

Before the young Indian could answer, Superintendent Halliday weighed in. "That's all very well," he said, full of foreboding as a farmer who sees thunderclouds building over his unharvested corn, "but Braeburn went out by the back gate. If he was heading for the King's Arms, he must have planned to go the long way around to avoid detection. For your sake, Dr. Jagai, we must hope he has not fallen off the city walls in a stupor, and broken his neck."

20

Mister Halliday went off to send his men out hunting for the drugged lawyer.

Seeing Dr. Jagai's appalled face, Daisy put her hand on his arm. "Don't forget, Braeburn killed Mr. McGowan," she said. "Otherwise he'd have stayed in the hotel as he was supposed to and he'd just have fallen asleep harmlessly in the bar-parlour."

"What made you think he was ready to scarper?" Alec asked again. "How did you know he was one of my two remaining suspects?"

"Speaking as the other," said Raymond, turning to Dr. Fraser, "if you're the police doctor, sir, as I assume, would you mind doing that wretched blood test while Chandra explains? It may look as if Braeburn's the murderer, but I want proof it wasn't me, and I'd like to get it out of the way."

"Certainly." Beckoning him over to the table, Dr. Fraser started taking odds and ends out of his black bag. "Go ahead, Dr. Jagai."

Daisy had no intention of watching the blood-drawing. She kept her gaze on Dr. Jagai. He still looked shaken as he began his story.

"Belinda told me Mr. Braeburn had frightened her. You, Mr. Fletcher, and Miss Dalrymple obviously took her fears seriously since you asked me not to let her out of my sight. And then Sergeant Tring brought her to me and she said her father was at that moment with Mr. Braeburn. Well, I knew at that point that the Chief Inspector was looking for scratches rather than information . . .

"Ouch!" Ray yelped. "No, it's all right, Judith, it didn't really hurt. Sorry to interrupt."

"So it seemed obvious," Dr. Jagai continued, "that Mr. Braeburn was under suspicion. I was going to ask Miss Dalrymple about him, but Mrs. Bretton bore her off. Belinda and I went into the bar-parlour."

"Dr. Jagai bought me ginger beer, Daddy. Miss Dalrymple said I could."

"That was kind of him." Alec smiled at the doctor.

"A little later," he resumed the tale, "Ray and Judith—Mr. Gillespie and Miss Smythe-Pike—joined us. Raymond told me Mr. Fletcher had advised him to consult me about a thorn broken off in his hand which was looking rather nasty. I went upstairs to fetch my bag, taking Belinda along with me, of course. When we returned to the bar-parlour, Kitty was with Ray and Judith."

"Mummy let me go to Ray and Judith," Kitty put in smugly. "She didn't know Dr. Jagai was sitting with them."

"Mr. Braeburn was there, too," Belinda said. "Not with the others, sitting at the bar. I pretended I didn't see him."

"Let Dr. Jagai tell his story, sweetheart," Alec admonished.

"I'd previously offered Kitty a ginger beer, so I went up to the bar to get it. I overheard Mr. Braeburn asking Briggs about ferries to the Continent. You can imagine I pricked up my ears. Briggs said the nearest ferry service was from Leith, Edinburgh's port, with sailings to Copenhagen. At that, Mr. Braeburn asked about cars for hire and Briggs directed him to the King's Arms Garage.

"I suppose I should have run to you, Chief Inspector. I wish I had. But there was my bag, with samples of several common drugs. I took the ginger beer back to Kitty, got out two bromide powders, and returned to the bar. I approached Mr. Braeburn with a request that he'd act for me in the matter of Mr. McGowan's will. By a stroke of luck, good or ill is yet to be seen, Mr. Bretton heard me. He promptly protested that Mr. Braeburn was the family lawyer while I was . . ." He hesitated, and Daisy wondered what offensive phrase Harold Bretton had used.

"I was only too obviously not one of the family," Dr. Jagai said ironically. "Mr. Braeburn turned towards him to make some response, giving me the opportunity to slip the powders into his whisky. I wish I had not, though as Miss Dalrymple says, had he stayed in the hotel, no harm would have been done."

"You couldn't guess he might go up on the walls," Daisy said. "In fact, maybe he hasn't. But if he has, it's very likely because he knows the way after following Belinda up there."

"And trying to kill her, as well as Albert McGowan," Alec said grimly, his arm around his daughter.

"Indeed!" exclaimed Dr. Fraser. "Well, to be sure, I'd not advise any man fuddled with whisky to go out on the city walls. If it comes to an autopsy, I see no need to look for other causes for a fall."

"*We're* not telling," Ray asserted. "Judith? Kitty?"

"Golly no," said Kitty, and Judith shook her head.

Everyone looked at Alec.

"I am a police officer," he said slowly, "sworn to

uphold the Law. But I'm a father, too. Close your ears, Tring and Piper! If Braeburn comes to grief, I'll do my best to square the Superintendent."

"Didn't hear a thing," said Tom Tring, his broad face bland.

"I also shall have a word with Halliday," Dr. Fraser said, turning back to the table. "He's a good fellow. Well, Mr. Gillespie, your blood is of a different group from that found under Mr. McGowan's fingernails. You are what we call a universal donor. Might I suggest your registering with your nearest hospital to be called upon in case of . . ."

"Ray, sit down!" Judith guided her suddenly ashen fiancé to the nearest chair. "Put your head down, darling."

"I thought"—he gulped—"I was still afraid I might have . . ."

"Don't try to talk," advised Dr. Jagai, who had sprung to his side. "Breathe deeply. Slowly in, hold it, slowly out. That's right. And again. In . . . hold . . . out. In . . . hold . . . out."

"Shouldn't he sit cross-legged?" Kitty said critically.

"Not just now. That's a long-term affair."

Daisy's curiosity reawakened. As a tinge of colour returned to Raymond's cheeks, she said, "You still haven't told me what you were all doing in Judith and Kitty's room."

"Yoga," said Belinda.

"It's an Indian thing," said Kitty. "For heaven's sake, don't tell Mummy I was doing it."

Raymond raised his head. "All for my benefit," he said wryly. "Frankly, Mr. Fletcher had rather upset me, and I was in a bit of a state still after Chandra treated my hand. He decided it was a good moment to teach me his tranquillizing exercise."

"Yoga is a complex physical, mental, and religious discipline," Dr. Jagai explained. "I know very little, just what I've learned from an Indian friend in London. This particular exercise, an adaptation and simplification, I have found to be calming to the stressed spirit. I hope that regular practice will prove useful to Ray." He smiled. "And that he'll let me study the results."

"Of course," Judith said warmly.

"Interesting," pronounced Dr. Fraser. "Well, Chief Inspector, if you've nothing more for me to do, I'll return to my patient patients."

"I'd still like Braeburn's blood tested, sir. If Dr. Jagai is right, they should be bringing him in very shortly."

"I shouldn't have done it." He shook his head, looking miserable.

"I'm glad you did," Belinda announced. "He was absolutely, awfully horrible. I hope he's broken his neck like he tried to make me break mine."

Daisy belatedly bethought herself that the child should have been removed long since. Meeting Alec's rueful glance, she guessed he felt likewise. She'd better take Belinda away before Braeburn's insensible body turned up.

"It must be nearly lunchtime," she said. "I'm starving. Belinda, let's go and wash our hands."

Reluctantly Belinda took her hand. At that moment, heavy footsteps were heard in the hall. Mr. Halliday put his head around the door.

"Got him!" he said. "Curled up like a dormouse on the steps down from the wall to the tunnel under it, and snoring fit to wake the dead."

Daisy glanced around the residents' lounge. Everyone was there, dressed for traveling but eager to hear

Alec's promised announcement before they hurried on to Dunston Castle and the miser's deathbed.

They all knew the police had taken in Alistair McGowan's solicitor for questioning.

"With Braeburn missing, the old man won't be changing his will after all," Jeremy Gillespie pointed out smugly to Harold Bretton. His parents looked equally smug.

"He's not dead yet," Bretton said, scowling. "Don't count your chickens before they're hatched."

Desmond Smythe-Pike stopped groaning about his painful gout to bark testily, "I've never balked at a fence in my life, by George! We'll find a lawyer in Edinburgh and take him with us. Any of those fellas can write up a simple will."

"Calm down, dear," his wife admonished him. "You know excitement only makes it worse." She turned back to chattering with her sister—she and Madame Pasquier were still catching up on the past thirty years.

Anne was giving Daisy the cold shoulder, offended at her lack of sympathy with the inhumane conditions the children had been forced to suffer for nearly twenty hours. After leaving them upstairs when they could quite well have come down, she now had them with her at a moment when they would surely have been better off with their nurse. She was showing off Baby to Matilda, while Belinda and Kitty entertained Tabitha.

Judith, sitting next to Daisy, glanced over to where Raymond and Dr. Jagai talked seriously together.

"That little Indian has given Ray hope," she said softly, "and I don't mean by failing to inherit the family fortune. He's a good man." Judith pondered a moment. "I don't know that I've ever met one before. We're getting married, you know, whether Grandfather leaves his money to Uncle Peter, or Mother, or Aunt Geraldine's sons, who are, after all, his grandsons, or a home for crippled cats. We'll manage somehow."

"I'm sure you will," said Daisy warmly, glad they weren't counting on old Alistair's vast wealth.

Judith resumed her customary drawl. "What about you and that gorgeous policeman of yours?" she asked with a teasing look. "I confess to moments when I've hated him, but I suppose he was only doing his job. Still, a copper and the Honourable Miss Dalrymple—even these days, it's not really on . . . or is it?"

Daisy's cheeks felt red-hot. "We're just friends. I've been involved in one or two of his cases."

"Aha!"Judith sobered again. "Anne said you lost your fiancée in the War. I'm sorry. What a foul business that was, enough to make a pacifist of one, whatever Daddy says about conchies."

"Michael was a conscientious objector." There were so few people Daisy could talk to about him with any hope of sympathy. "He was a Quaker. He drove a Friends' ambulance."

"I wish Ray had! The worst of his waking nightmares come from having had to kill. That's part of the reason the possibility that he'd murdered Uncle Albert without being aware of it hit him so hard, even though he knew he'd scratched himself during one of his turns. You won't let him know I've told you, will you? He's fearfully ashamed of it."

"Of course not. So that was it! May I tell Alec, if he swears on his honour never to breathe a word to another soul? I'm sure he's dying to know what led him astray. Oh, here he is now."

Alec came into the lounge, flanked by Tring and Piper. As an expectant silence fell, Belinda slipped across to Daisy's side.

"Ladies and gentlemen," Alec began, "I want to thank you all for consenting to break your journey here in Berwick to assist . . ."

"Didn't know we had a choice!" trumpeted Smythe-Pike.

Alec wondered just how forcefully Superintendent Halliday had worded his request for the family to stay. However, he continued smoothly, ". . . to assist the police in investigating this heinous crime. In view of your cooperation—some more, some considerably less—I feel it right to confirm formally what I imagine you have already heard informally: Donald Braeburn has been arrested for the murder of Albert McGowan."

Braeburn was still sleeping off the bromide behind bars. Since he had previously given permission for a blood test, Dr. Fraser had not bothered to wait until he awoke to draw a sample. The lawyer's blood group, a comparatively rare one, matched the blood under the old man's fingernails and on the pillow-case.

"But dash it all, my dear chap," said Bretton plaintively, "what I can't see is why the deuce he did it."

Scanning all the puzzled, curious, expectant faces, Alec decided Braeburn's plea of confidence no longer held water.

"He was afraid. Mr. McGowan confided his plans for the fortune he was about to inherit, and Braeburn told him his brother had, in the past few years, squandered the greater part of that fortune."

"Stuff and nonsense!" roared Smythe-Pike. "Dammit, Alistair McGowan wouldn't know how to squander a penny if he tried."

Alec raised a hand to still the mounting murmur. "So we gathered," he said dryly. "We surmise that Albert McGowan held the same opinion, and that he accused Braeburn of embezzlement and threatened an audit. In fact, Braeburn's partners have already called in the accountants. By his own statement to me, it seems probable that there's nothing left of Alistair McGowan's fortune but a few thousand. A very few thousand. I don't know what can be salvaged, but you'd better not count on more."

Above the ensuing pandemonium rose Enid Gillespie's screech. "A few paltry thousands! Much good that will do us. He counted on your bungling incompetence, Peter. He knew you'd never realize you'd been swindled!"

A quiet voice behind Alec said, "Oh dear!"

He swung round. A drab, tired, middle-aged woman had entered the lounge unnoticed. "Can I help you, madam?" he asked.

"You're the chief detective?" she said, flustered. With a doubtful glance at the tumultuous group behind him, she continued, "I'm sorry to interrupt your meeting, but I'm Julia Gillespie."

"I'd say my meeting has come to an undignified end, Miss Gillespie. Was your family expecting you?"

"No. They sent a telegram, but I didn't have time when the boy brought it from the Post Office to search for the key to Uncle Alistair's cash-box to get a shilling for an answer. There's no telephone at Dunston Castle, you see. Uncle Alistair considered them nothing but a new-fangled way to waste money. I knew once I'd left I'd never want to go back, so I brought the news myself."

Alec could think of only one item of news the miser's unpaid skivvy might bring. "Let me get their attention for you, ma'am," he suggested, "and you can make your announcement."

"Thank you," she accepted with a grateful smile.

Turning, Alec clapped his hands and said in a voice

which, though nowhere near as loud as Smythe-Pike's, cut through the babble like a policeman's whistle. "Ladies and gentlemen, your attention please!"

"Julia!"

"Aunt Julia!"

"What the . . . ?"

"Don't tell me . . . !"

Alec frowned and glared. "Go ahead, ma'am." He moved aside with Tom and Piper.

Miss Gillespie quailed a little under the barrage of eyes. Clearing her throat, she said, "I'm sorry to tell you . . . No! I'm not a bit sorry! I know it's dreadfully unChristian of me but I'm glad! Uncle Alistair has passed away. He died yesterday, at a few minutes past noon."

The horrified silence was broken by a shout of laughter from Raymond. He clapped Dr. Jagai on the back. "So you get the lot after all, Chandra," he cried. "What's left of it, anyway. Congratulations, old chap."

The sun shone down upon Berwick station. Today it was almost possible to believe Spring was on its way to this most northerly outpost of England.

The relatives of the deceased McGowan twins had already departed for London, with varying degrees of fury, disgruntlement, resignation, amusement and, in Kitty's case, delight. "Now Mummy will have to let me be a writer," she had told Daisy, "or a nurse. Acksherly, I think I'd like to be a detective, but I don't s'pose they let girls."

The detectives from Scotland Yard, accompanied by Belinda, would follow later. In the meantime, Alec and Belinda had come to see off Daisy and Dr. Jagai on the next train to Edinburgh.

Belinda hung on Daisy's arm. "Thank you for looking after me, Miss Dalrymple," she said. "I wish you were coming back to London with us."

"I have work to do, darling. But I'll only be gone a few days."

"Unless you stumble across another body," Alec observed ironically.

Daisy laughed. "If so, I'll ignore it, since Scotland Yard doesn't operate in Scotland. Odd, isn't it?"

"Not as odd as your making the acquaintance of the late Albert McGowan shortly before he departed this life. Do you know, I still have no idea how you came to meet him?"

"Oh, that wasn't Miss Dalrymple, Daddy, it was me."

"Not another female sleuth in the making," Alec groaned, "as if one wasn't enough! Here comes the train. Doctor, my hearty thanks for your help. I hope we'll be seeing you in town."

He shook Chandra Jagai's hand and Belinda turned to the Indian to say good-bye.

While his daughter was occupied, Alec said softly to Daisy, "I owe you more than I can ever repay."

"Bosh," said Daisy, holding out her hand. "She's a pet. It's been a pleasure—when I wasn't absolutely terrified for her."

He took her hand as a whistle announced the train approaching across the bridge. A hasty glance at Belinda showed her still absorbed in earnest conversation with Jagai.

The engine puffed into the station. Belinda, her hand on the doctor's arm, stood on tiptoe and leaned forward to whisper in his ear.

"Did you see?" she asked joyfully. "He kissed her!"

Please turn the page for
an exciting sneak peak at
Carola Dunn's next
Daisy Dalrymple mystery

DAMSEL IN DISTRESS

coming from Kensington Books
in March 2002!

1

Phillip strained his ears. Yes, there it was, that sinister knocking noise again.

The aging engine of his Swift two-seater made a deuce of a racket going up the steepish hill, and odd squeaks and raffles from chassis and body were inevitable. He worked the old bus pretty hard. For every joint oiled, for every bolt tightened, another loosened. But the knocking was new, different, and bally sinister.

Safely over the crest of the Surrey Downs, he pulled off the "B" road into a convenient gateway. A cow looked at him over the five-barred gate and mooed.

"I'll be gone long before milking time," he assured her, jumping out.

Taking off his blazer, he dropped it on the seat and rolled up his sleeves before he opened up the bonnet. As he peered into the oily depths, the hum of a well-tuned engine approached along the road. He glanced round to see a scarlet Aston Martin zip past, stop, reverse, and come to a halt beside him.

"Say, are you stuck?" enquired the girl behind the wheel, putting back her dust-veil to reveal a pretty face surrounded by blond curls. "Can I give you a ride?"

"Thanks awfully, but I'm not exactly stuck."

"Oh." The American girl—Phillip was sure she must

be American—looked enquiringly at the Swift. "You have the hood up."

"The hood?" He glanced at the hood, folded down on this mild, dry spring day. Ah, but she was American, she probably called it the roof. "You mean the bonnet? Something's knocking in the engine," he explained, "but if a few minutes' tinkering with my own tools won't solve it, I'll drive on to the next garage and borrow their tools."

"You fix your own automobile? Gee, that's real smart."

"Nothing much to boast about," Phillip said modestly. On a closer inspection those curls were gold, not mere blond, and her face was the prettiest he'd seen in years, not smothered in powder and paint, either, like most these days. "I like messing about with motor-cars," he confessed, glad that he hadn't yet got around to crawling underneath and getting oil on his face. "Just wish I could spend more time at it."

"I've always wanted to take a whack at it." She was a girl in a million! "But Poppa won't let me. He says it's not ladylike. Real set on me acting ladylike, Poppa is. Why, it took me years to talk him into letting me drive. Now I test automobiles for him, just motoring around to check out how they feel to an amateur driver."

"Is that what you're doing with this beauty? Don't see many of them on the roads."

"It runs swell. Poppa's thinking of investing a few bucks so they can raise production. That's what we're doing in England, looking for up-and-coming auto manufacturers for Poppa to invest in. I guess you can tell I'm not English?" she asked wistfully.

"I think your accent's absolutely ripping."

"Honest Injun? And there I was wanting to learn to

talk like a proper English lady. I just love England, the quaint little villages and the history and flowers everywhere."

She waved her hand at the verge and hedge-bank. Phillip suddenly noticed the April profusion of primroses, violets, celandines, and stitchwort, hitherto unobserved.

"But gee," the girl continued, sounding quite regretful, "I mustn't keep you from your tinkering. The truth is, I'm kinda lost. The signposts all point to places I don't want to go. Can you direct me to the main London road?"

Phillip opened his mouth to say, "Second to the right and straight on till morning," or whatever the directions were, when he was struck by a brain-wave. At least, he rather thought it might be a brain-wave. The Honourable Phillip Petrie was not sufficiently acquainted with the bally things to be quite sure at first sight. In fact, he was all too accustomed to being regarded by family and friends alike as a bit of a chump.

Still, it did look awfully like a brain-wave. "It's rather complicated," he lied, "from here to the London road. If you're not in a frightful hurry, if you wouldn't mind waiting a few minutes, you could follow me."

The girl's dazzling smile made him blink. "What a swell idea," she exclaimed.

Much heartened, Phillip produced the second part of his inspiration. "I don't know about you," he said recklessly, "but I'm getting jolly peckish. It's nearly teatime and there's a frightfully good little tea-shop in Purley. Would you . . . Do you think you might consider joining me for tea?"

"Golly gee, I'd love to," said the wonderful girl. "We don't have anything like the English afternoon tea, but when I get home I'm surely going to keep it up. I'm Gloria Arbuckle, by the way." She held out her hand.

"Phillip Petrie." Shaking hands, he frowned. "You shouldn't accept invitations from strangers, you know, Miss Arbuckle. Come to that, your father shouldn't let you drive around the countryside alone. What if you broke down?"

"I'm supposed to take Poppa's assistant with me," she admitted, "but he was busy, and on the first fine day in ages, I wanted to get out of that smoky city. As for the invitation, it's not like you asked me to go drinking and dancing in some speakeasy. You don't even have speakeasies over here."

"No," said Phillip, rocked by another brain-wave, "but we have jolly good dance floors, perfectly respectable, and I'd be most frightfully bucked if, one of these days, you'd go dancing with me?"

"We'll see," she said, but she smiled.

"What-ho, old thing!"

At this unceremonious greeting, Daisy looked up in annoyance from her second-hand Underwood. She had assumed the footsteps in the hall were someone calling on Lucy, who shared the "bijou" residence with her.

"Oh, it's you, Phillip. What do you want? I told Mrs. Potter I can't see anyone. I'm busy."

"She said you were just writing," Phillip said defensively, dropping his grey Homburg hat on the desk.

"*Just* writing! I'll have to have a word with her."

"Well, perhaps I put the 'just' in. No need to rag the poor old dear."

"For heaven's sake, Phillip, writing is how I make my living and I've two articles due. I keep forgetting to allow for how long the post takes to New York. The

American magazine pays jolly well and I don't want to risk losing the work by being late. So unless you've got something urgent to say . . ."

"Not exactly urgent, but it won't take a minute, honestly." With a diffident gesture, Phillip smoothed his sleek, fair hair. His conventionally good-looking face bore such an appealing look that Daisy gave in.

"All right," she sighed. "Let's hear it."

Perching his loose-limbed frame on the corner of her desk, he swung a long leg clad in pin-stripe trousering and contemplated the well-polished tip of his shoe. She swivelled her chair to face him.

"Well," he said, a faint flush creeping up his cheeks, "it's like this. Er . . ."

"Philip, get a move on!"

"Yes, well, dash it, this is a bit difficult, old bean."

"Is it *necessary?*"

"I should ruddy well think so. A proper cad I'd look if I didn't. . . . You see, the thing is. . . . I say, Daisy, you know I've proposed to you once or twice?"

"At least half a dozen times."

"That many?" he said, rather aghast.

"And I've turned you down just as many. I know you only ask because you feel Gervaise would expect you to take care of me." Daisy's brother, killed in the Great War, had been Phillip's best pal since childhood, growing up on a neighboring estate. "Which is rubbish, so out with it. You've found someone else, haven't you? Someone you really want to marry?"

"By Jove, how did you guess?" Phillip's patent relief almost made Daisy laugh.

She managed to control herself. "Who is it? Someone I know? One of the latest crop of debs?"

"As a matter of fact, she's American. You like Americans, don't you?" he asked anxiously.

"I've met some charming Americans. The one who especially springs to mind is Mr. Thorwald, my editor." Daisy looked longingly at the half-typed sheet of paper in the typewriter. "Tell me about her," she said, resigned.

"Her name's Gloria—Gloria Arbuckle. She's a poppet."

Daisy had expected a "stunner," an "angel," or a "jolly good sport." The old-fashioned word Phillip chose to describe his beloved impressed her even more than the glow in his blue eyes. Unlike others she could name, he wasn't given to falling for pretty girls, so perhaps he really had found his true love. She hoped so.

"Miss Arbuckle is here with her family?" she asked.

"Her father. Her mother died a couple of years ago, and she's an only child. Mr. Arbuckle's a millionaire. I know what people will think, Daisy," he said earnestly, "but you don't believe I care about the shekels, do you?"

"Of course not, old dear, not when I haven't a bean and you've been proposing to me regularly once a month forever. I take it Miss Arbuckle's convinced of your unmercenary nature, but what about her father?"

"He's a good sort and he seems to rather like me. In fact, Gloria says he's taken to me in a big way, but he doesn't know yet that I want to marry her."

"Does he know your father's a lord?" Daisy asked. Republicans though they were, quite a lot of Americans seemed to consider a title for their daughters well worth the price of purchase.

"Yes, but I don't think he has a frightfully high opinion of the peerage. Besides, I've explained it all, that I'm a younger son with no chance of inheriting the title, and I'll never be more than an 'Hon.' or have more than a small allowance." He grimaced. "My people haven't met them yet."

"Aha! You're expecting a ragging from . . . What is it, Mrs. Potter?"

Breathing heavily, the stout charwoman beamed as she set a tray of tea-things on the desk. "The kettle were just on the boil, miss, so I thought I'd bring up a nice cuppa for you and the gentleman. No biscuits," she added regretfully. "We finished 'em up for elevenses, miss, remember?"

"Yes," Daisy said guiltily. Though no slimming diet could possibly make her rounded figure fashionably boyish, she really ought to make an effort. At least, Lucy said so. Frequently. "Thank you, Mrs. Potter."

"I'll pour," Phillip offered, leaving his perch and pulling the other chair up to the desk. "The typewriter is in your way."

"This is *not* turning into a tea-party! One cup, and off you go. Happy as I am to hear your news, I've work to do."

"You'll be free this weekend, won't you?" he asked hopefully, passing her a steaming cup. "I want you to meet Gloria and Arbuckle, and . . . well, actually, I hoped you'd go with me when I take them to meet my people. Lend your support, and all that."

"You're going to brace up and bite the bullet? I could spare a couple of hours, if you really think my presence would help. Are Lord and Lady Petrie coming up to town specially to meet them?"

"Lord no! The Arbuckles are staying in Great Malvern, at the Abbey Hotel. Gloria wanted to get out of town—she adores the English countryside—so I persuaded Arbuckle that Malvern's convenient for his business doings in Oxford and Coventry and Birmingham."

"Hardly! And apart from the Malvern Hills, the countryside isn't anything special."

"It's easy to drive to both the Cotswolds and the Welsh mountains," Phillip argued, "and none of those cities is more than fifty miles away. Not to mention the concerts and tennis and golf . . ."

"You needn't go on," said Daisy, laughing. "I've read the adverts. 'Healthiest of health resorts, lowest death rate in the kingdom, purest water in the world.' "

"I threw all that guff at him, but the clincher was the Morgan Motor Company being in the town. Arbuckle's looking to invest in British motor manufacturers to diversify his holdings. He made his packet by selling out his railway stocks—railroad, they call it—and going into automobiles, in America, at just the right moment."

"Stocks and shares, just your line."

Shaking his head, Phillip pulled a face. "I can't stand the perishing City much longer. I'm an absolute duffer at it. If Gloria will marry me, I hope her father will find me a job in the technical end of the motor-car business, but I'm going to tell the pater I'm getting out anyway."

"You've always hated it," Daisy sympathized. "Like me and stenography."

"I'd rather be a common-or-garden hired motor mechanic, greasy overalls and all, and what's more, I'd make more money at it. I'd even rather sell second-hand cars. If that don't suit the pater's notions of consequence, he can jolly well cough up the ready to set up my own business. I know a fellow who's dying to go into partnership, and . . ."

"Not now, Phillip. I can't make it to Malvern this weekend, but if you can wait till next, I'll come along to hold your hand."

"Will you? You're a real brick, Daisy!"

"I owe Mother a visit. She's feeling neglected, as she never hesitates to let me know."

"I'll pop in and see her. I'm buzzing down on Saturday anyway—I've been home every weekend since Gloria left town. There's a chappie staying at the hotel," he added darkly, "who's been making a dead set at her. I get down as much as I can."

"Your parents must be a bit surprised by the sudden excess of filial devotion, and the Arbuckles that you haven't yet introduced them. You've only just plucked up the nerve?"

Phillip was indignant. "Not at all. It's only last week I began to think I had a real chance with Gloria, and then I had to talk to you first. The mater . . . All right," he said hastily, standing up as she thrust his hat at him, "I've talked. I'm going. You'll like her, Daisy. She's got golden curls and the bluest eyes you ever saw, and . . ."

"Toodle-oo, Phillip," said Daisy, cutting short the rhapsody.

"Oh, right-ho, pip-pip. And you honestly don't mind?"

"I honestly don't mind a bit."

Phillip went off at last with an air of enormous relief.

Her fingers resting on the typewriter keys, Daisy pondered a moment before taking up her interrupted train of thought. So Gloria had golden curls and blue eyes, did she? And no doubt a million-dollar wardrobe. Well, her own eyes were blue, but her shingled hair was an intermediate brown and her wardrobe mostly last year's, if not older, and bought at Selfridge's Bargain Basement.

Not that she was jealous. Phillip was an honorary brother. He had never even pretended to be in love with her. She was just afraid the dear old ass might have fallen for a pretty face without considering what was behind it.

But he had described Gloria as a poppet, not a stunner. Daisy could only hope she was going to like the American girl.

Occasional gateways in the hedges revealed Bredon Hill on the horizon to the right; the Malvern Hills loomed ahead. From a cloudless sky the sun shone down on drought-parched fields and orchards, rotten luck for the farmers but perfect for a fellow in love.

" 'It's three o'clock in the morning,' " Phillip warbled merrily, if inaccurately and off-key, as he tootled along the narrow, winding lane across the Severn plain. " 'We've danced the whole night through.' "

Nearly home. He'd have a quick wash and brush-up, change his clothes, and then drive into Great Malvern, stopping at Violet's for a box of chocs. After tea with the Arbuckles at the Abbey Hotel, he and Gloria would stroll by the swan pool in Priory Park. Later they might go to the pictures, if there was anything decent showing, or dance at the Winter Gardens ballroom to the music of Billy Gammon's All-Star Players.

Dancing, he hoped. If there was any bliss greater than doing the Charleston, tango, or fox-trot with Gloria, it was waltzing with Gloria.

Lost in a dream, he zipped round a bend and jammed on his brakes. A large motor-car, though pulled into a gateway, blocked half the lane.

"By Jove!" Phillip muttered. "It's a good job I overhauled the brakes the other day. What the deuce . . . Oh!" His irritation with the idiot who'd stopped in such a spot vanished as he recognized Arbuckle's vast blue Studebaker touring car.

Arbuckle, sitting in the back seat, turned and waved. And there was Gloria, perched on the top bar of the gate, slim, silk-clad ankles very much in evidence, golden hair outshining the stubble of the hayfield behind her.

"Phil . . . Mr. Petrie," she cried, "aren't you just an angel? A regular White Knight rushing to the rescue!" She started to climb down.

Phillip leapt from the Swift, squeezed between Studebaker and hedge, and arrived just in time to catch her as she jumped the last two bars.

"Careful," he said breathlessly, his arms about her waist. She gazed up at him, eyes blue as the sky, rosy lips parted. Overhead a lark poured out a burst of melody, and the air was full of the fragrance of wild roses.

Mr. Arbuckle coughed. Phillip and Gloria sprang apart.

"Waal now," said her father, a short, spare man with a long face lengthened by a receding hairline, "if this isn't quite a coincidence."

"You've broken down, sir?" Phillip asked, at last noticing the Studebaker's bonnet open on both sides. "I'll have a look, shall I?"

"It's mighty kind of you to offer, young fella, but I guess it's not something that can be fixed on the spot. Me, I'm the financial wizard, don't pretend to understand the mechanical stuff, but Crawford, my technical man, was driving us. Say, you've met him."

"Yes, you introduced us." He hadn't pursued the acquaintance, not having taken to the American engineer, despite his enviably extensive knowledge of motor-cars' design and manufacture.

"Crawford knows autos if anyone does. He went off with some broken part or other to hike to the nearest garage."

"I might as well have a dekko." Phillip already had his aged tweed jacket off. He tossed it into the Studebaker and rolled up his sleeves. He wasn't about to pass up a good excuse to examine an unfamiliar engine.

Gloria came and stood beside him. "Mr. Crawford said something about the radiator," she said uncertainly. "Didn't he, Poppa?"

"Beats me, honey."

"That's it." Phillip pointed. "Look, the hose is gone. It must have split. I think I have a spare in my tool-box which just might fit. Let's give it a try."

"Atta-boy!" said Mr. Arbuckle with a nod of approval. "That's what I like to hear. Be Prepared. It's a wunnerful motto, yes sirree, and not just for Boy Scouts."

"Yes, sir." Phillip grinned at him. He was growing quite fond of the old bird.

He fetched a couple of lengths of different-sized hose, a knife, spanner, and screwdriver from the toolkit attached to the Swift's running board. As he bent over the Studebaker, a brown Ford motor-van with FARRIS, BUTCHERS painted on the side panel came along the lane and stopped.

A burly man, shabbily dressed, stepped down. Touching his cap to Arbuckle and Gloria, he addressed Phillip. "Wotcher, cock. Need an 'and?"

"No, thanks. It's just a matter of getting a new radiator hose clamped in."

The man leaned with meaty hands on the Studebaker's nose. "Yer'll need water to fill 'er up, gov'nor," he pointed out.

"True," Phillip agreed. "I'll buzz over to the nearest farm in my bus." Gesturing with the screwdriver towards the Swift, he turned his head slightly. From the corner of his eye he caught a sudden motion.

Arbuckle cried out. Phillip swung round. Heavy

boots thudded on the dry, packed earth of the lane as four men masked with handkerchiefs rushed around the front of the van.

Two dived over the side of the Studebaker, reaching for Arbuckle. One grabbed Gloria. The fourth swung a crowbar at Phillip.

He ducked the blow.

"Gloria!" he shouted, and went for her attacker with the screwdriver.

The van's driver caught him from behind and wrenched the screwdriver from his grasp. A second swing of the crowbar caught him on the side of the head.

Exploding stars blinded him. His ears rang. Distantly aware of a heavy, sweetish odour, he sank into darkness.

ABOUT THE AUTHOR

Born and raised in England, Carola Dunn now lives in Eugene, Oregon. Her next Daisy Dalrymple mystery, DAMSEL IN DISTRESS, will be published by Kensington Publishing in March, 2002. You can visit her Web site at http://www.geocities.com/CarolaDunn.